ROMEO AND JULIET

ILLUSTRATED BY
SONIA LEONG

Amulet Books, New York

PUBLISHER'S NOTE: This is a work of fiction. Names, characters, places, and incidents are either the product of the author's imagination or are used fictitiously, and any resemblance to actual persons, living or dead, business establishments, events, or locales is entirely coincidental.

Cataloging-in-Publication Data has been applied for and may be obtained from the Library of Congress.
ISBN 13: 978-0-8109-9325-9
ISBN 10: 0-8109-9325-2

Originally published in the U.K. by SelfMadeHero
(www.selfmadehero.com)

Illustrator: Sonia Leong
Text Adaptor: Richard Appignanesi
Designer: Andy Huckle
Textual Consultant: Nick de Somogyi
Originating Publisher: Emma Hayley

Published in 2007 by Amulet Books, an imprint of Harry N. Abrams, Inc.

Printed and bound in China
10 9 8 7 6 5 4 3 2 1

HNA
harry n. abrams, inc.
a subsidiary of La Martinière Groupe
115 West 18th Street
New York, NY 10011
www.hnabooks.com

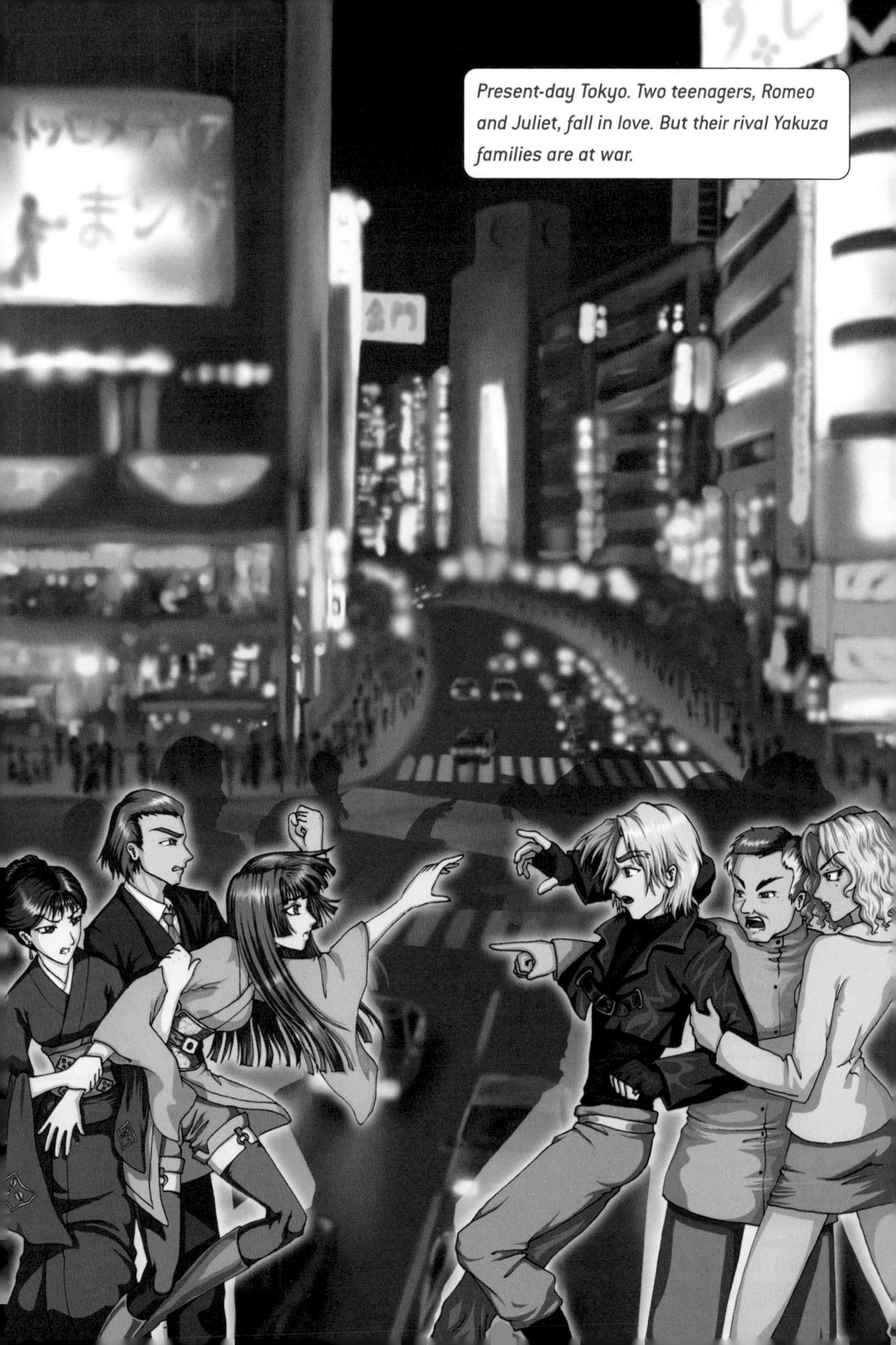
Present-day Tokyo. Two teenagers, Romeo and Juliet, fall in love. But their rival Yakuza families are at war.

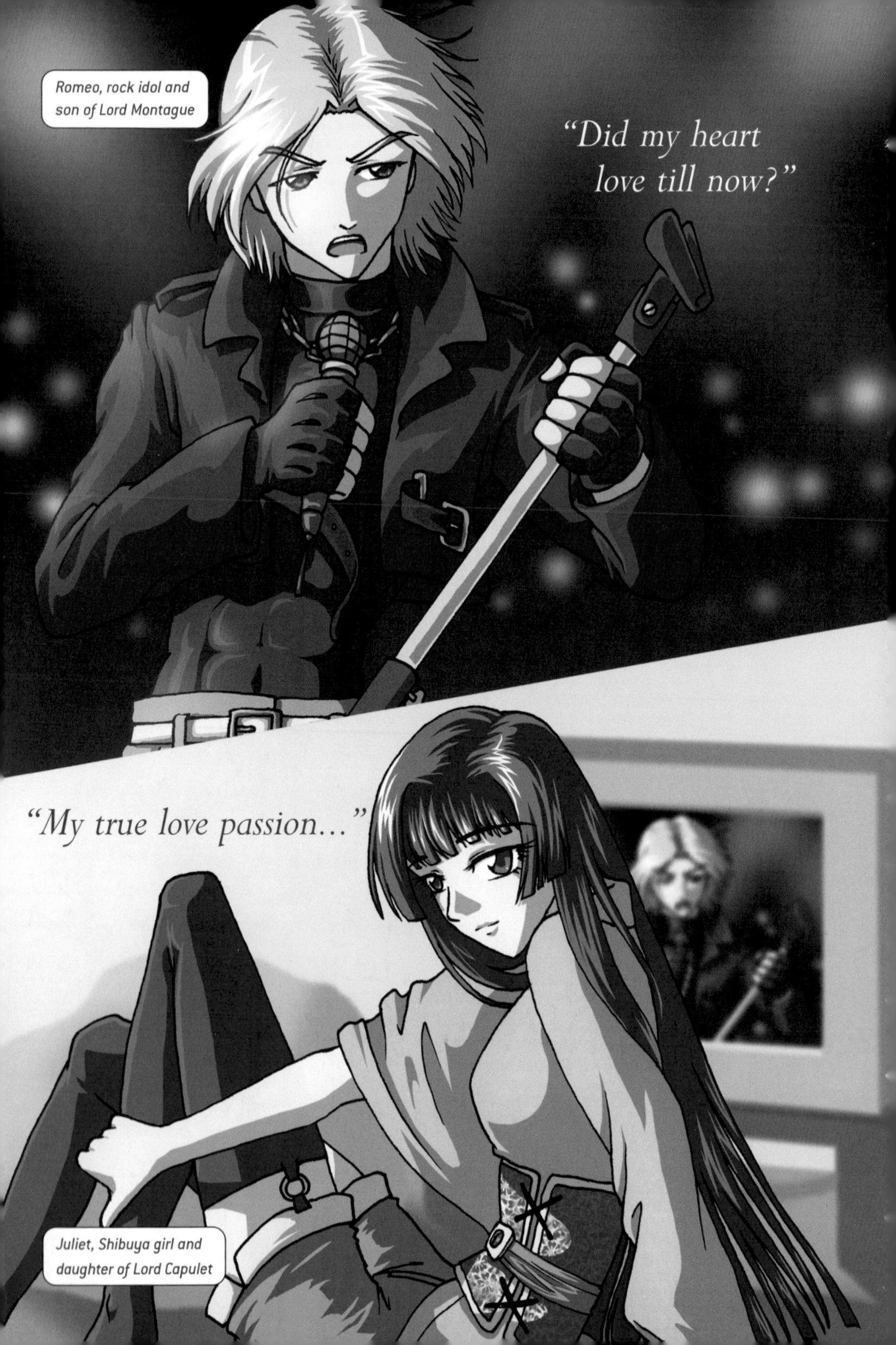
Romeo, rock idol and son of Lord Montague
"Did my heart love till now?"
"My true love passion..."
Juliet, Shibuya girl and daughter of Lord Capulet

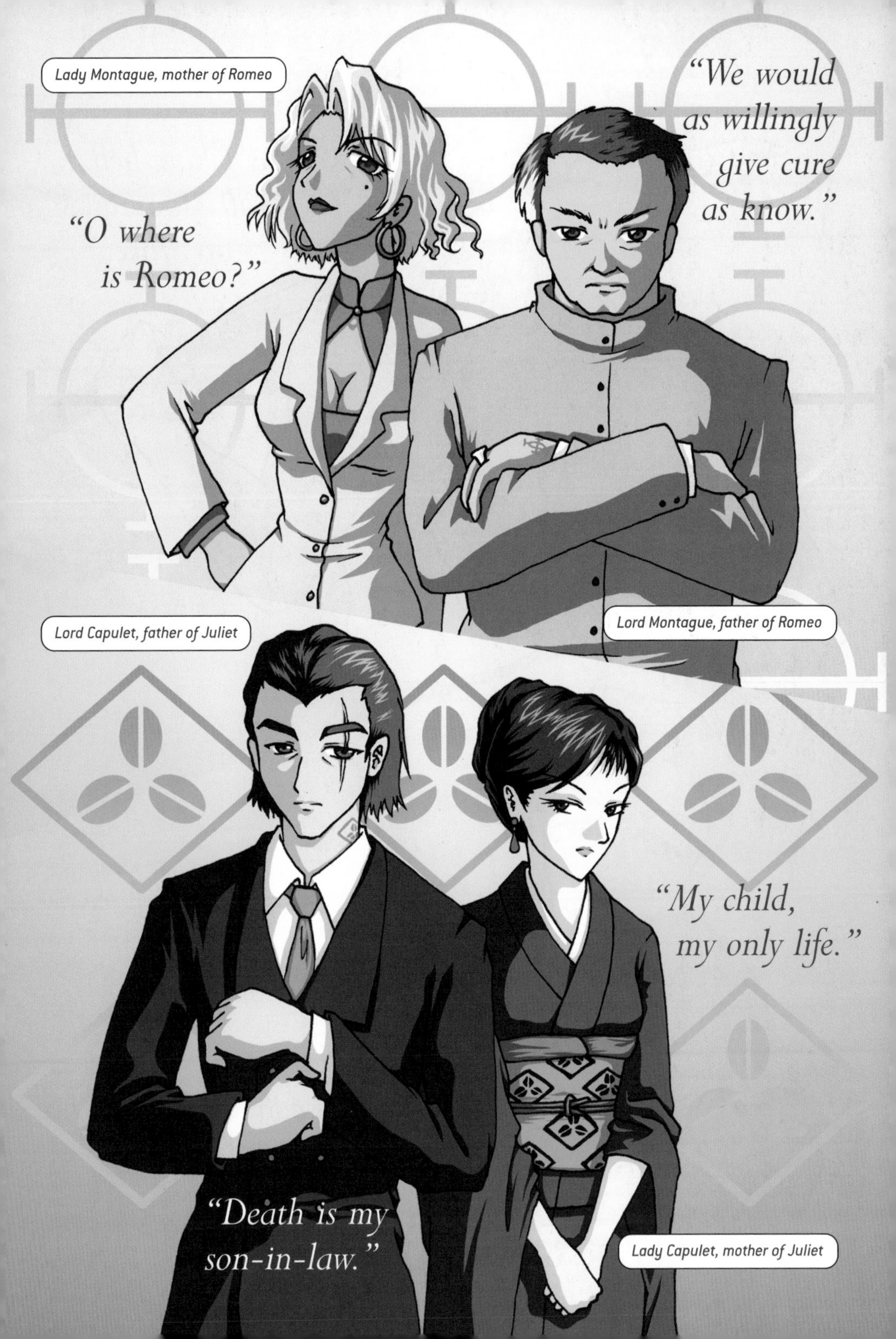
Lady Montague, mother of Romeo
"O where is Romeo?"
"We would as willingly give cure as know."
Lord Montague, father of Romeo
Lord Capulet, father of Juliet
"My child, my only life."
"Death is my son-in-law."
Lady Capulet, mother of Juliet

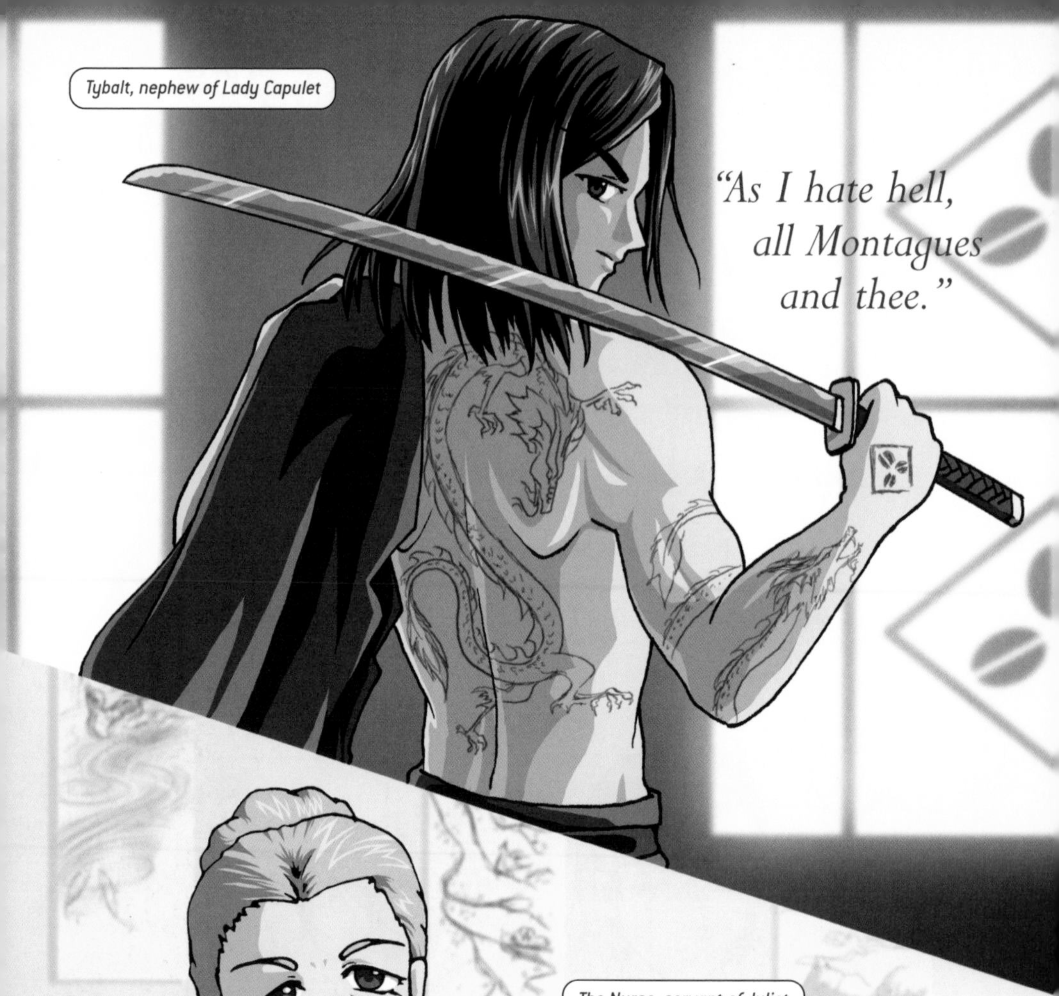
Tybalt, nephew of Lady Capulet
"As I hate hell, all Montagues and thee."
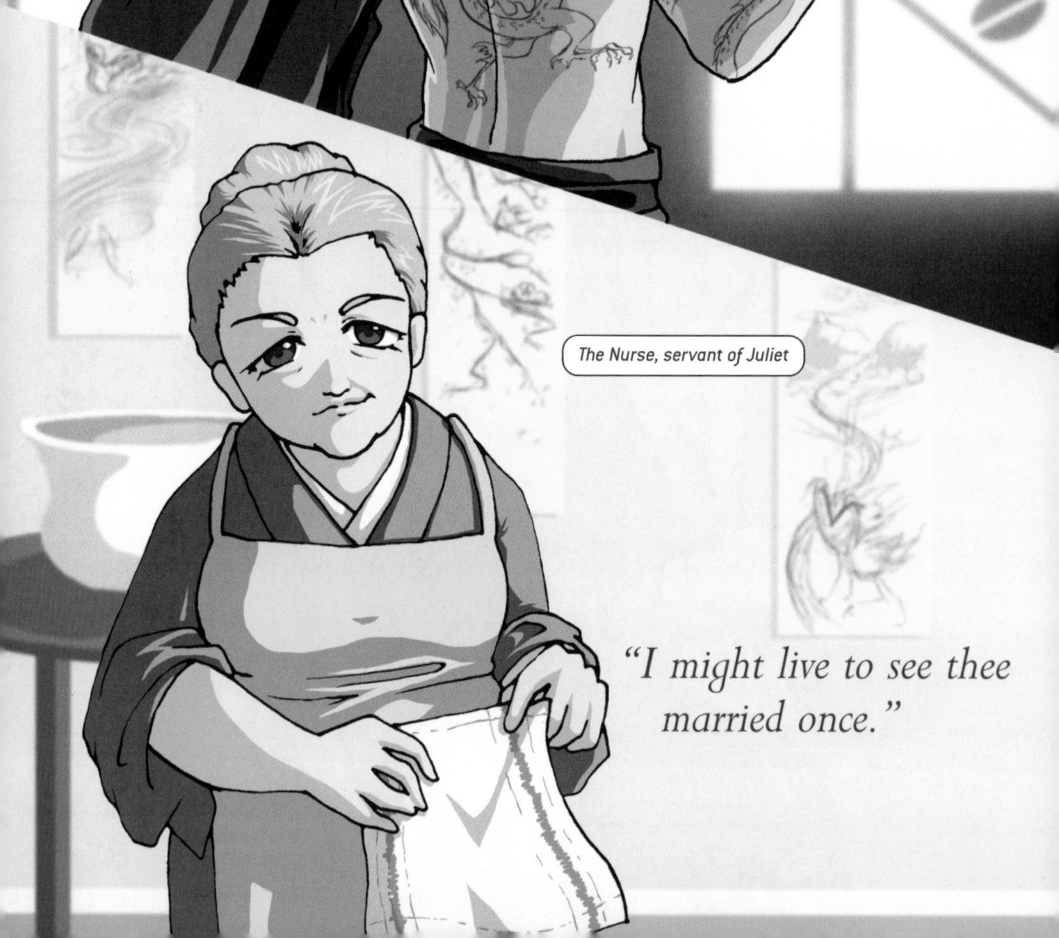
The Nurse, servant of Juliet
"I might live to see thee married once."

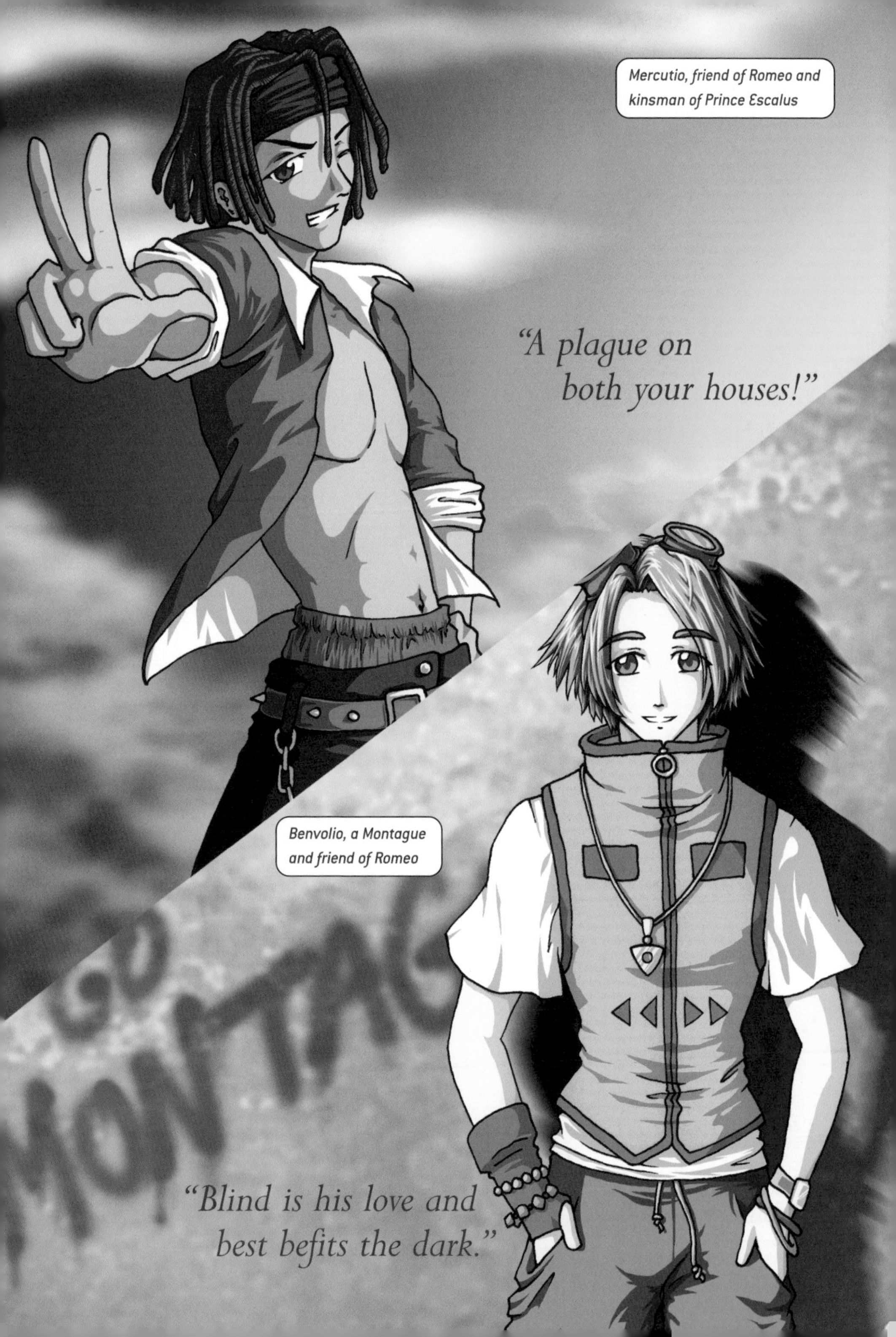
Mercutio, friend of Romeo and kinsman of Prince Escalus
"A plague on both your houses!"
Benvolio, a Montague and friend of Romeo
"Blind is his love and best befits the dark."

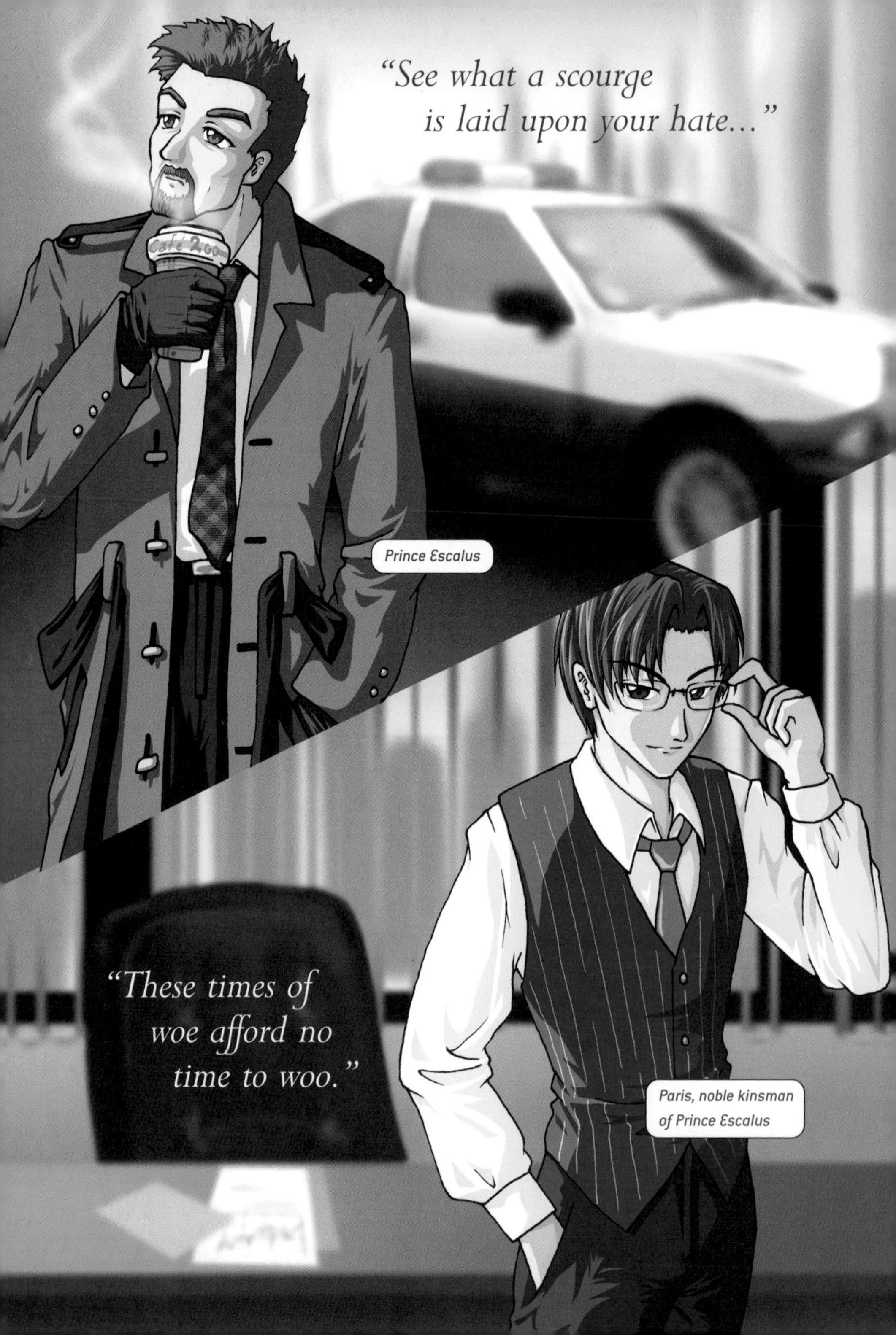
"See what a scourge is laid upon your hate..."
Café 2 Go
Prince Escalus
"These times of woe afford no time to woo."
Paris, noble kinsman of Prince Escalus

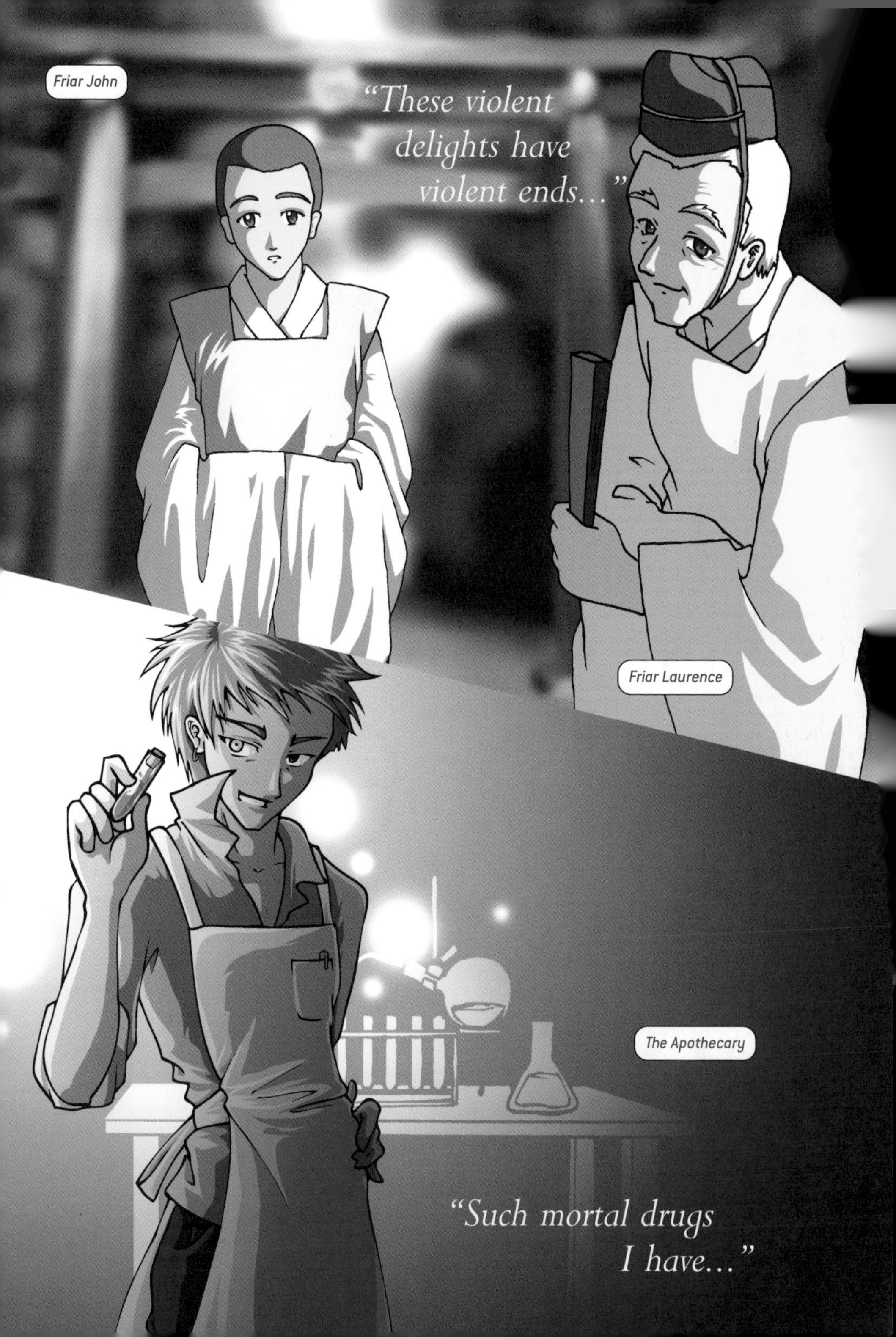
Friar John
"These violent delights have violent ends..."
Friar Laurence
The Apothecary
"Such mortal drugs I have..."

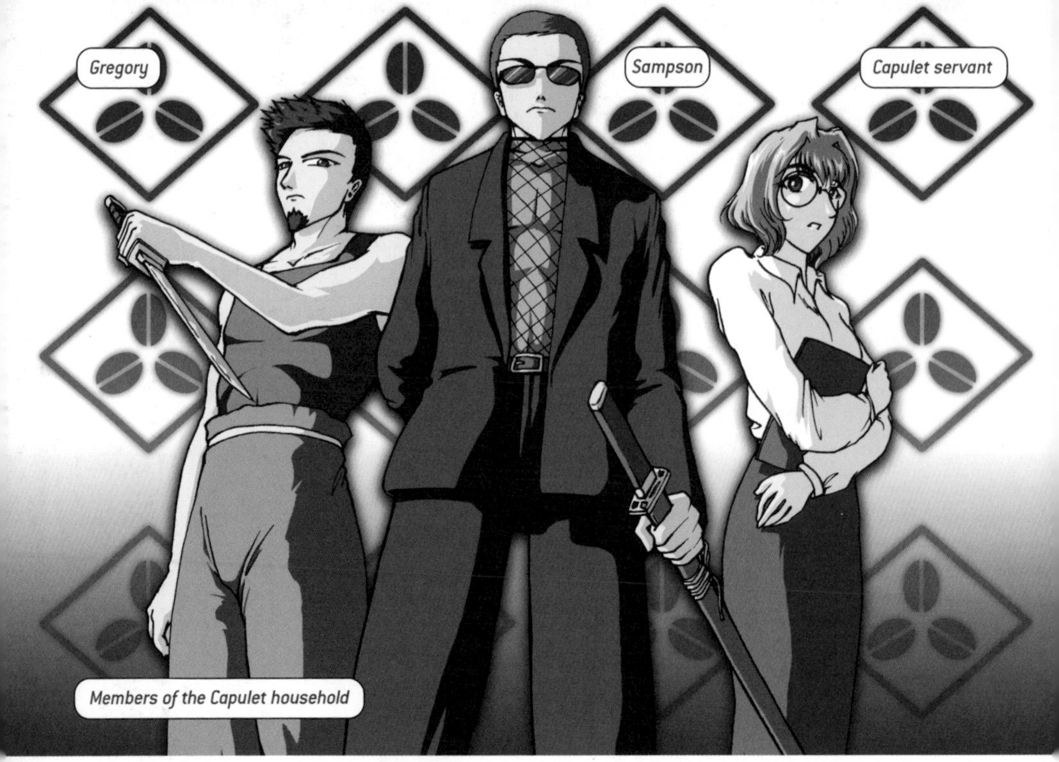
Gregory
Sampson
Capulet servant
Members of the Capulet household

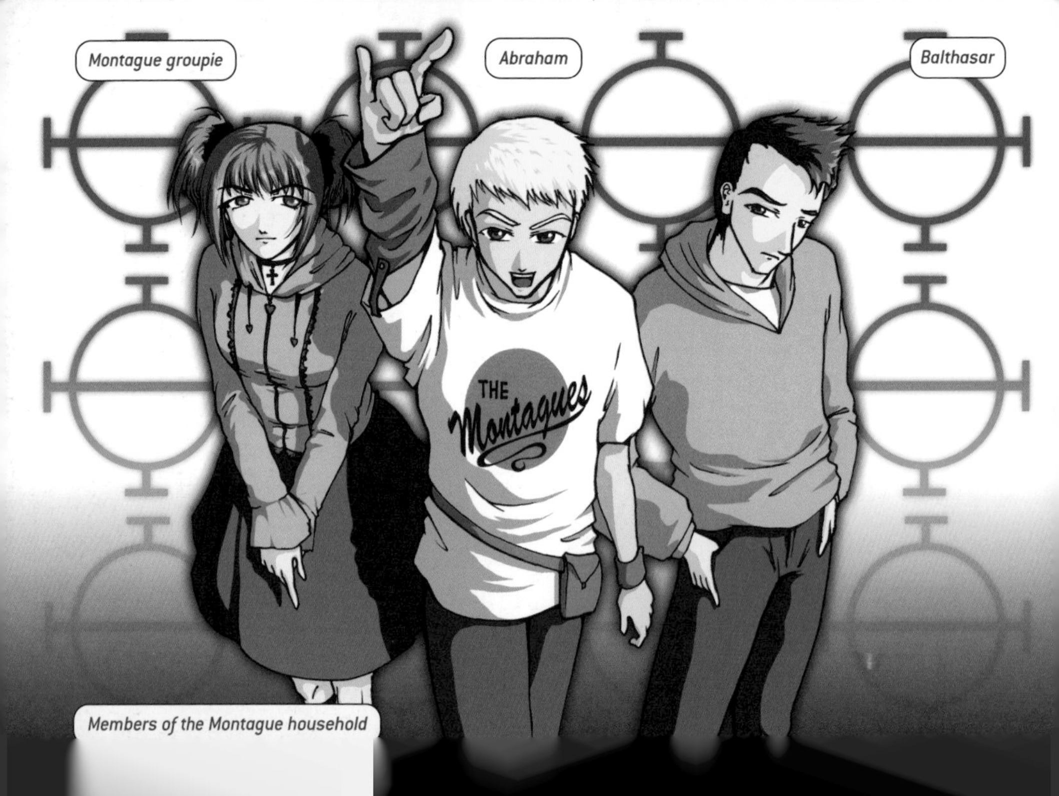
Montague groupie
Abraham
Balthasar
THE Montagues
Members of the Montague household

The Most Excellent and Lamentable Tragedy of

ROMEO AND JULIET

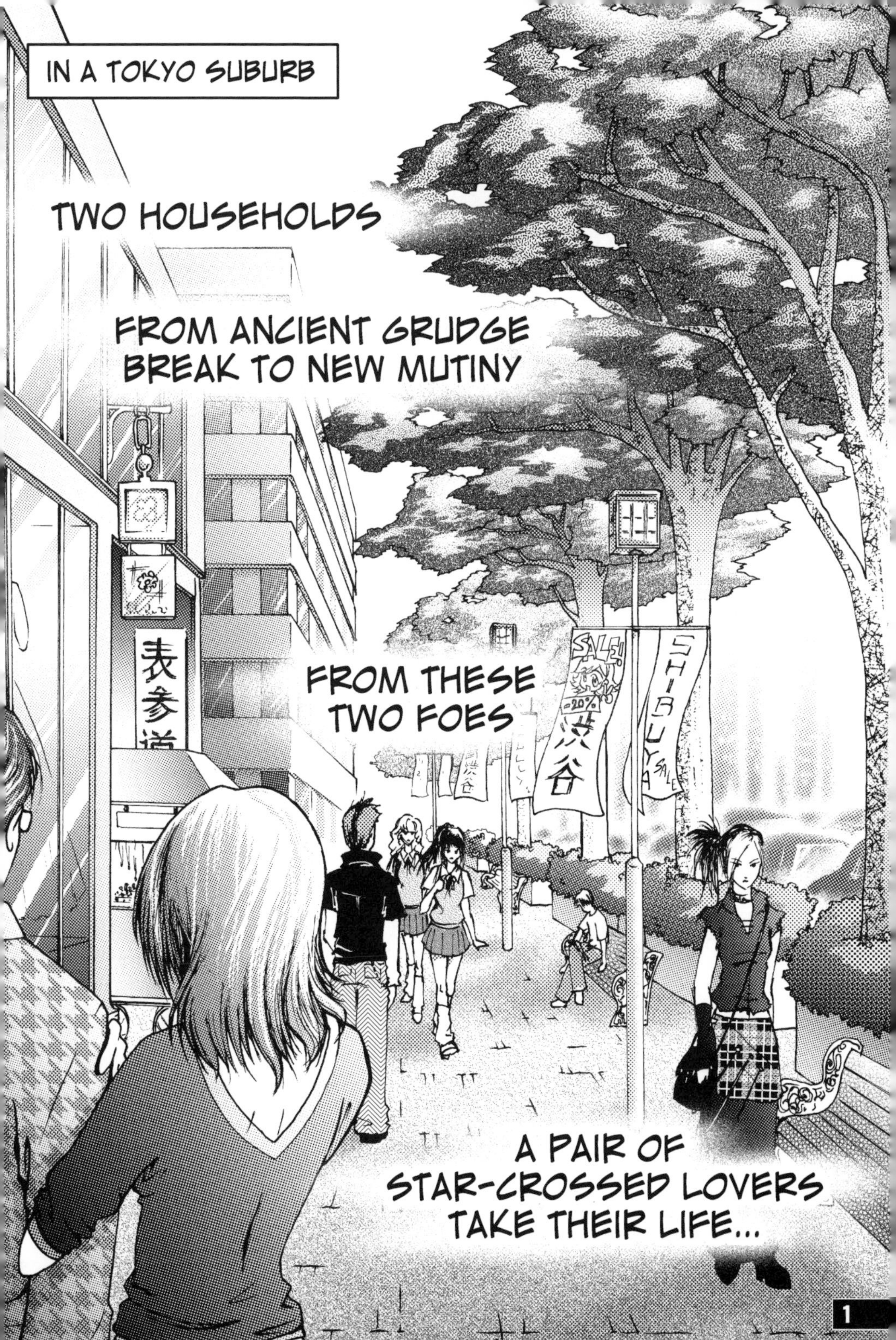
IN A TOKYO SUBURB
TWO HOUSEHOLDS
FROM ANCIENT GRUDGE BREAK TO NEW MUTINY
表参道
SALE!
-20%
渋谷
SHIBUYA
SALE
FROM THESE TWO FOES
A PAIR OF STAR-CROSSED LOVERS TAKE THEIR LIFE...

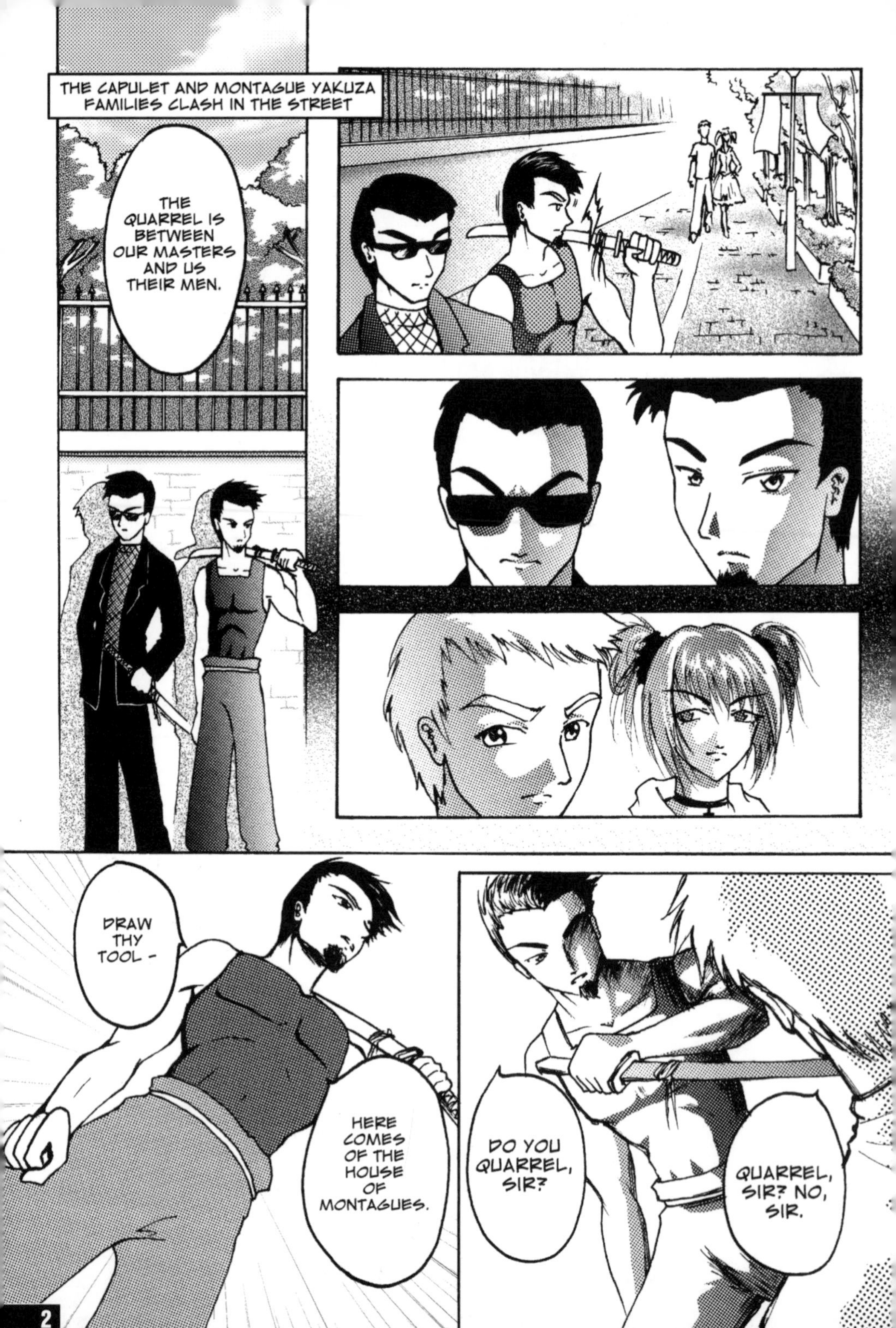
THE CAPULET AND MONTAGUE YAKUZA FAMILIES CLASH IN THE STREET
THE QUARREL IS BETWEEN OUR MASTERS AND US THEIR MEN.
DRAW THY TOOL -
HERE COMES OF THE HOUSE OF MONTAGUES.
DO YOU QUARREL, SIR?
QUARREL, SIR? NO, SIR.

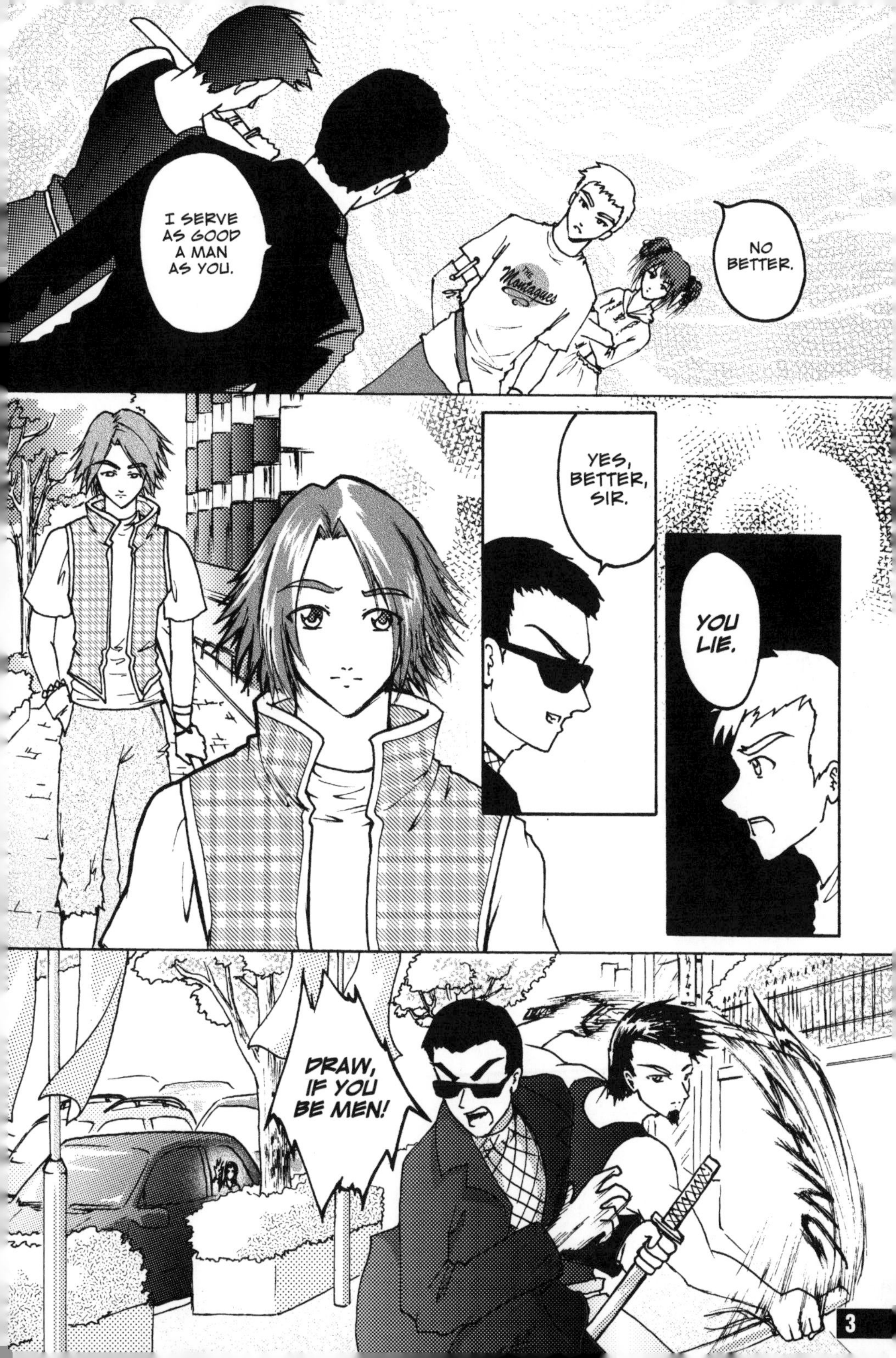
I SERVE AS GOOD A MAN AS YOU.
THE Montagues
NO BETTER.
YES, BETTER, SIR.
YOU LIE.
DRAW, IF YOU BE MEN!

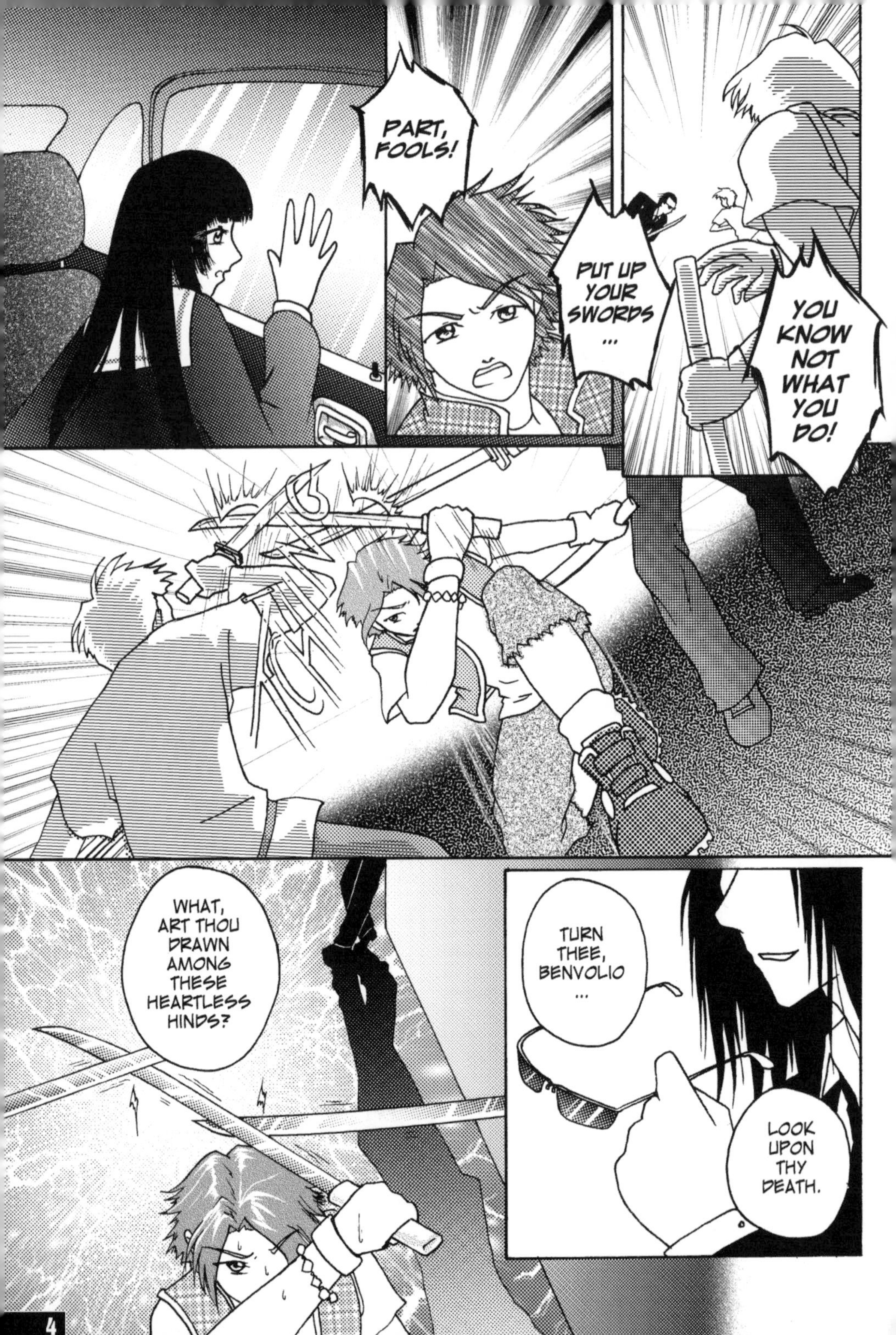
PART, FOOLS!
PUT UP YOUR SWORDS ...
YOU KNOW NOT WHAT YOU DO!
WHAT, ART THOU DRAWN AMONG THESE HEARTLESS HINDS?
TURN THEE, BENVOLIO ...
LOOK UPON THY DEATH.

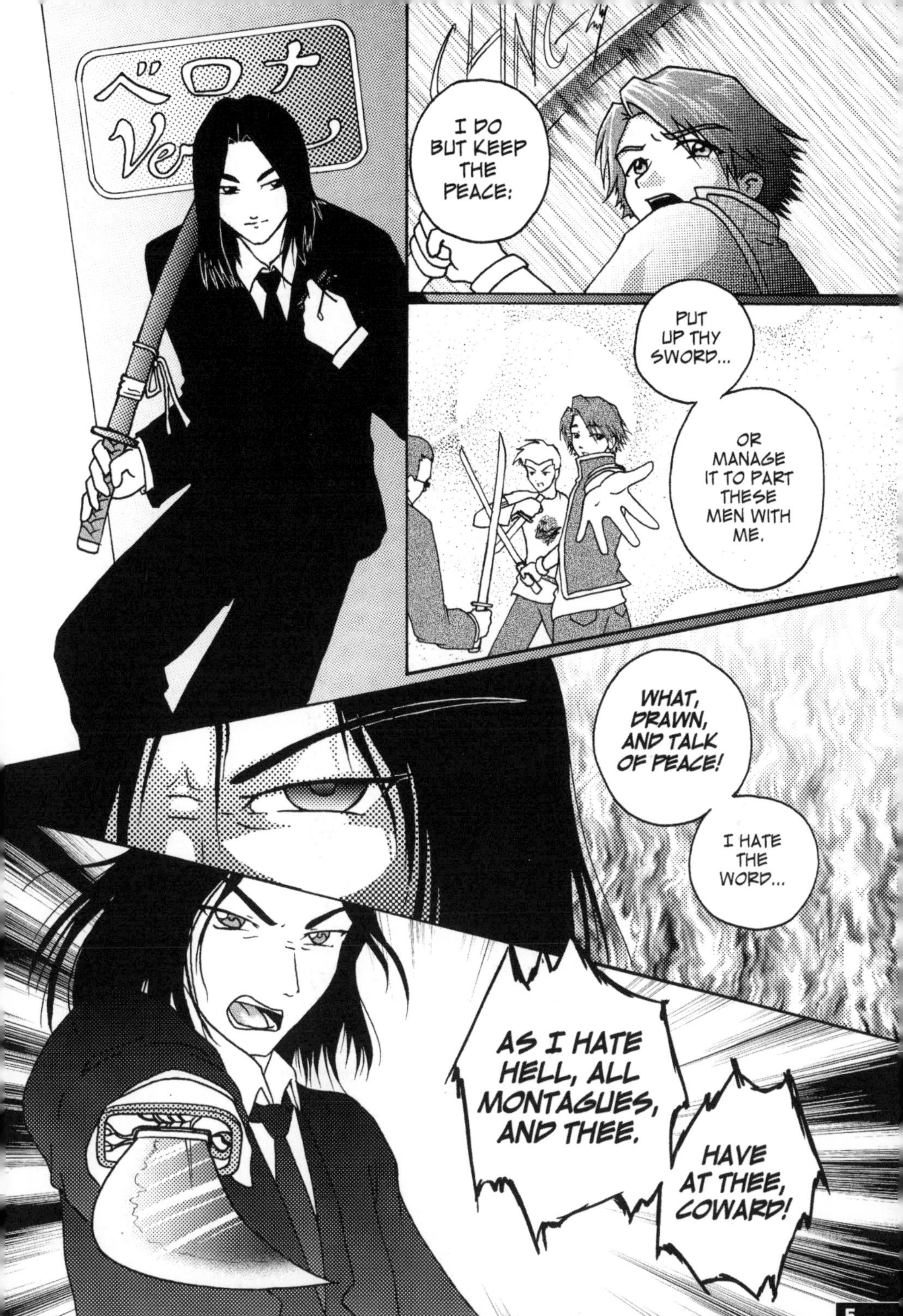
ベロナ
CLING
I DO BUT KEEP THE PEACE:
PUT UP THY SWORD...
OR MANAGE IT TO PART THESE MEN WITH ME.
WHAT, DRAWN, AND TALK OF PEACE!
I HATE THE WORD...
AS I HATE HELL, ALL MONTAGUES, AND THEE.
HAVE AT THEE, COWARD!

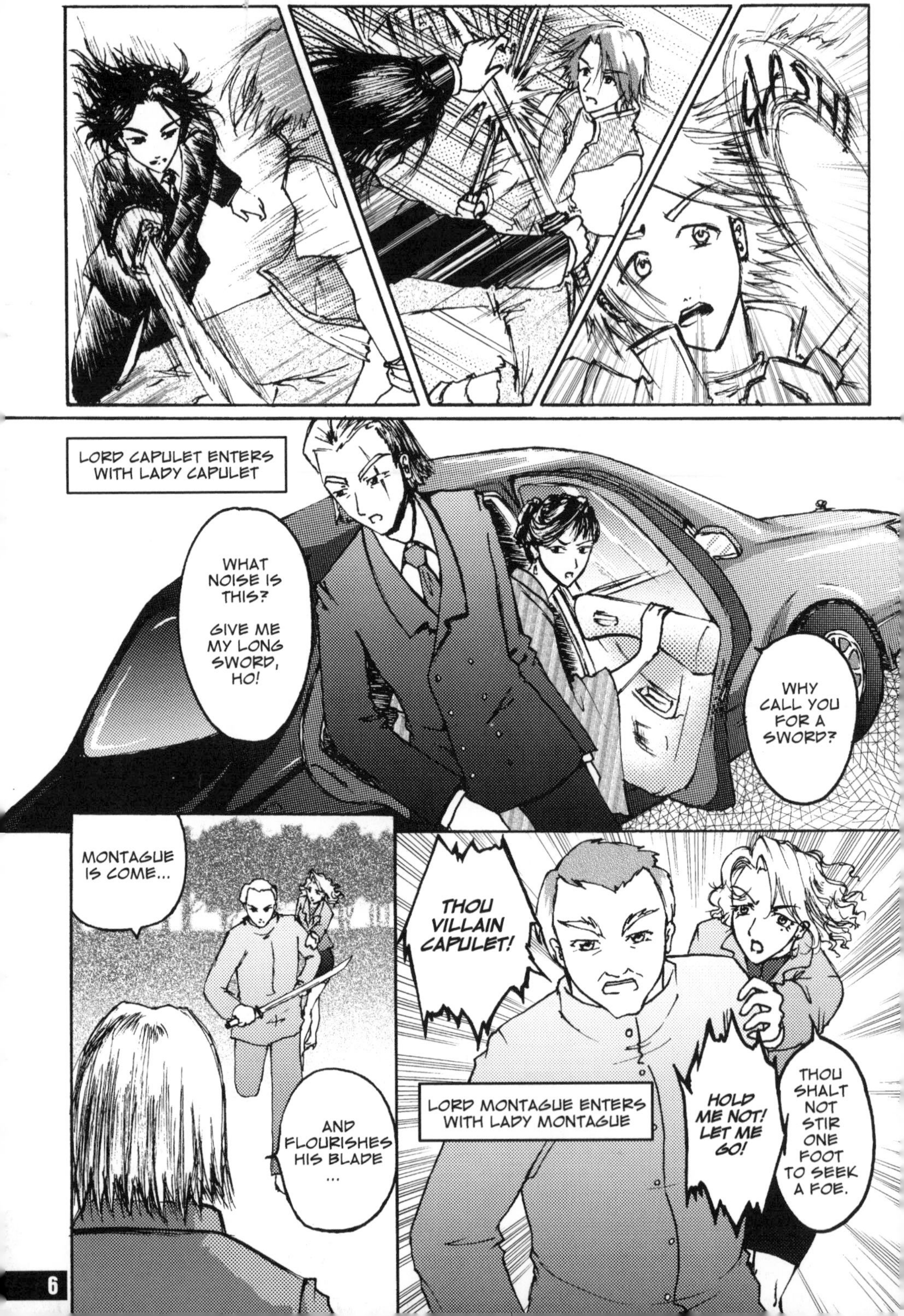
GASH!
LORD CAPULET ENTERS WITH LADY CAPULET
WHAT NOISE IS THIS? GIVE ME MY LONG SWORD, HO!
WHY CALL YOU FOR A SWORD?
MONTAGUE IS COME...
AND FLOURISHES HIS BLADE ...
THOU VILLAIN CAPULET!
LORD MONTAGUE ENTERS WITH LADY MONTAGUE
HOLD ME NOT! LET ME GO!
THOU SHALT NOT STIR ONE FOOT TO SEEK A FOE.

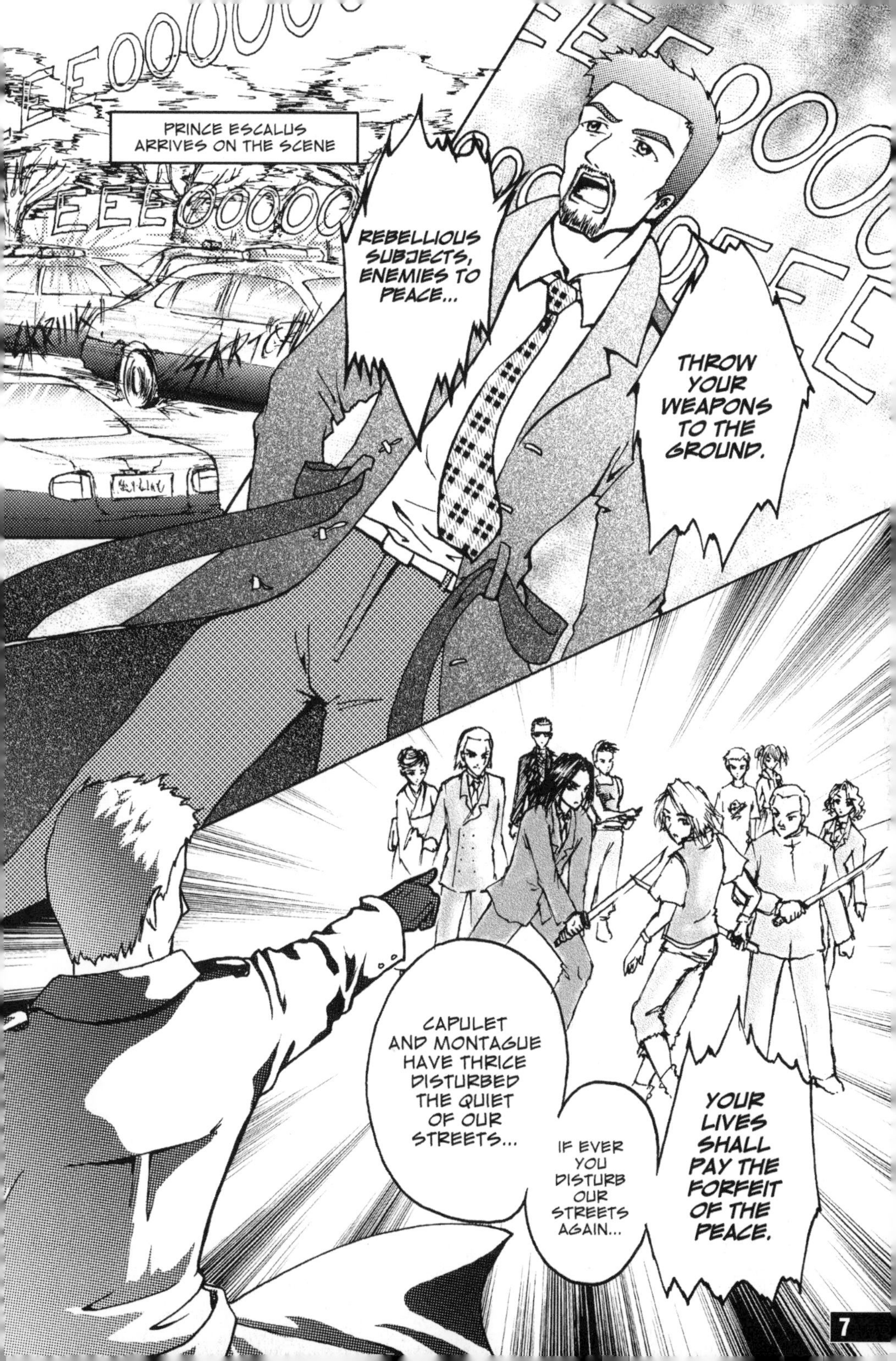
EEEOOOOO
PRINCE ESCALUS ARRIVES ON THE SCENE
EEEOOOOO
EEEOOOOO
REBELLIOUS SUBJECTS, ENEMIES TO PEACE...
THROW YOUR WEAPONS TO THE GROUND.
CAPULET AND MONTAGUE HAVE THRICE DISTURBED THE QUIET OF OUR STREETS...
IF EVER YOU DISTURB OUR STREETS AGAIN...
YOUR LIVES SHALL PAY THE FORFEIT OF THE PEACE.

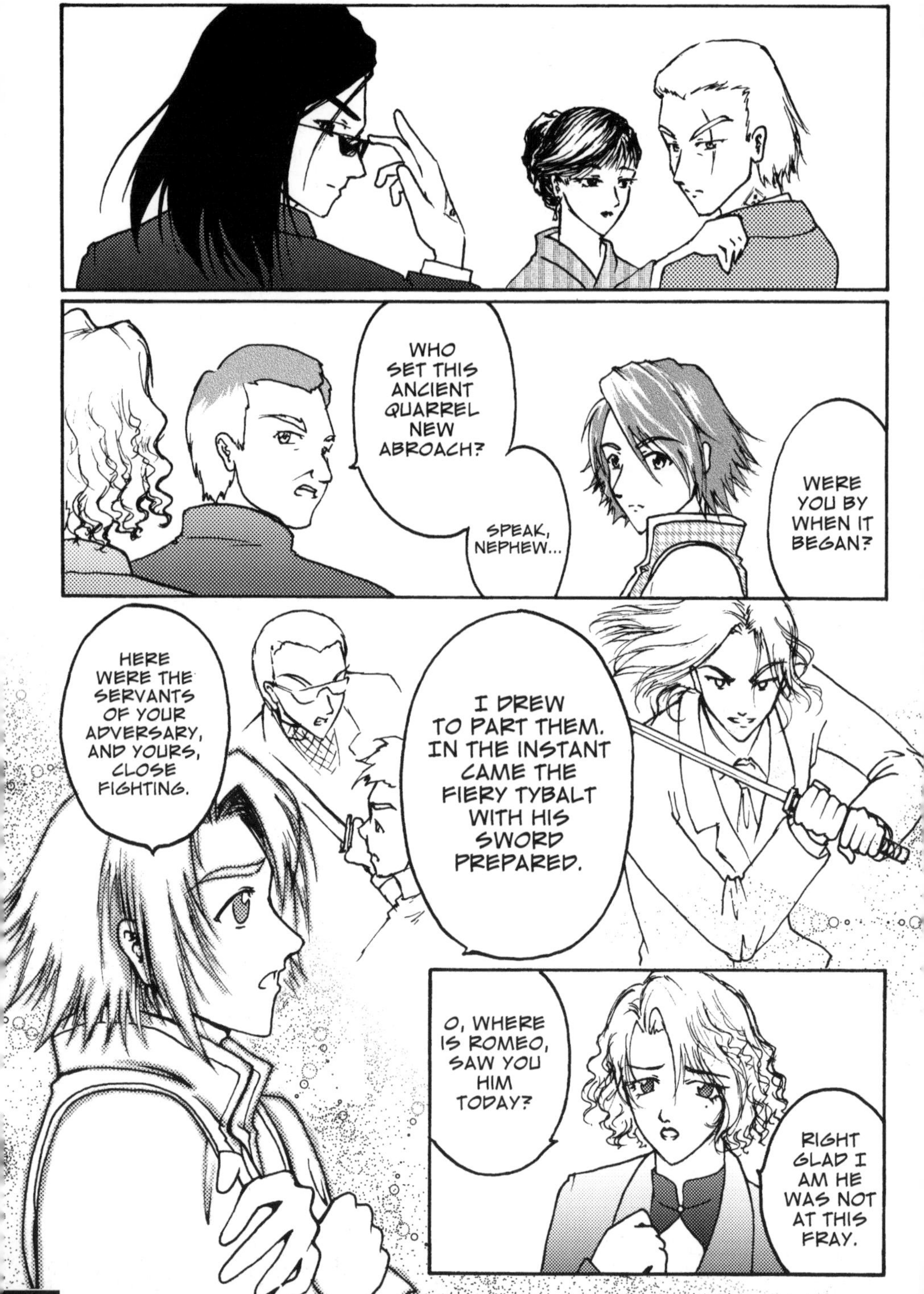
WHO SET THIS ANCIENT QUARREL NEW ABROACH?
SPEAK, NEPHEW...
WERE YOU BY WHEN IT BEGAN?
HERE WERE THE SERVANTS OF YOUR ADVERSARY, AND YOURS, CLOSE FIGHTING.
I DREW TO PART THEM. IN THE INSTANT CAME THE FIERY TYBALT WITH HIS SWORD PREPARED.
O, WHERE IS ROMEO, SAW YOU HIM TODAY?
RIGHT GLAD I AM HE WAS NOT AT THIS FRAY.

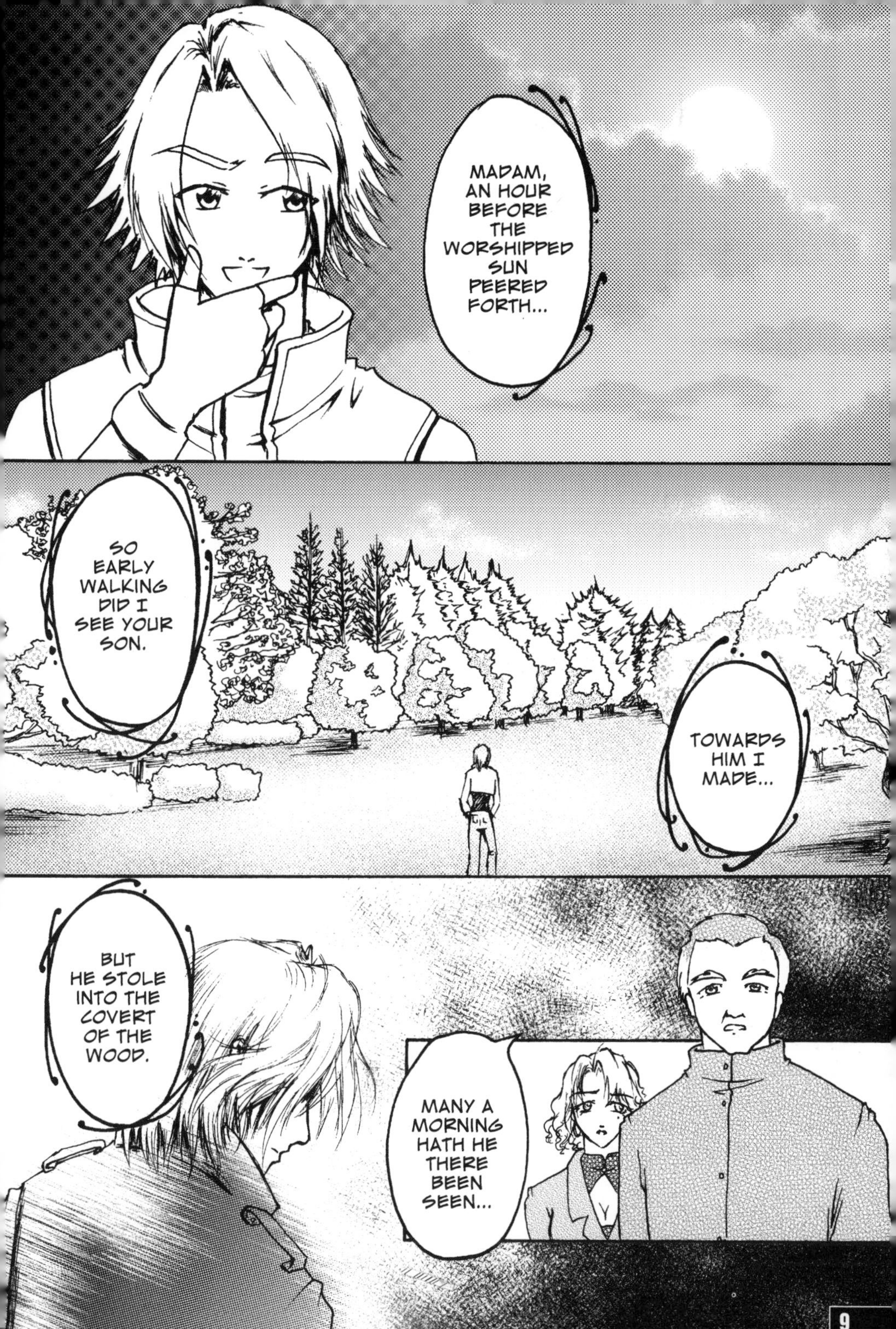
MADAM, AN HOUR BEFORE THE WORSHIPPED SUN PEERED FORTH...
SO EARLY WALKING DID I SEE YOUR SON.
TOWARDS HIM I MADE...
BUT HE STOLE INTO THE COVERT OF THE WOOD.
MANY A MORNING HATH HE THERE BEEN SEEN...

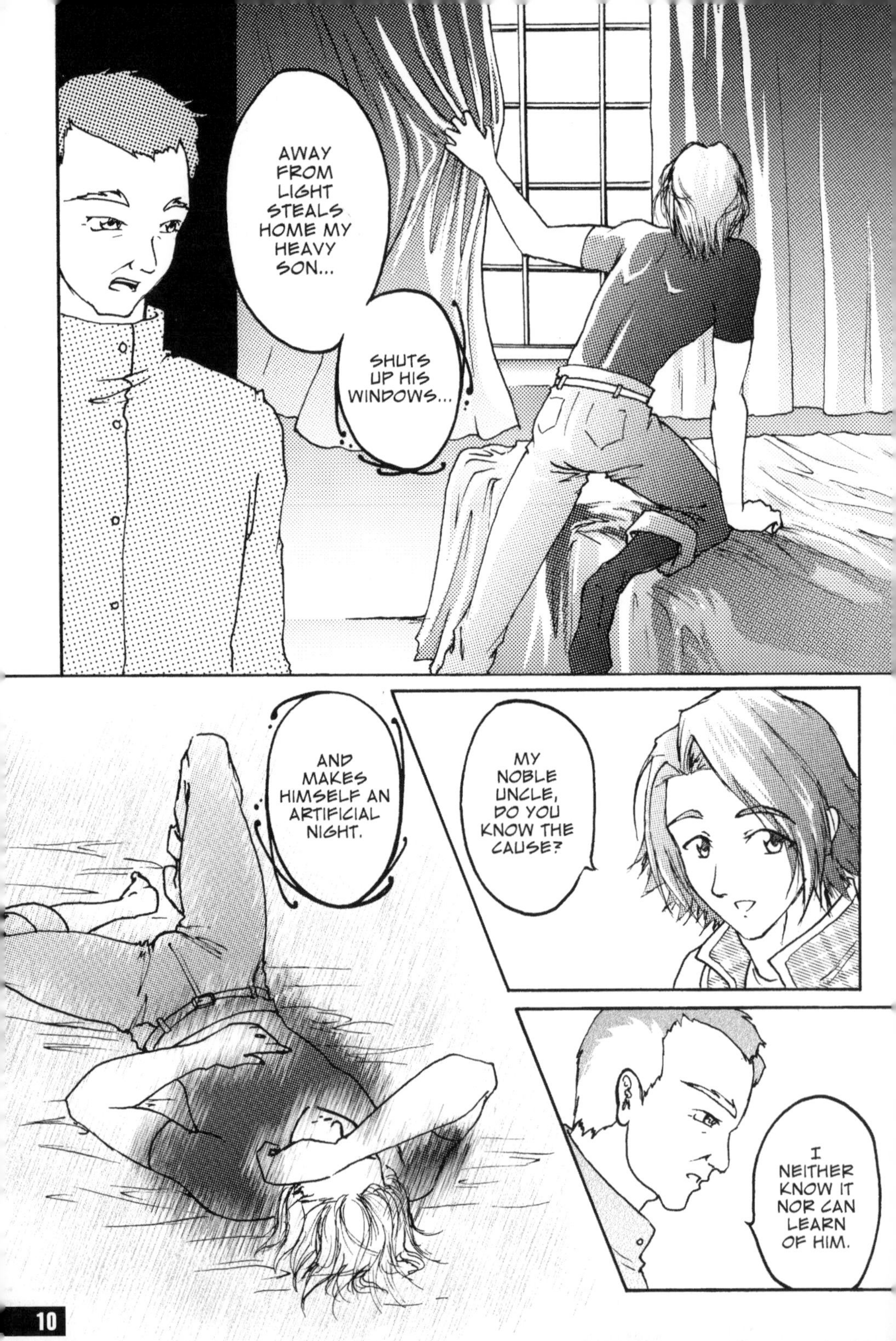
AWAY FROM LIGHT STEALS HOME MY HEAVY SON...
SHUTS UP HIS WINDOWS...
AND MAKES HIMSELF AN ARTIFICIAL NIGHT.
MY NOBLE UNCLE, DO YOU KNOW THE CAUSE?
I NEITHER KNOW IT NOR CAN LEARN OF HIM.

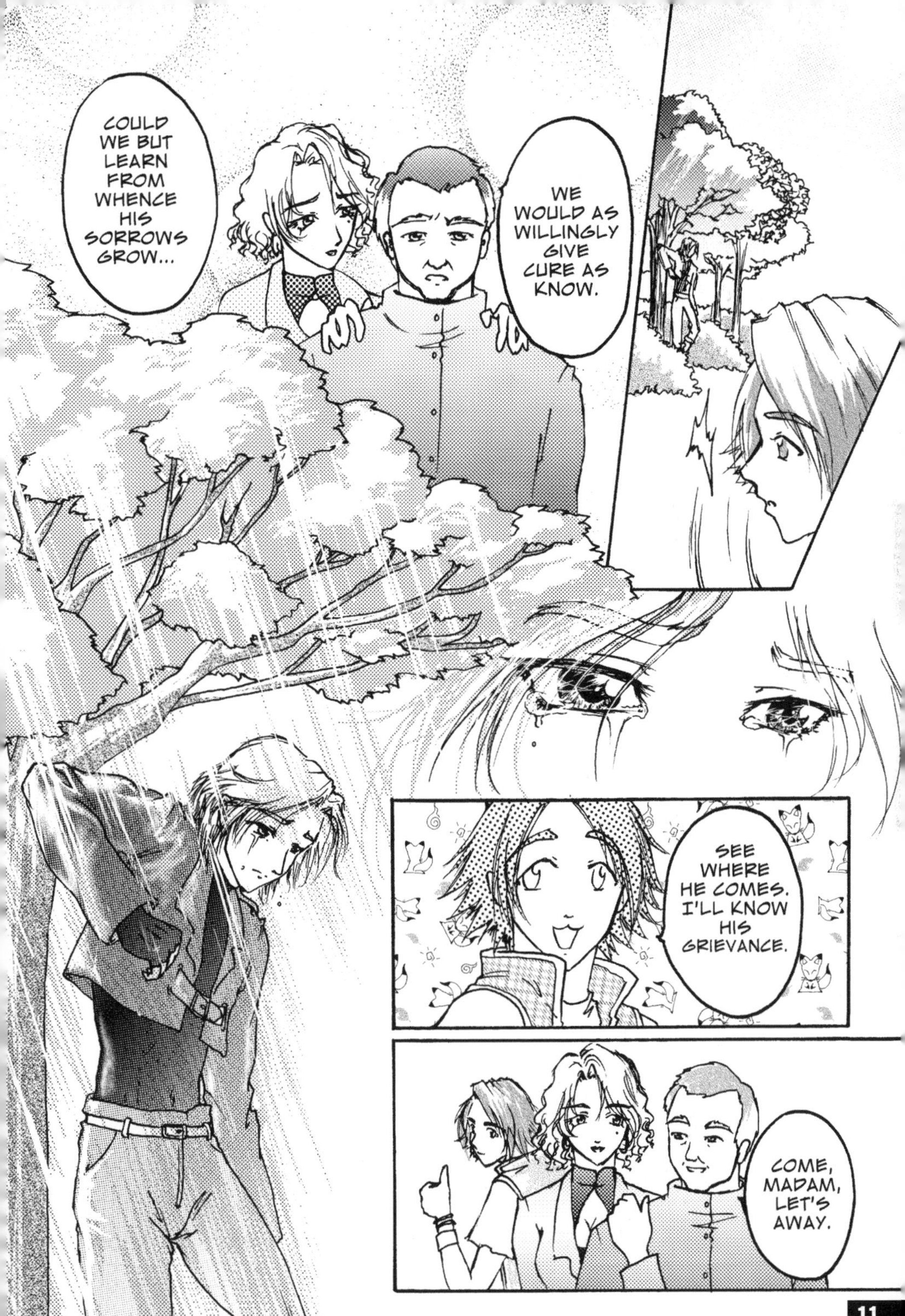
COULD WE BUT LEARN FROM WHENCE HIS SORROWS GROW...
WE WOULD AS WILLINGLY GIVE CURE AS KNOW.
SEE WHERE HE COMES. I'LL KNOW HIS GRIEVANCE.
COME, MADAM, LET'S AWAY.

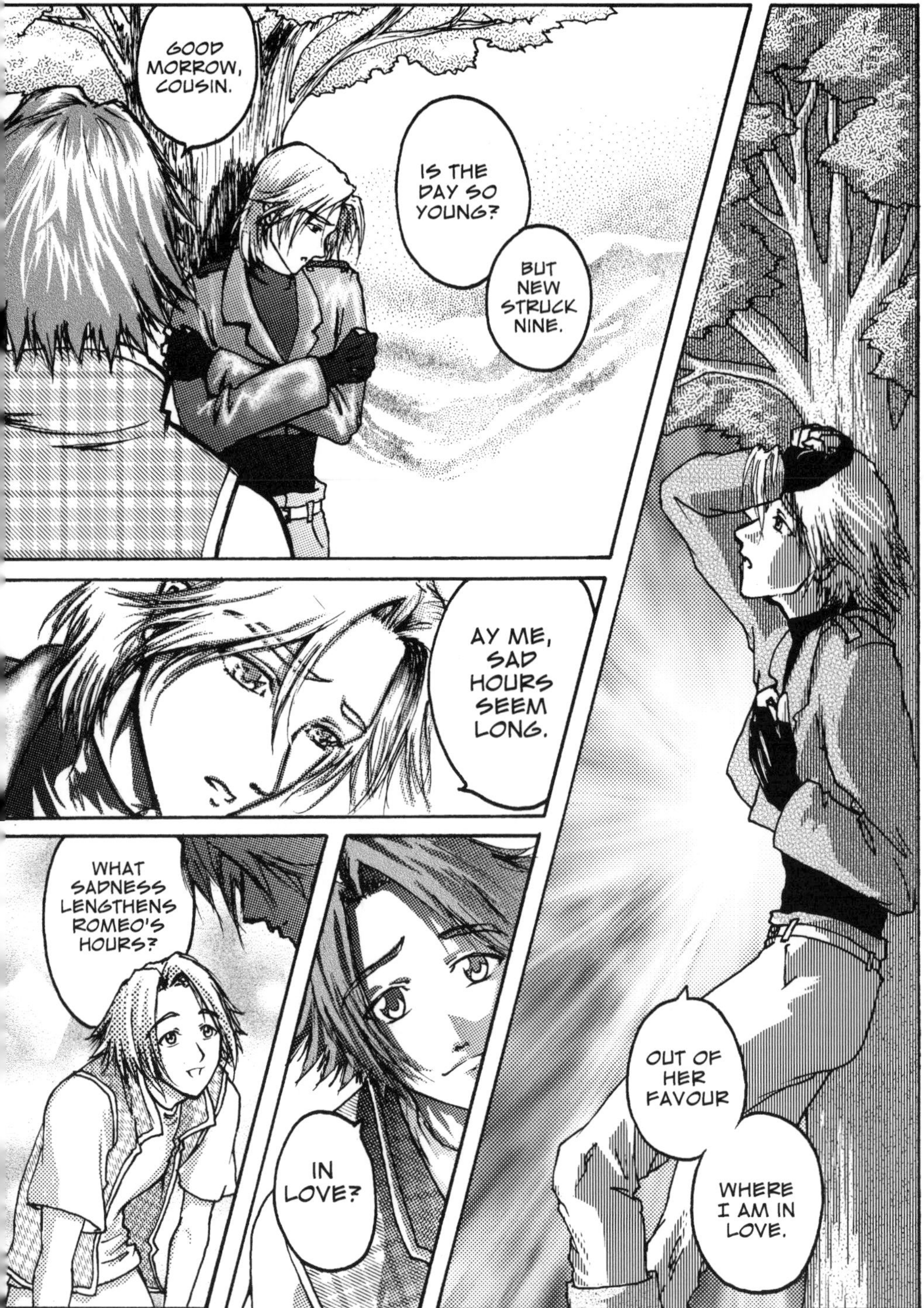
GOOD MORROW, COUSIN.
IS THE DAY SO YOUNG?
BUT NEW STRUCK NINE.
AY ME, SAD HOURS SEEM LONG.
WHAT SADNESS LENGTHENS ROMEO'S HOURS?
IN LOVE?
OUT OF HER FAVOUR
WHERE I AM IN LOVE.

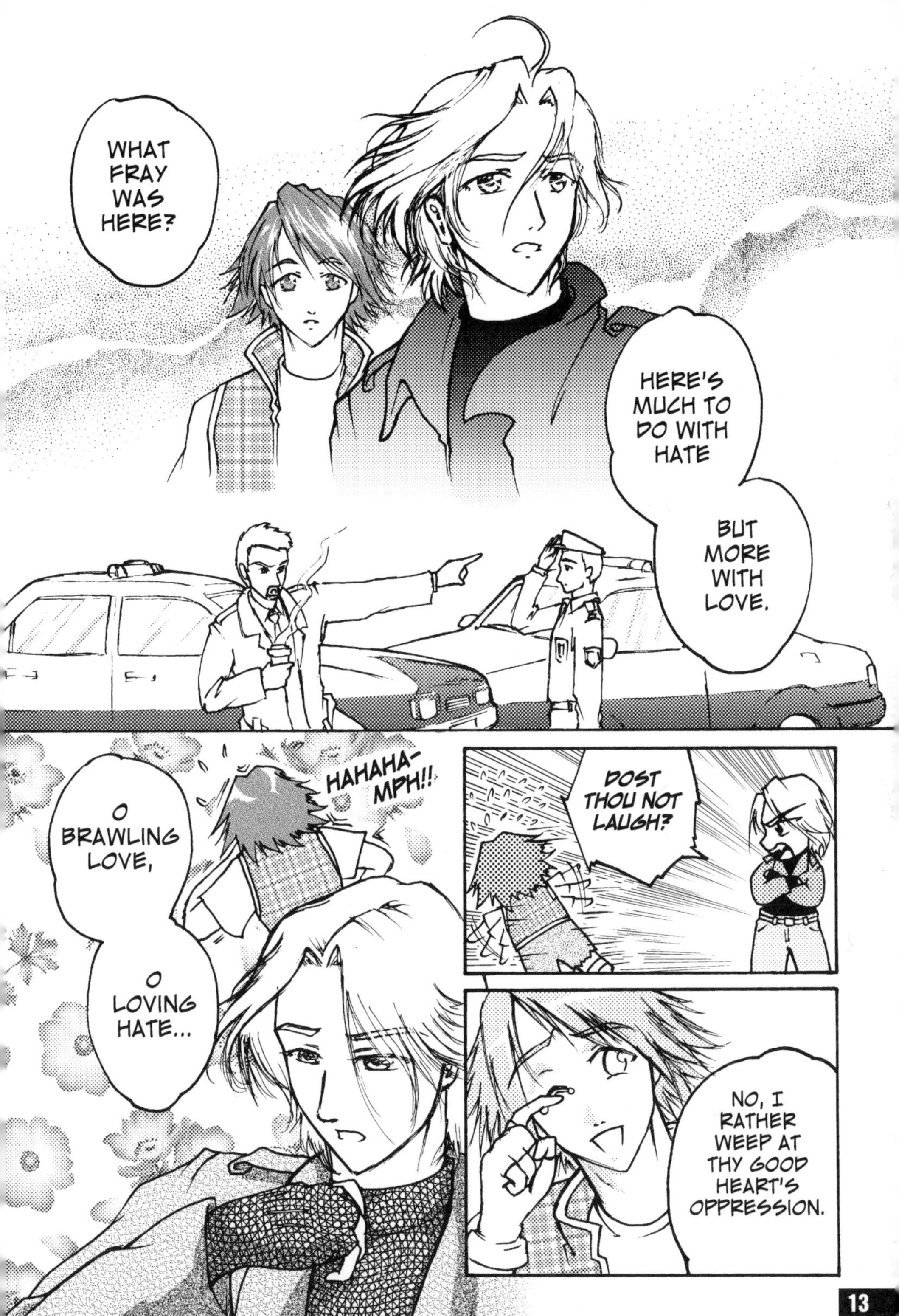
WHAT FRAY WAS HERE?
HERE'S MUCH TO DO WITH HATE
BUT MORE WITH LOVE.
O BRAWLING LOVE,
HAHAHA-MPH!!
O LOVING HATE...
DOST THOU NOT LAUGH?
NO, I RATHER WEEP AT THY GOOD HEART'S OPPRESSION.

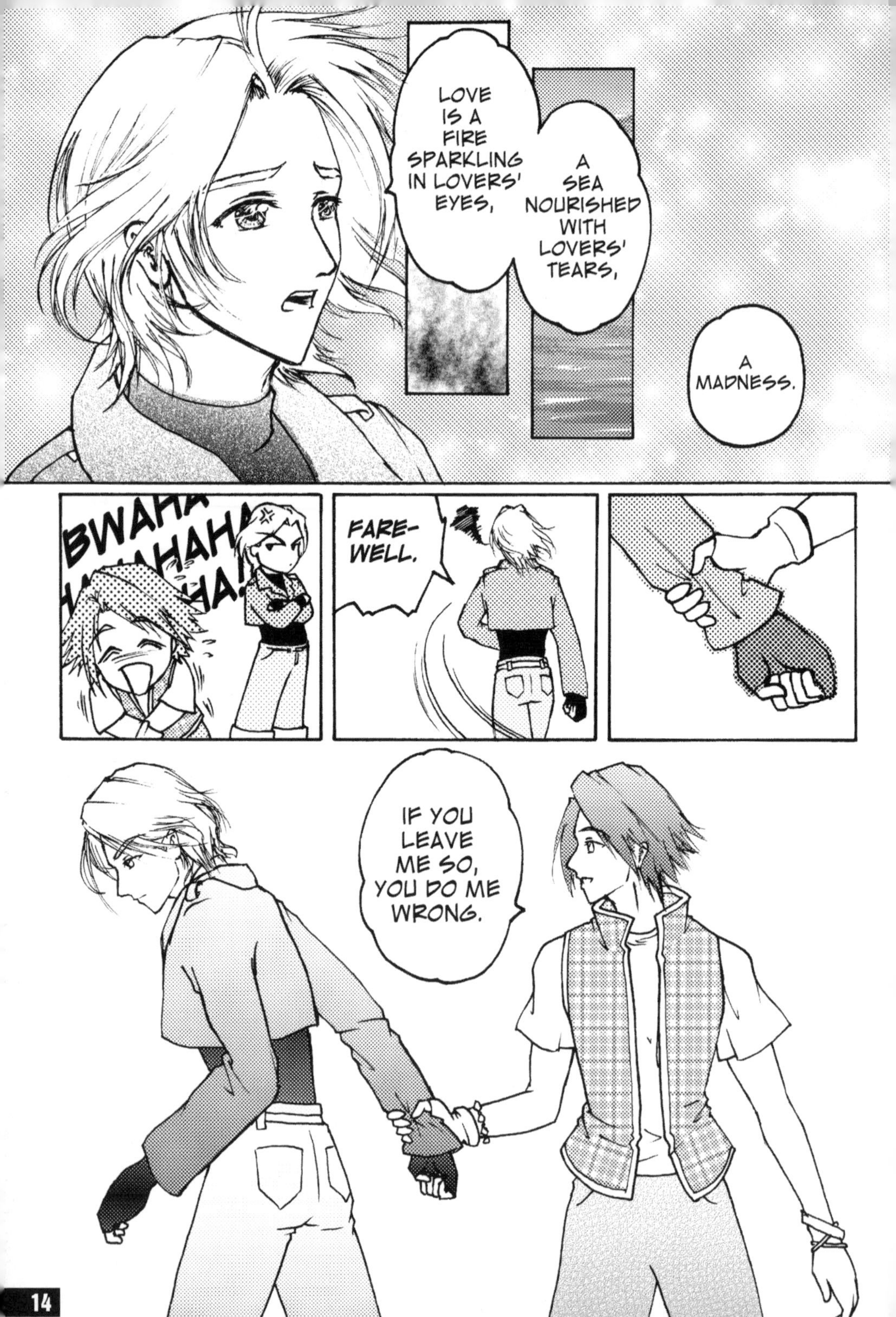
LOVE IS A FIRE SPARKLING IN LOVERS' EYES,
A SEA NOURISHED WITH LOVERS' TEARS,
A MADNESS.
BWAHAHAHAHAHAHA!
FARE-WELL.
IF YOU LEAVE ME SO, YOU DO ME WRONG.

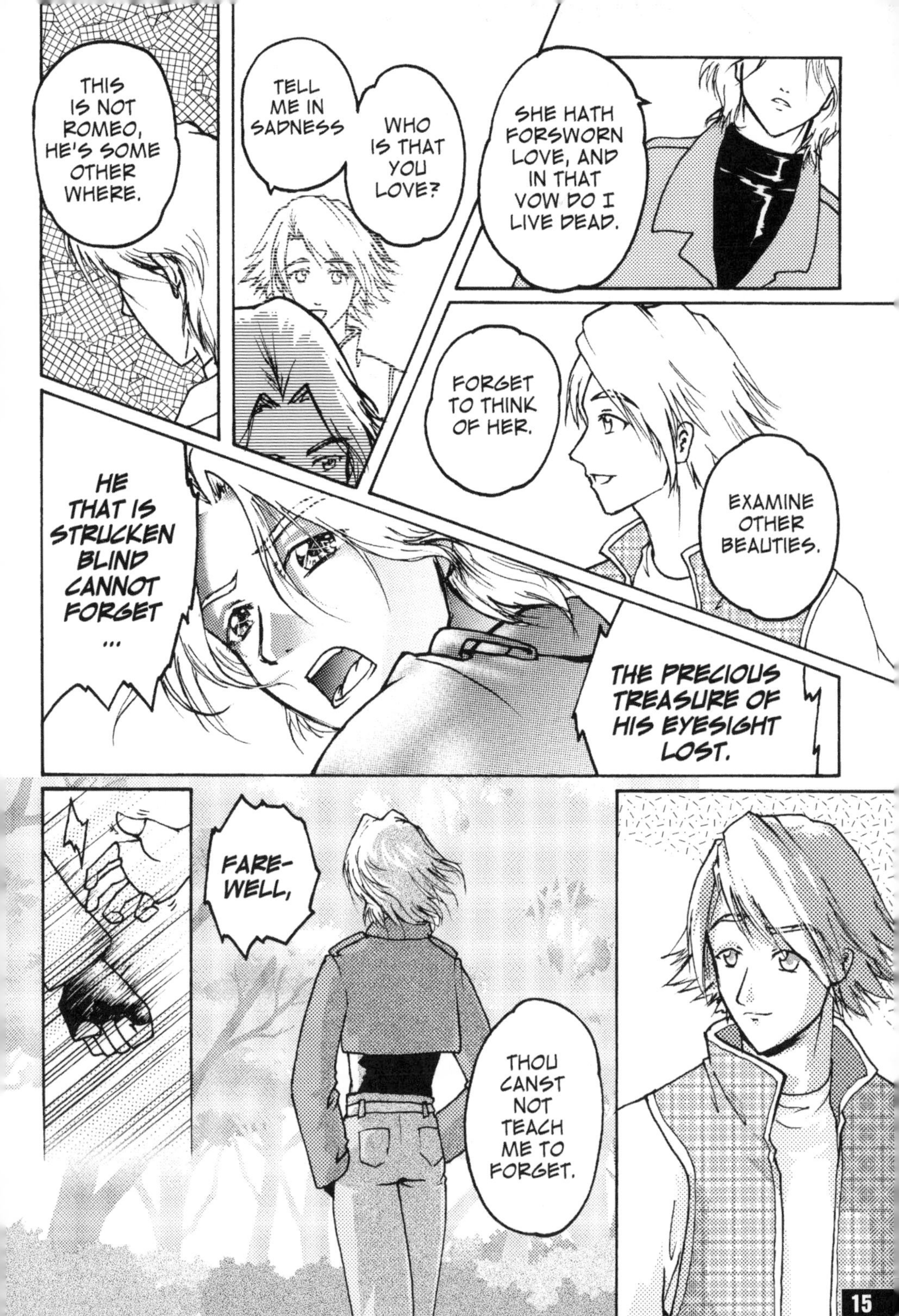
THIS IS NOT ROMEO, HE'S SOME OTHER WHERE.
TELL ME IN SADNESS
WHO IS THAT YOU LOVE?
SHE HATH FORSWORN LOVE, AND IN THAT VOW DO I LIVE DEAD.
FORGET TO THINK OF HER.
EXAMINE OTHER BEAUTIES.
HE THAT IS STRUCKEN BLIND CANNOT FORGET ...
THE PRECIOUS TREASURE OF HIS EYESIGHT LOST.
FARE-WELL,
THOU CANST NOT TEACH ME TO FORGET.

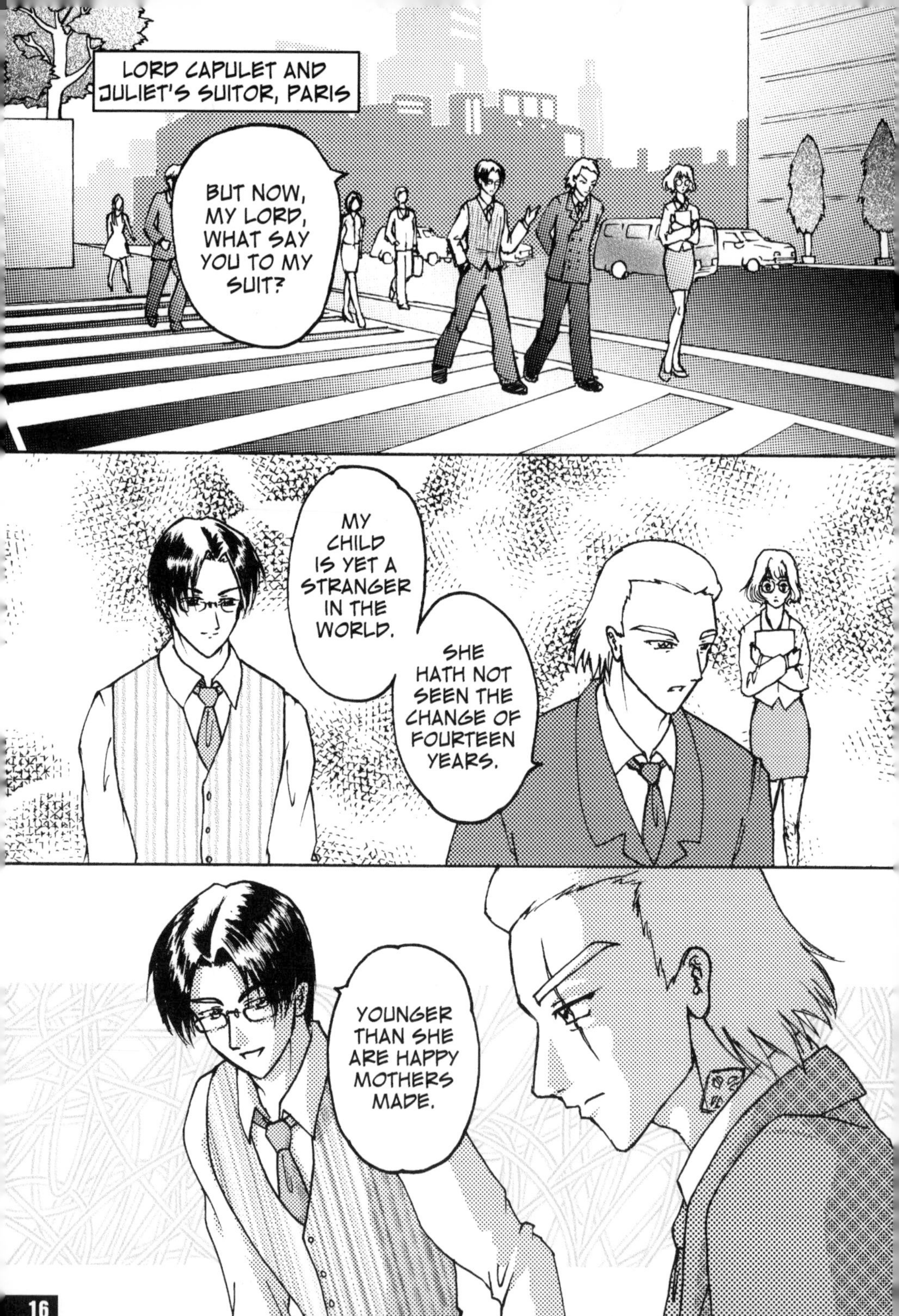
LORD CAPULET AND JULIET'S SUITOR, PARIS
BUT NOW, MY LORD, WHAT SAY YOU TO MY SUIT?
MY CHILD IS YET A STRANGER IN THE WORLD.
SHE HATH NOT SEEN THE CHANGE OF FOURTEEN YEARS.
YOUNGER THAN SHE ARE HAPPY MOTHERS MADE.

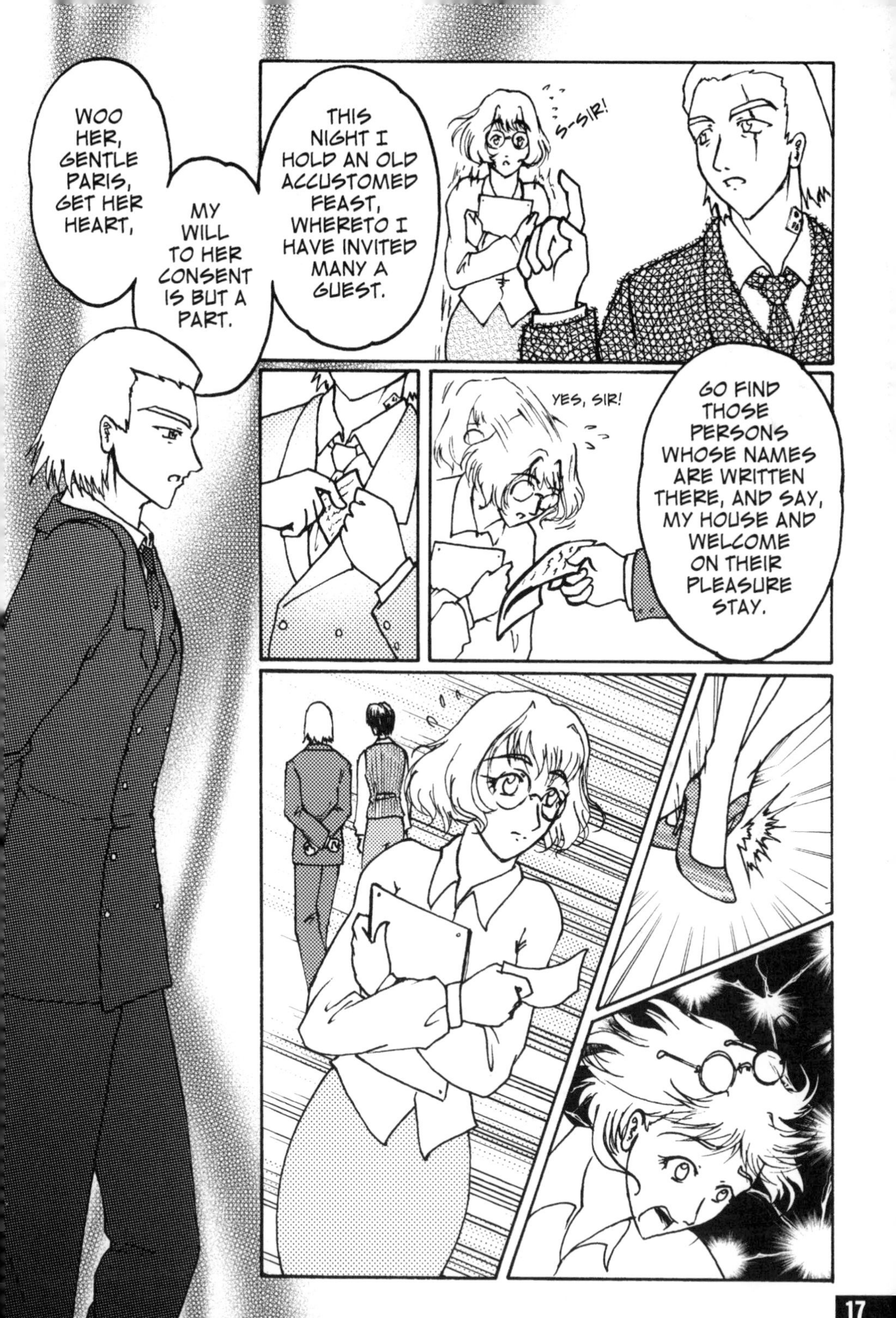
WOO HER, GENTLE PARIS, GET HER HEART,
MY WILL TO HER CONSENT IS BUT A PART.
THIS NIGHT I HOLD AN OLD ACCUSTOMED FEAST, WHERETO I HAVE INVITED MANY A GUEST.
S-SIR!
YES, SIR!
GO FIND THOSE PERSONS WHOSE NAMES ARE WRITTEN THERE, AND SAY, MY HOUSE AND WELCOME ON THEIR PLEASURE STAY.

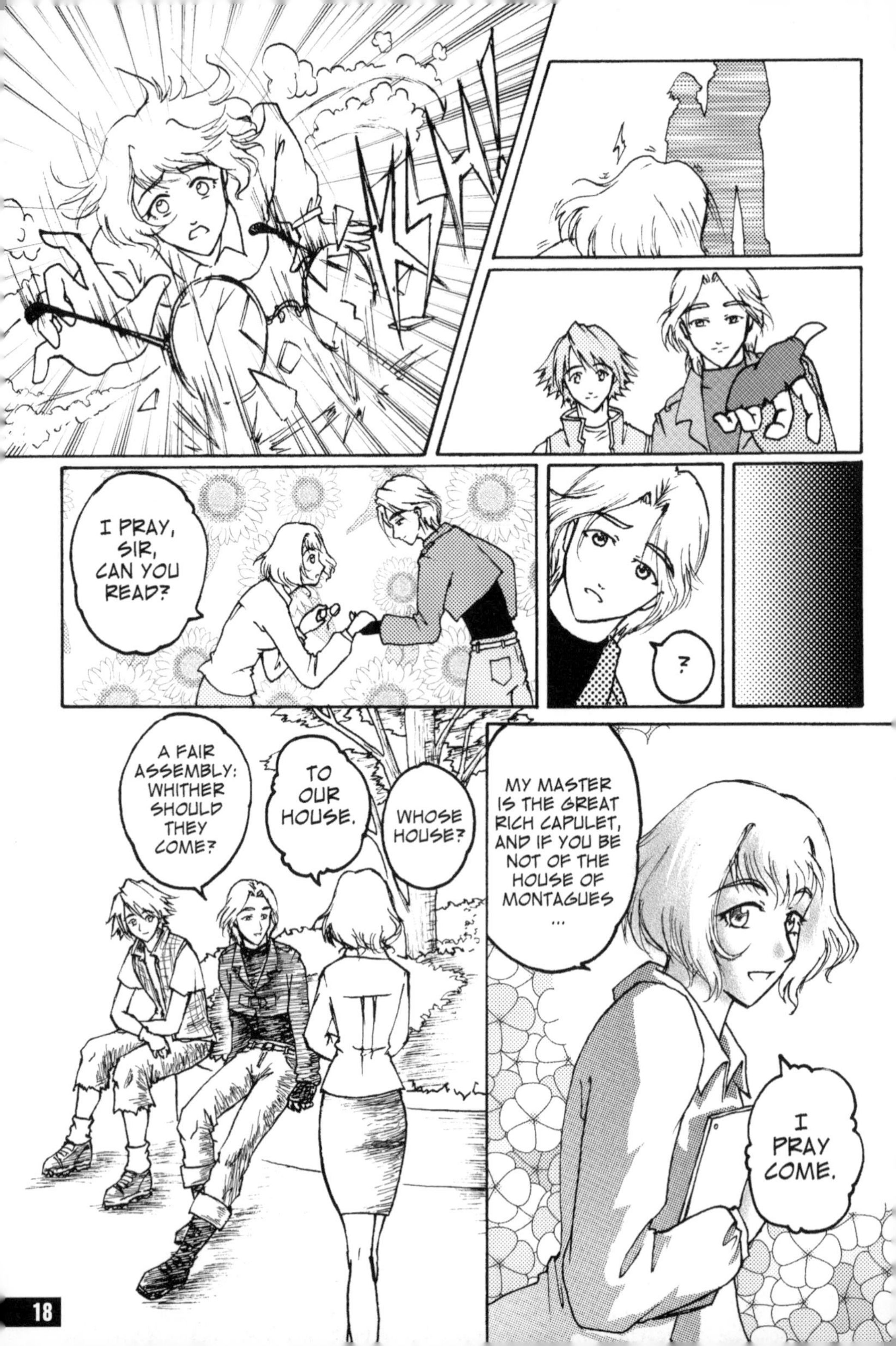
I PRAY, SIR, CAN YOU READ?
?
A FAIR ASSEMBLY: WHITHER SHOULD THEY COME?
TO OUR HOUSE.
WHOSE HOUSE?
MY MASTER IS THE GREAT RICH CAPULET, AND IF YOU BE NOT OF THE HOUSE OF MONTAGUES ...
I PRAY COME.

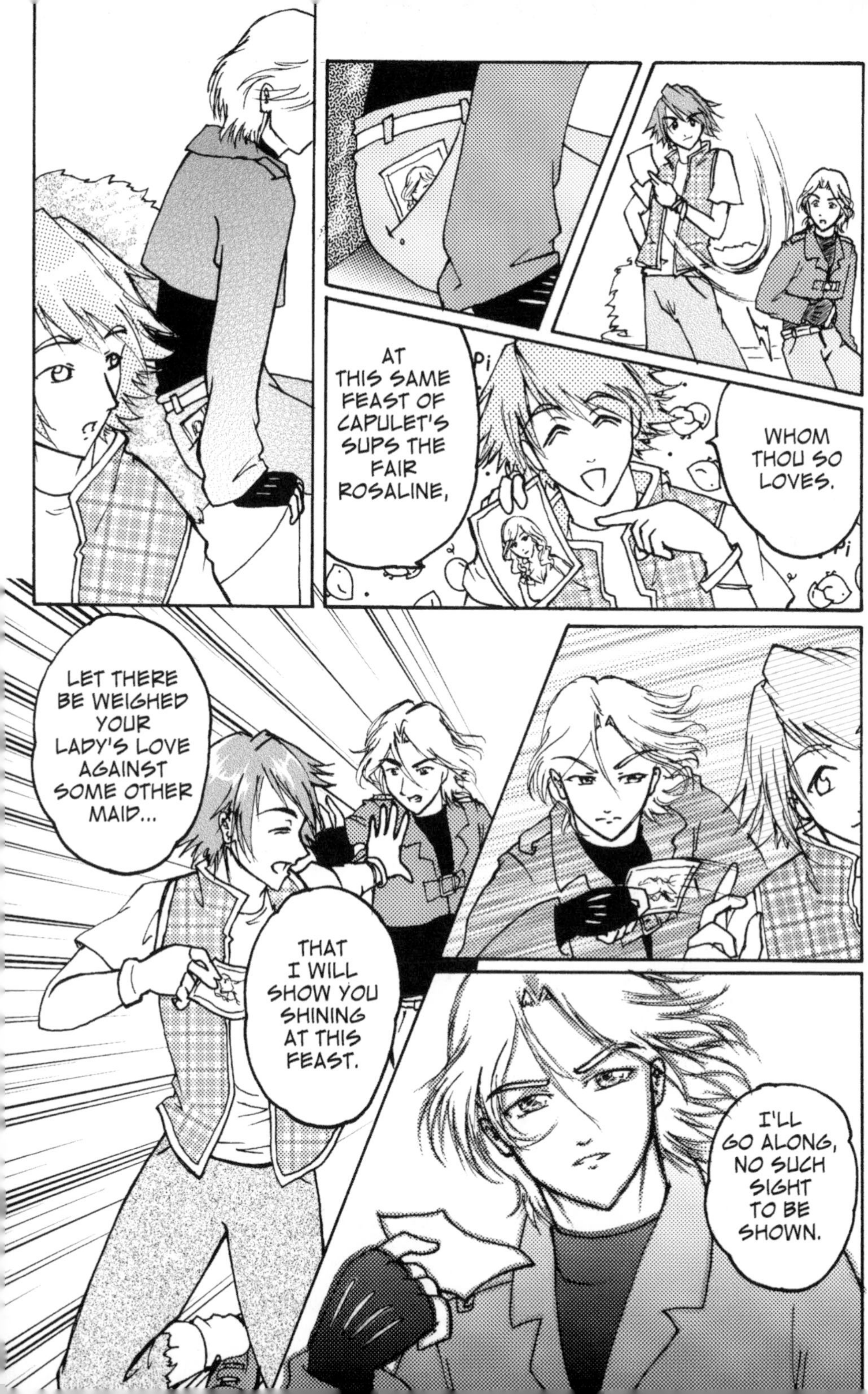
AT THIS SAME FEAST OF CAPULET'S SUPS THE FAIR ROSALINE,
Pi
WHOM THOU SO LOVES.
Pi
LET THERE BE WEIGHED YOUR LADY'S LOVE AGAINST SOME OTHER MAID...
THAT I WILL SHOW YOU SHINING AT THIS FEAST.
I'LL GO ALONG, NO SUCH SIGHT TO BE SHOWN.

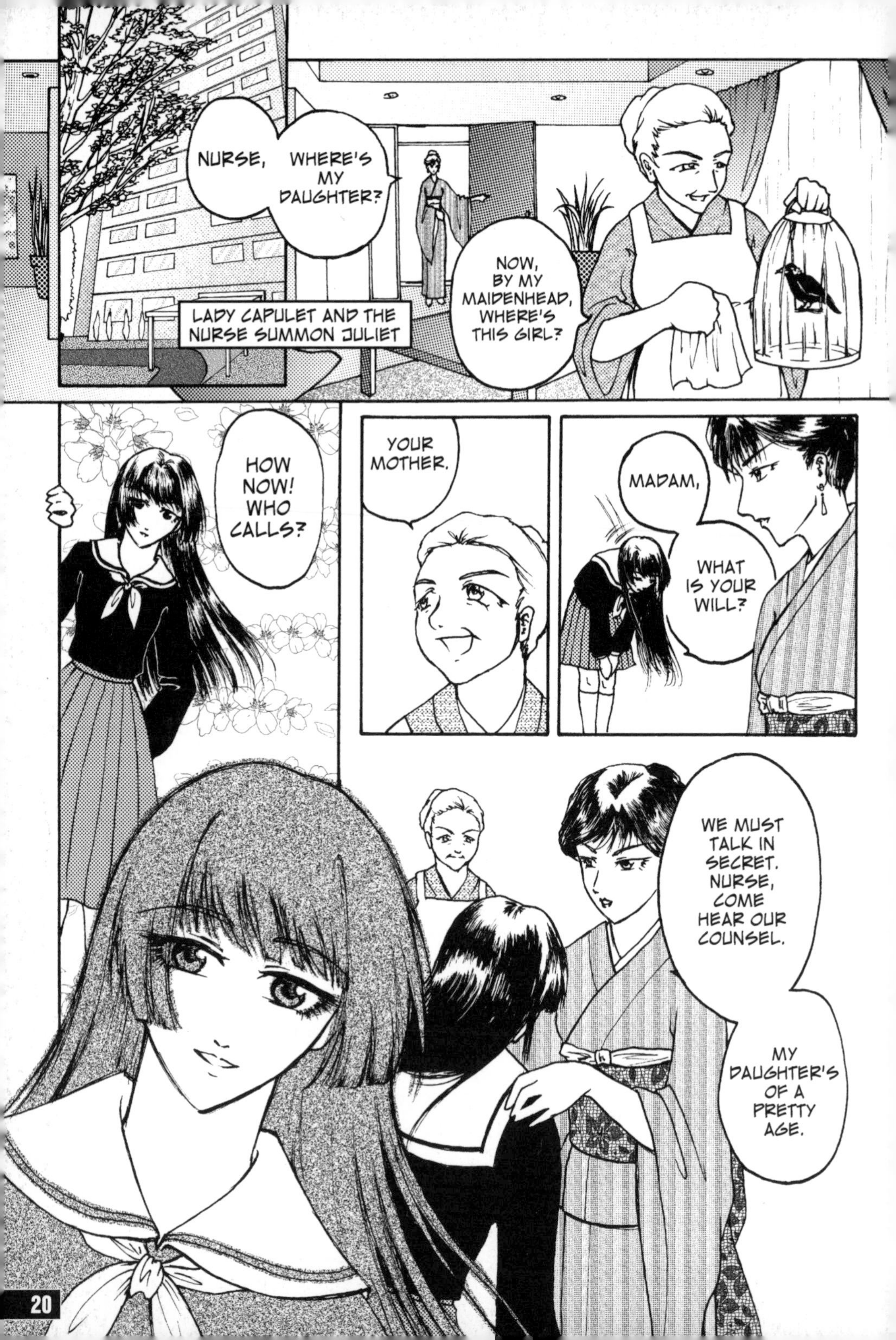
NURSE, WHERE'S MY DAUGHTER?
LADY CAPULET AND THE NURSE SUMMON JULIET
NOW, BY MY MAIDENHEAD, WHERE'S THIS GIRL?
HOW NOW! WHO CALLS?
YOUR MOTHER.
MADAM,
WHAT IS YOUR WILL?
WE MUST TALK IN SECRET. NURSE, COME HEAR OUR COUNSEL.
MY DAUGHTER'S OF A PRETTY AGE.

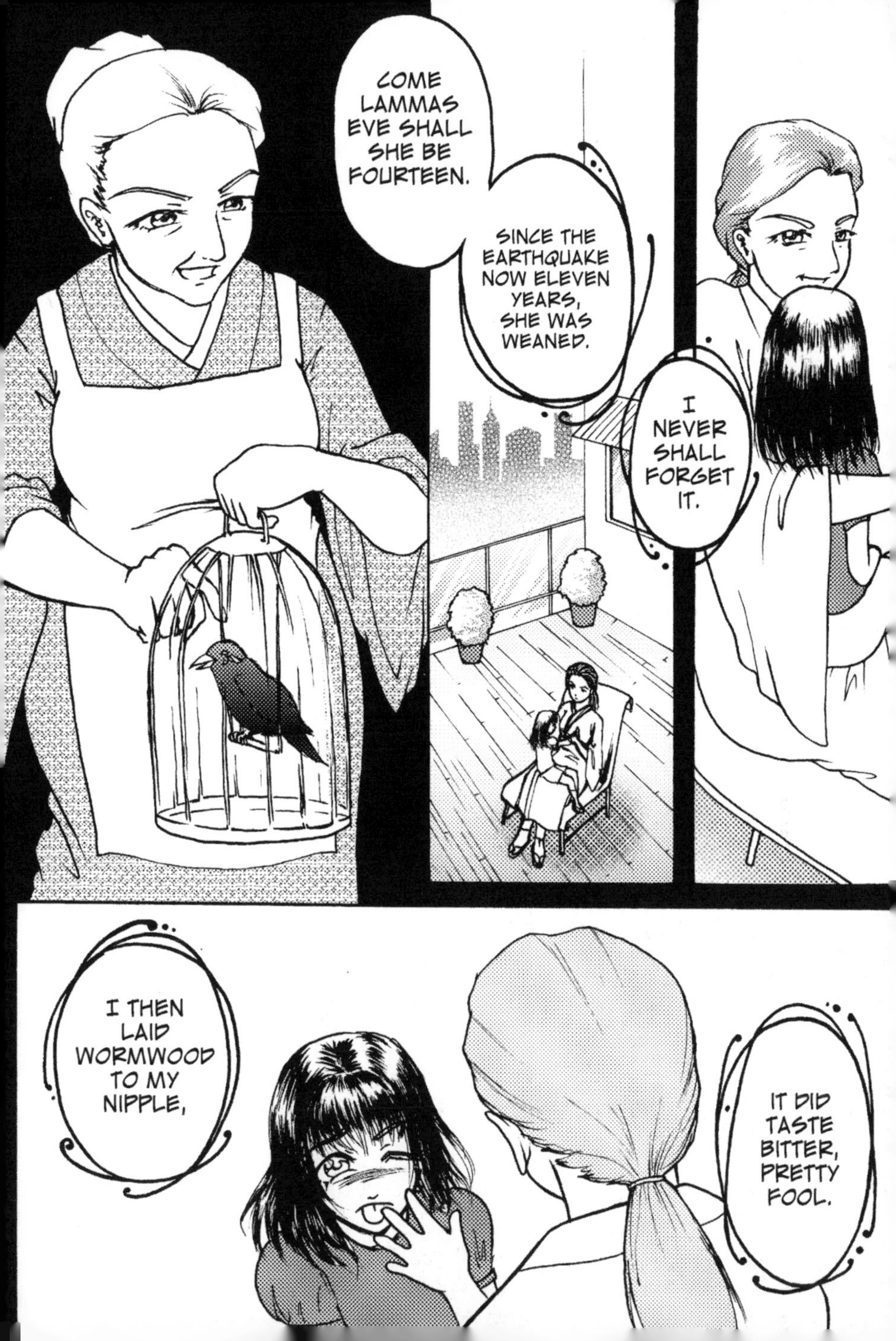
COME LAMMAS EVE SHALL SHE BE FOURTEEN.
SINCE THE EARTHQUAKE NOW ELEVEN YEARS, SHE WAS WEANED.
I NEVER SHALL FORGET IT.
I THEN LAID WORMWOOD TO MY NIPPLE,
IT DID TASTE BITTER, PRETTY FOOL.

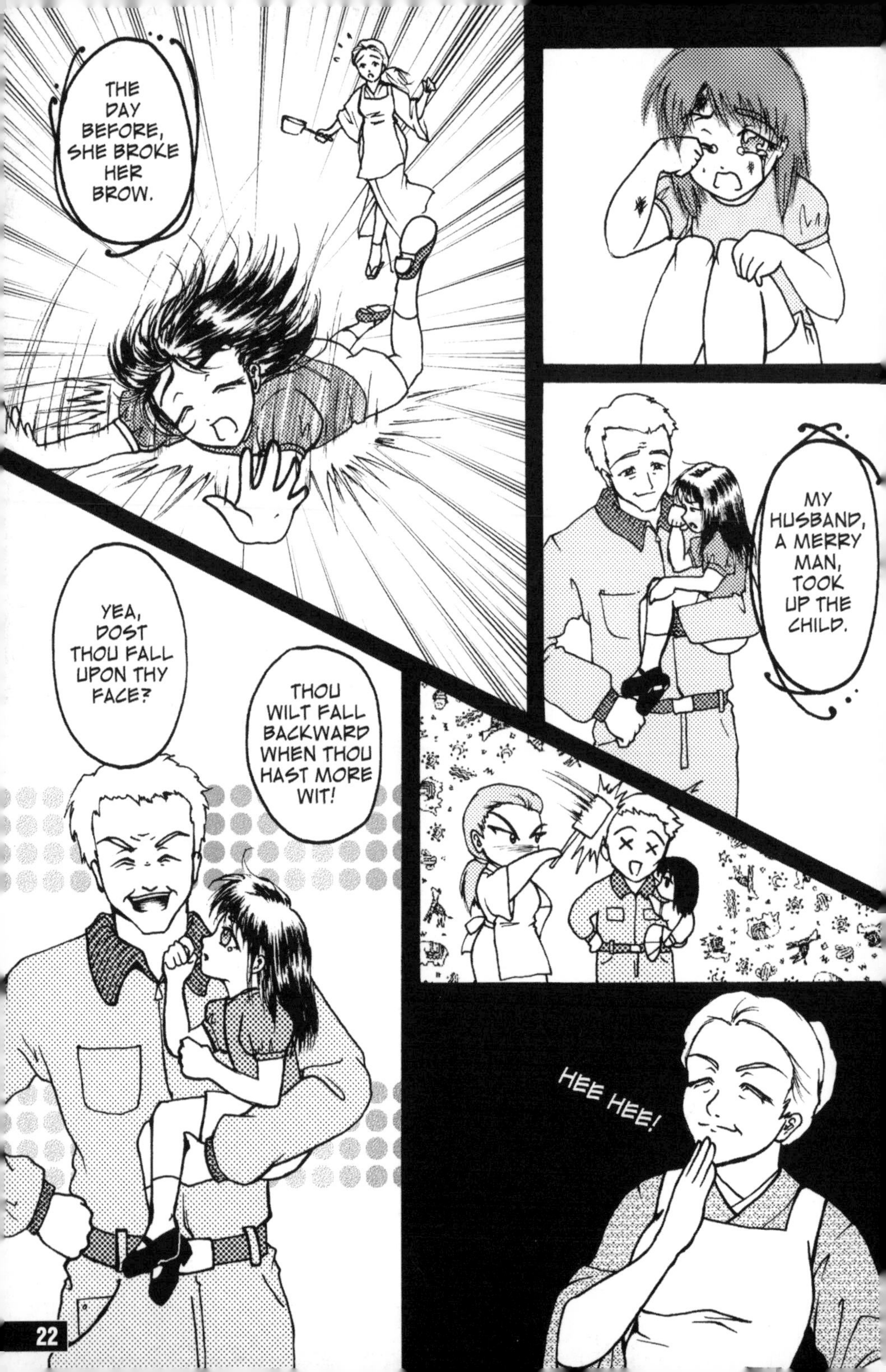
THE DAY BEFORE, SHE BROKE HER BROW.
MY HUSBAND, A MERRY MAN, TOOK UP THE CHILD.
YEA, DOST THOU FALL UPON THY FACE?
THOU WILT FALL BACKWARD WHEN THOU HAST MORE WIT!
HEE HEE!

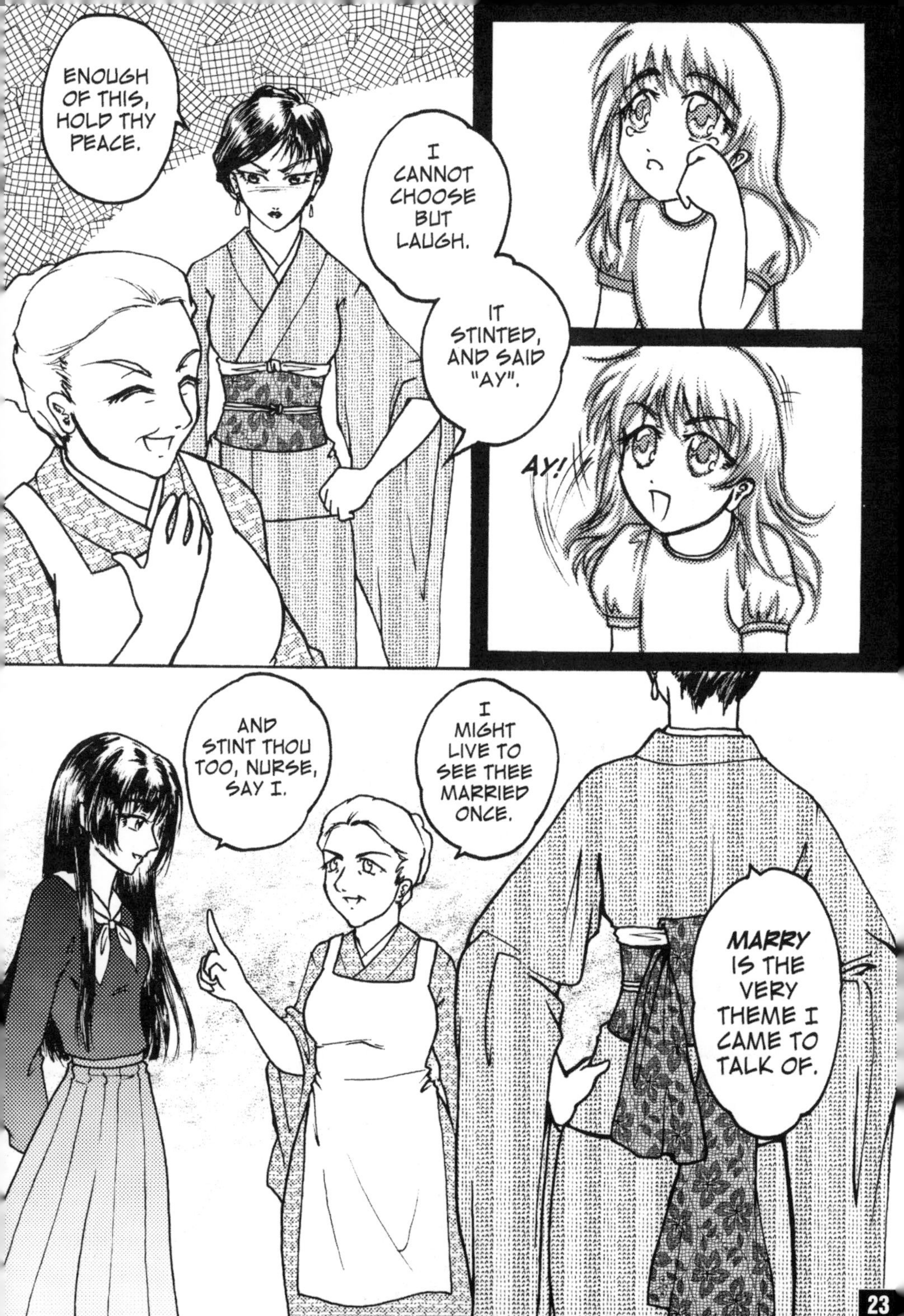
ENOUGH OF THIS, HOLD THY PEACE.
I CANNOT CHOOSE BUT LAUGH.
IT STINTED, AND SAID "AY".
AY!
AND STINT THOU TOO, NURSE, SAY I.
I MIGHT LIVE TO SEE THEE MARRIED ONCE.
MARRY IS THE VERY THEME I CAME TO TALK OF.

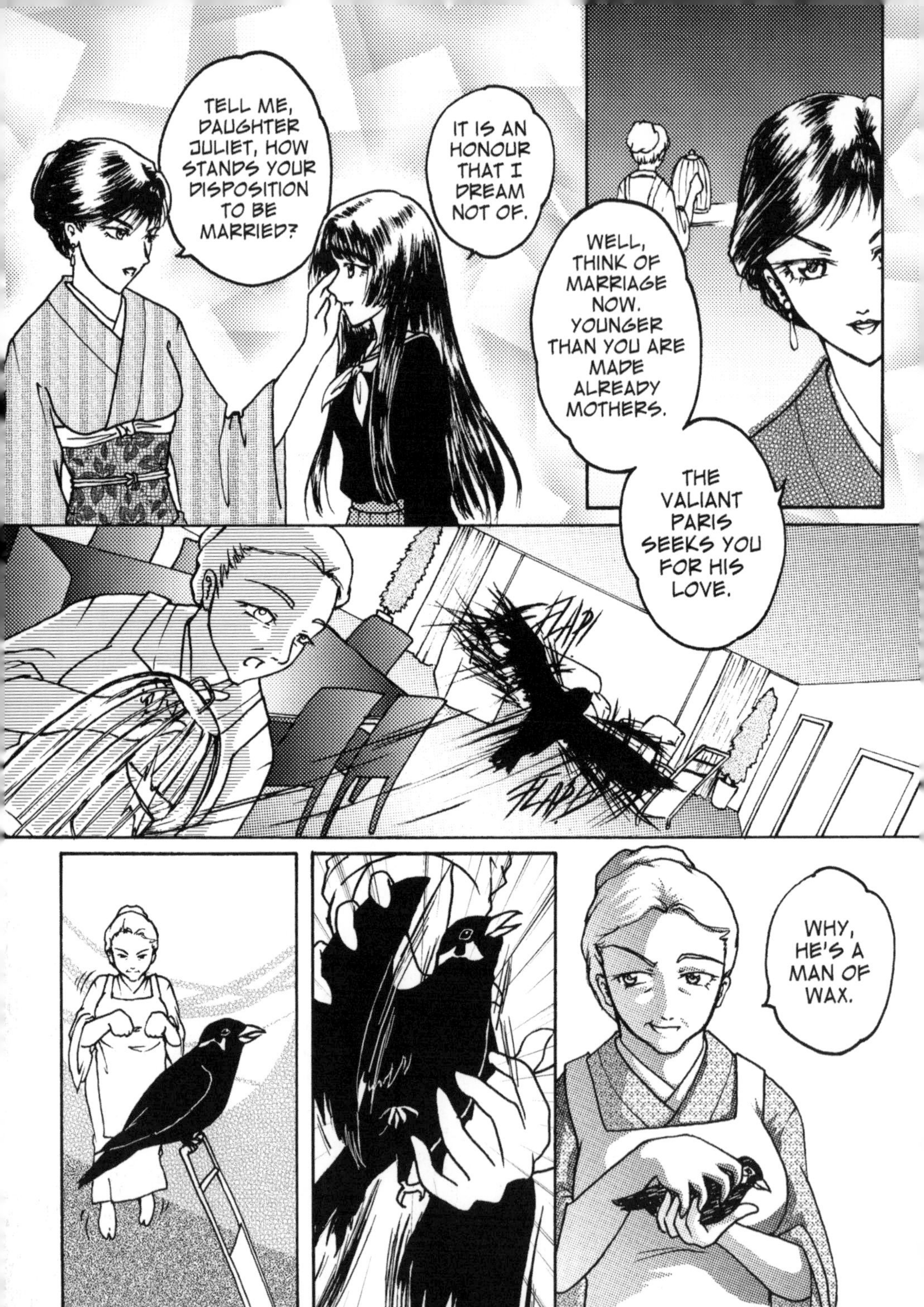
TELL ME, DAUGHTER JULIET, HOW STANDS YOUR DISPOSITION TO BE MARRIED?
IT IS AN HONOUR THAT I DREAM NOT OF.
WELL, THINK OF MARRIAGE NOW. YOUNGER THAN YOU ARE MADE ALREADY MOTHERS.
THE VALIANT PARIS SEEKS YOU FOR HIS LOVE.
FLAP!
FLAP!
WHY, HE'S A MAN OF WAX.

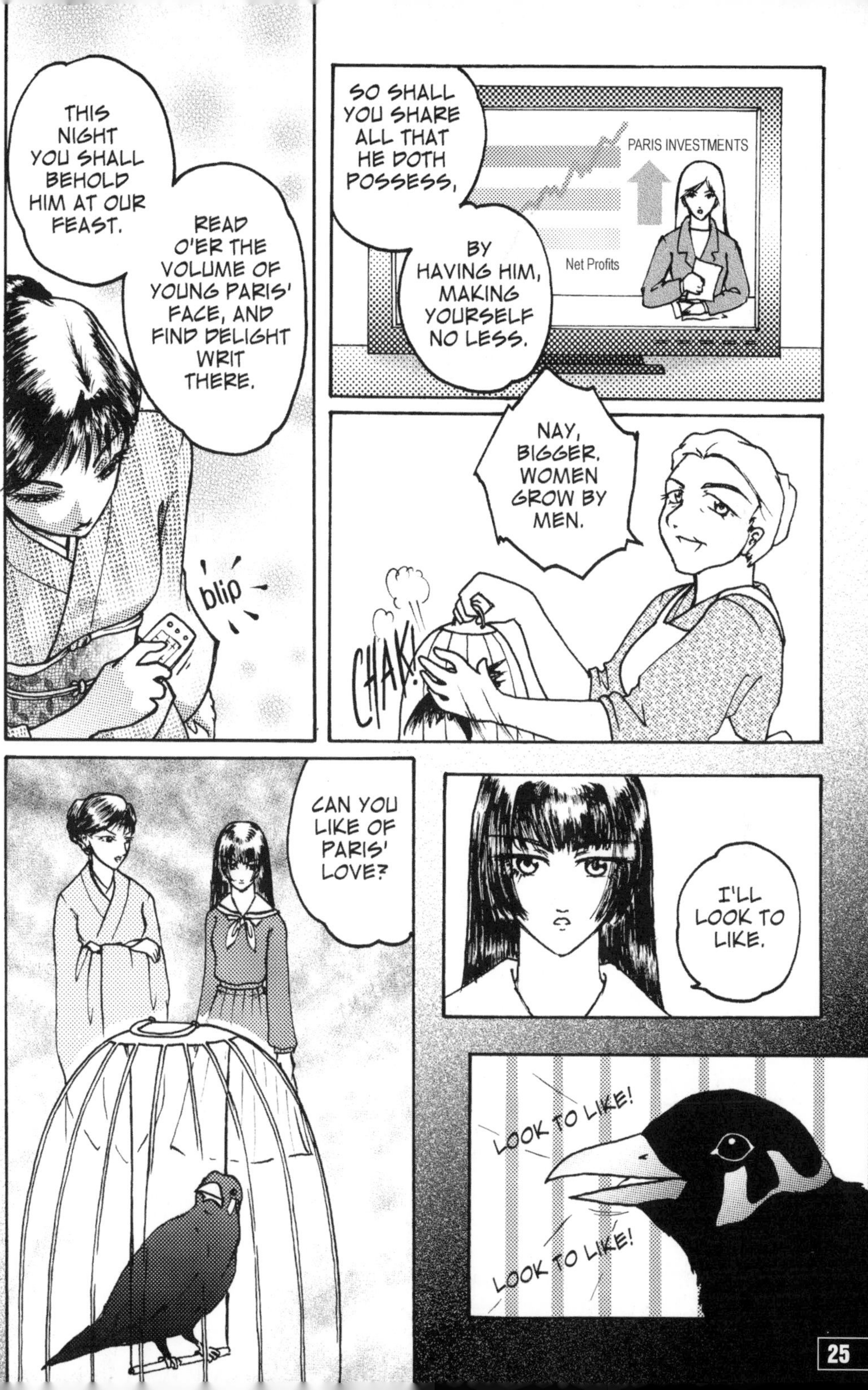

THIS NIGHT YOU SHALL BEHOLD HIM AT OUR FEAST.
READ O'ER THE VOLUME OF YOUNG PARIS' FACE, AND FIND DELIGHT WRIT THERE.
blip
SO SHALL YOU SHARE ALL THAT HE DOTH POSSESS,
PARIS INVESTMENTS
Net Profits
BY HAVING HIM, MAKING YOURSELF NO LESS.
NAY, BIGGER. WOMEN GROW BY MEN.
CHAK!
CAN YOU LIKE OF PARIS' LOVE?
I'LL LOOK TO LIKE.
LOOK TO LIKE!
LOOK TO LIKE!

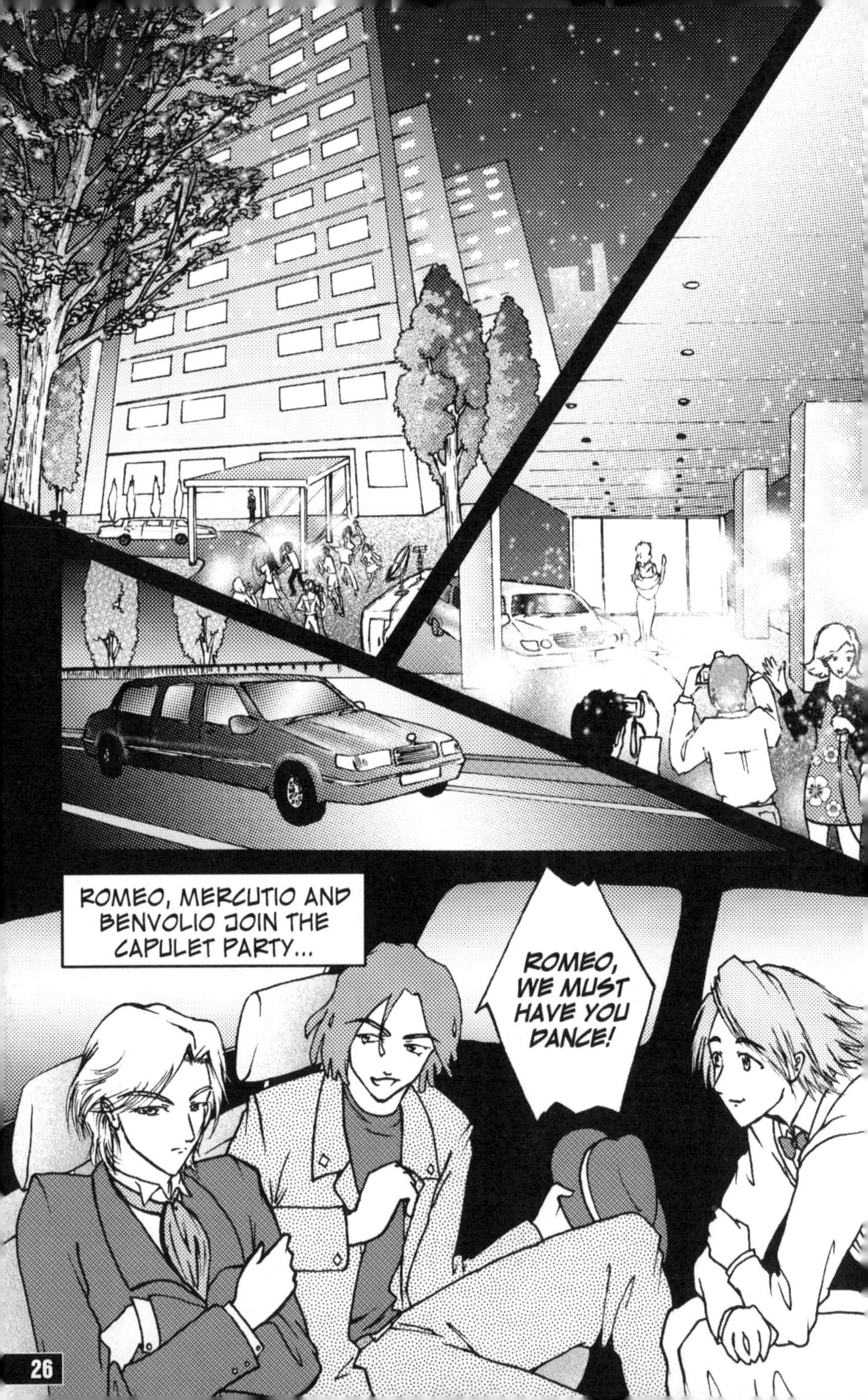
ROMEO, MERCUTIO AND BENVOLIO JOIN THE CAPULET PARTY...
ROMEO, WE MUST HAVE YOU DANCE!

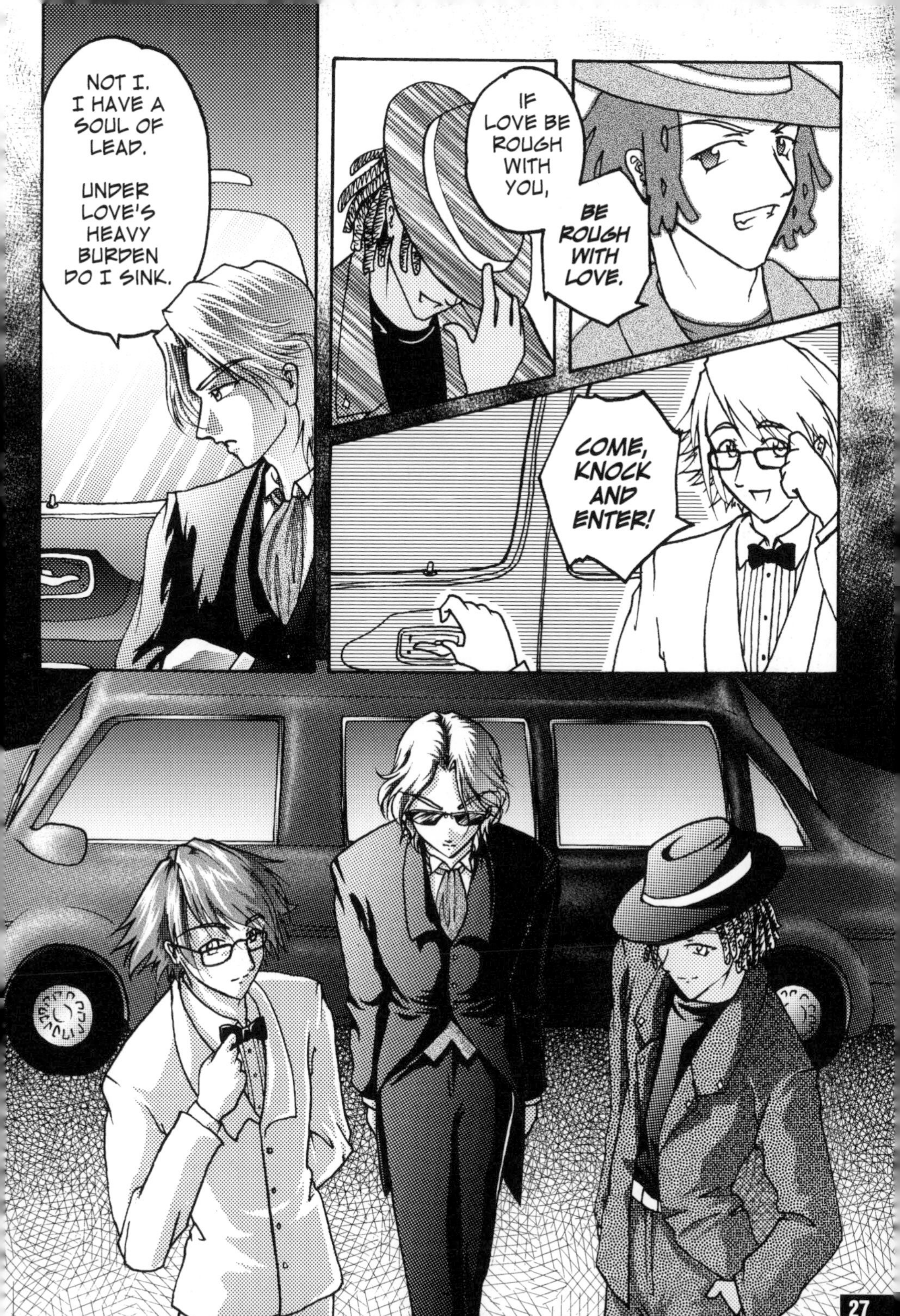
NOT I. I HAVE A SOUL OF LEAD.
UNDER LOVE'S HEAVY BURDEN DO I SINK.
IF LOVE BE ROUGH WITH YOU,
BE ROUGH WITH LOVE.
COME, KNOCK AND ENTER!

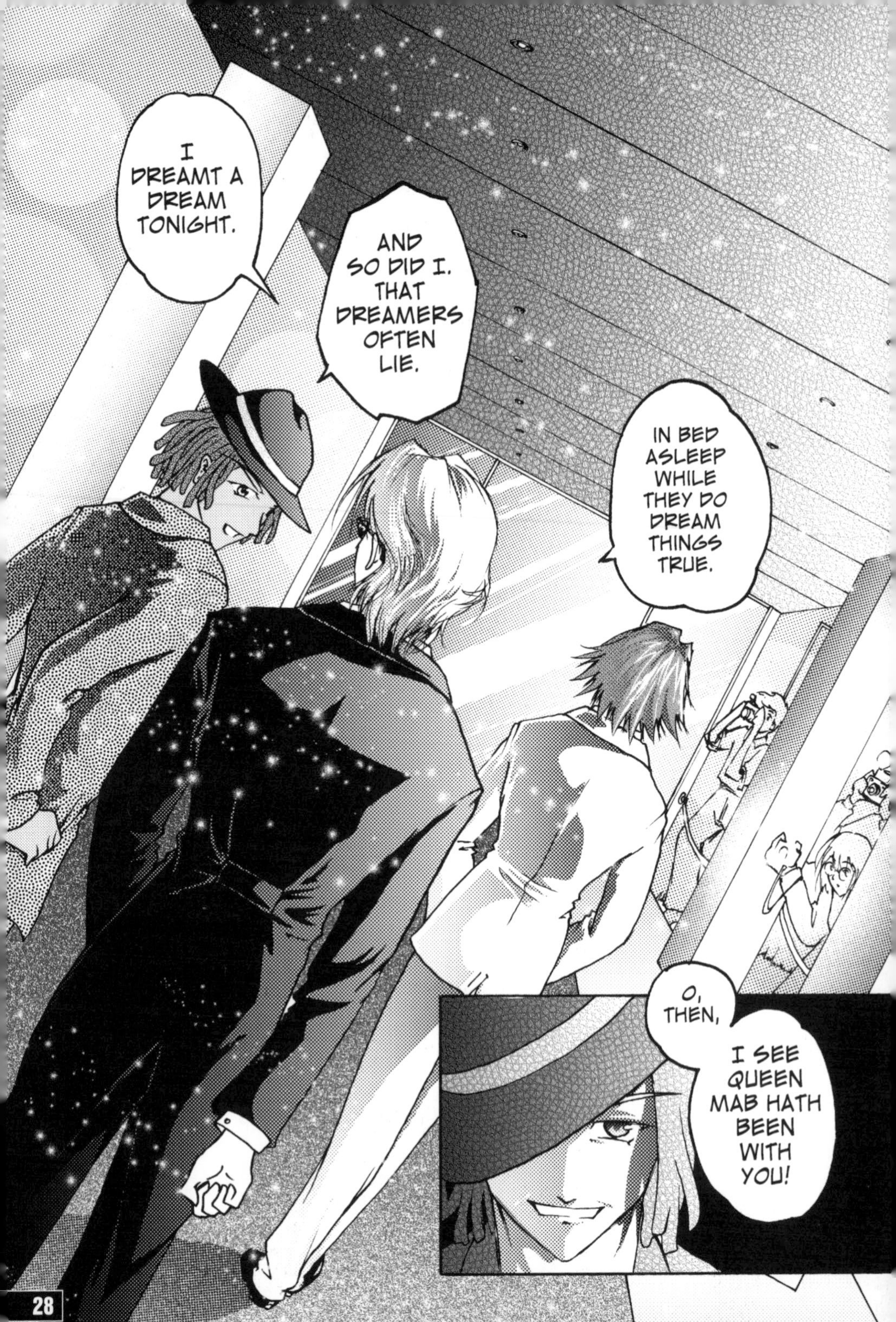
I DREAMT A DREAM TONIGHT.
AND SO DID I. THAT DREAMERS OFTEN LIE.
IN BED ASLEEP WHILE THEY DO DREAM THINGS TRUE.
O, THEN,
I SEE QUEEN MAB HATH BEEN WITH YOU!

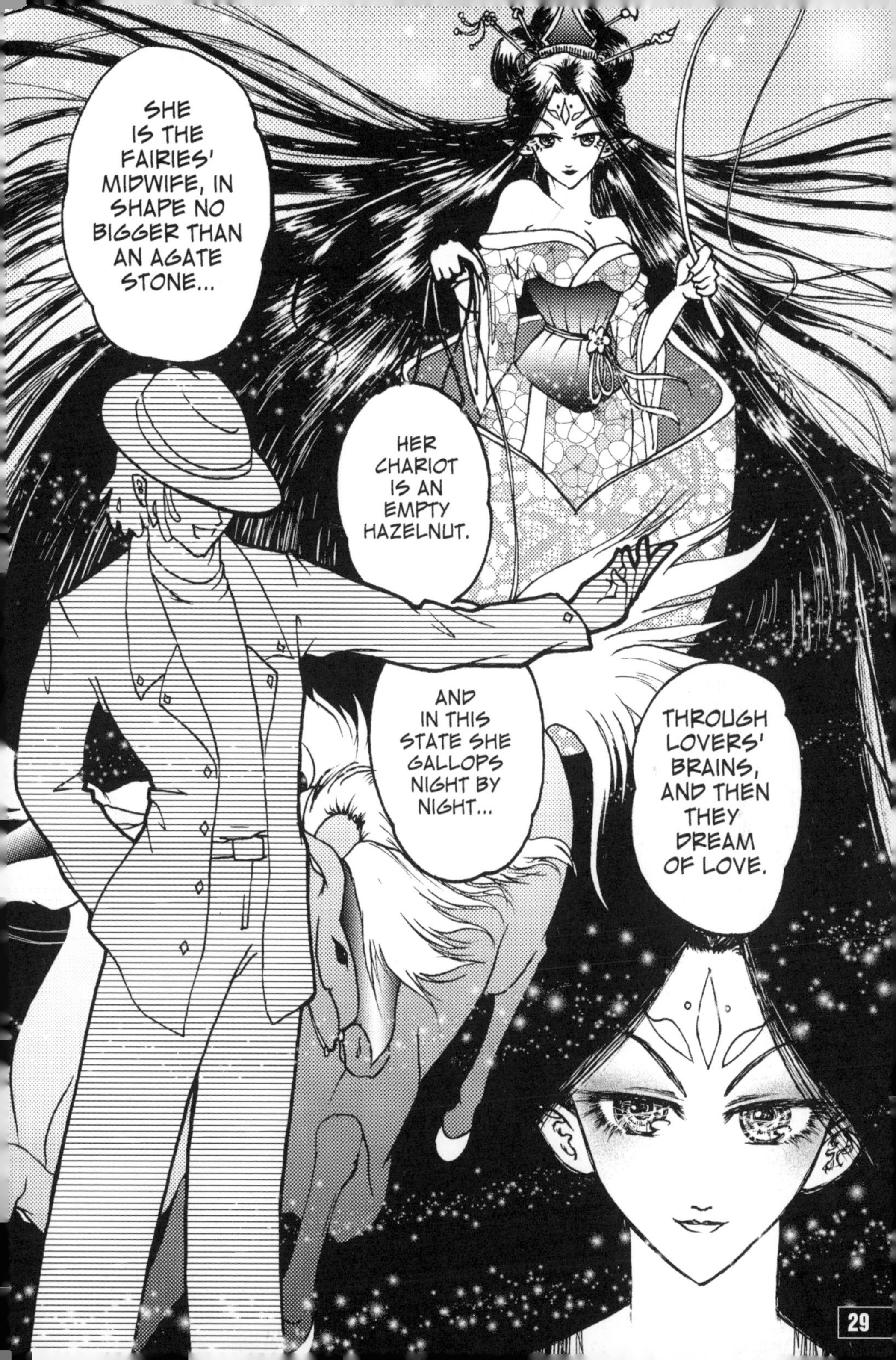
SHE IS THE FAIRIES' MIDWIFE, IN SHAPE NO BIGGER THAN AN AGATE STONE...
HER CHARIOT IS AN EMPTY HAZELNUT.
AND IN THIS STATE SHE GALLOPS NIGHT BY NIGHT...
THROUGH LOVERS' BRAINS, AND THEN THEY DREAM OF LOVE.

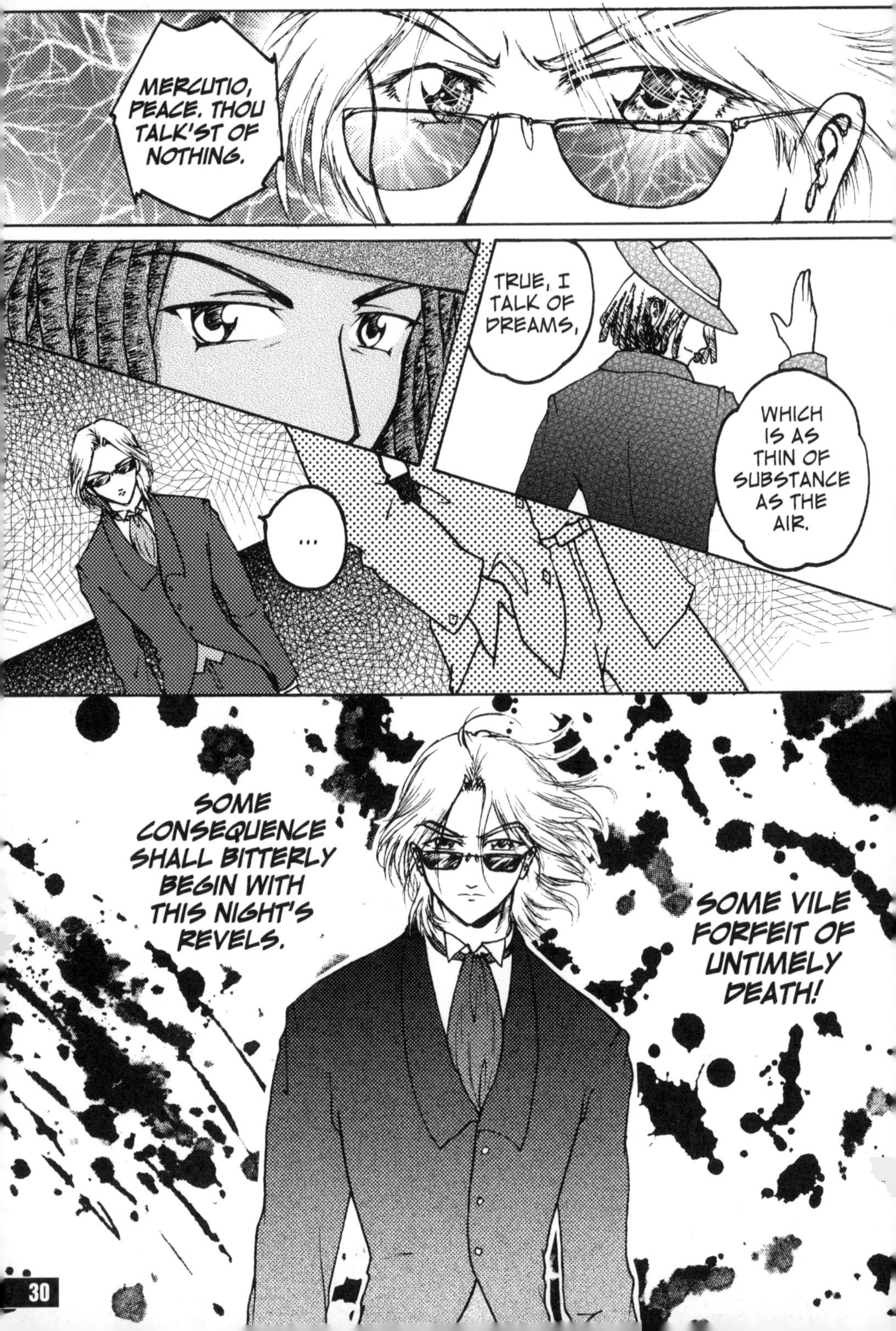
MERCUTIO, PEACE. THOU TALK'ST OF NOTHING.
TRUE, I TALK OF DREAMS,
WHICH IS AS THIN OF SUBSTANCE AS THE AIR.
...
SOME CONSEQUENCE SHALL BITTERLY BEGIN WITH THIS NIGHT'S REVELS.
SOME VILE FORFEIT OF UNTIMELY DEATH!

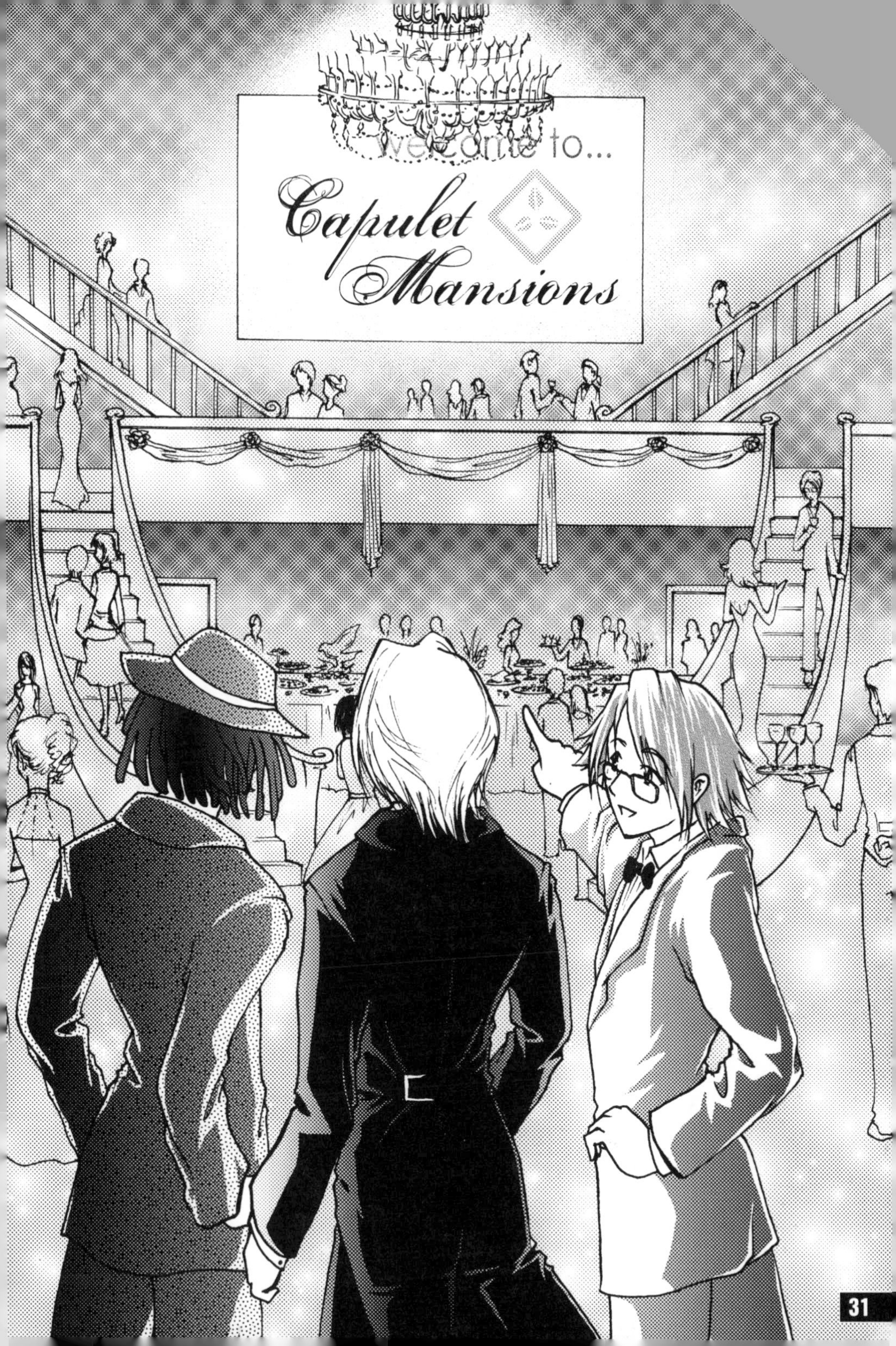
welcome to...
Capulet Mansions

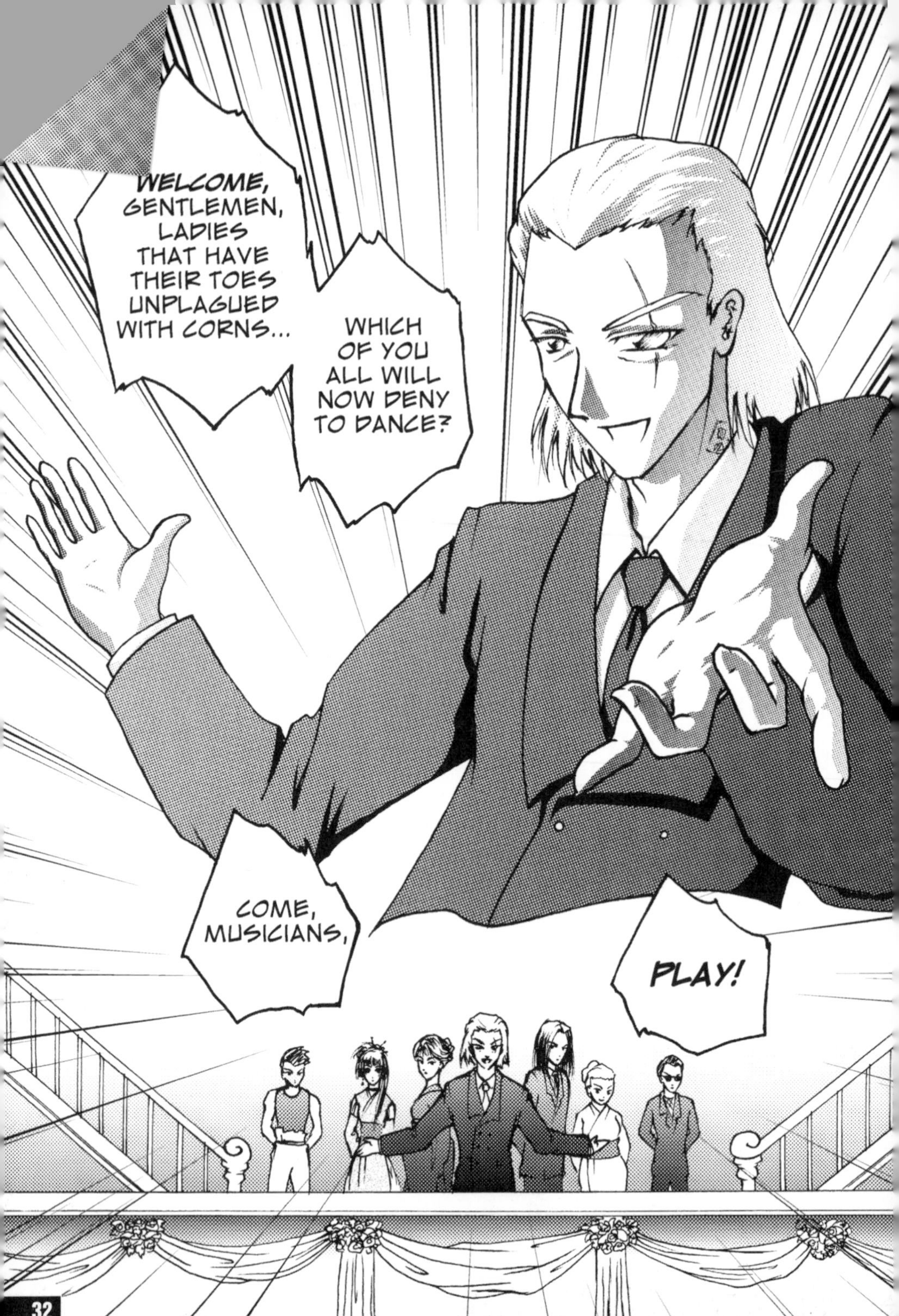
WELCOME, GENTLEMEN, LADIES THAT HAVE THEIR TOES UNPLAGUED WITH CORNS...
WHICH OF YOU ALL WILL NOW DENY TO DANCE?
COME, MUSICIANS,
PLAY!

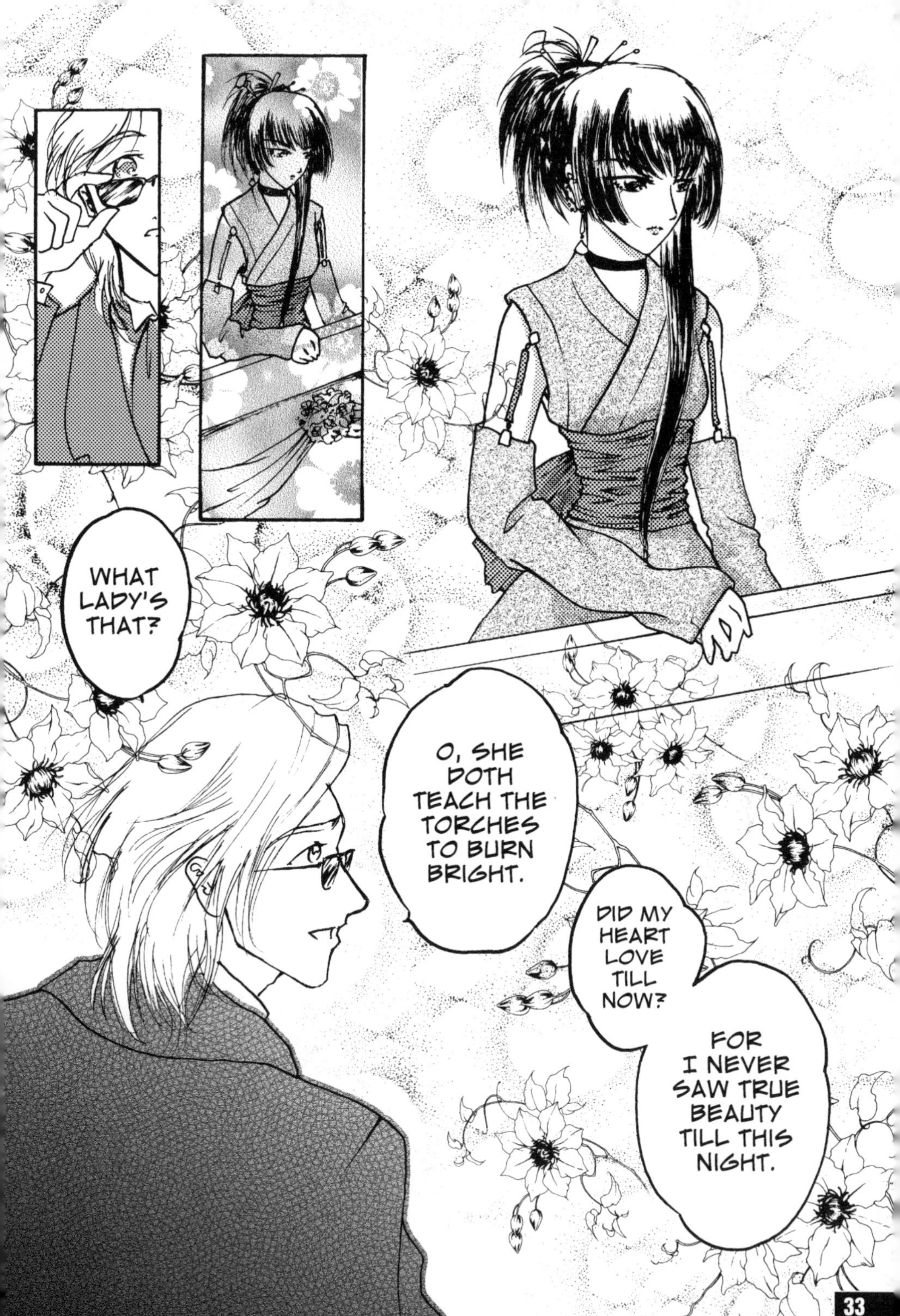
WHAT LADY'S THAT?
O, SHE DOTH TEACH THE TORCHES TO BURN BRIGHT.
DID MY HEART LOVE TILL NOW?
FOR I NEVER SAW TRUE BEAUTY TILL THIS NIGHT.

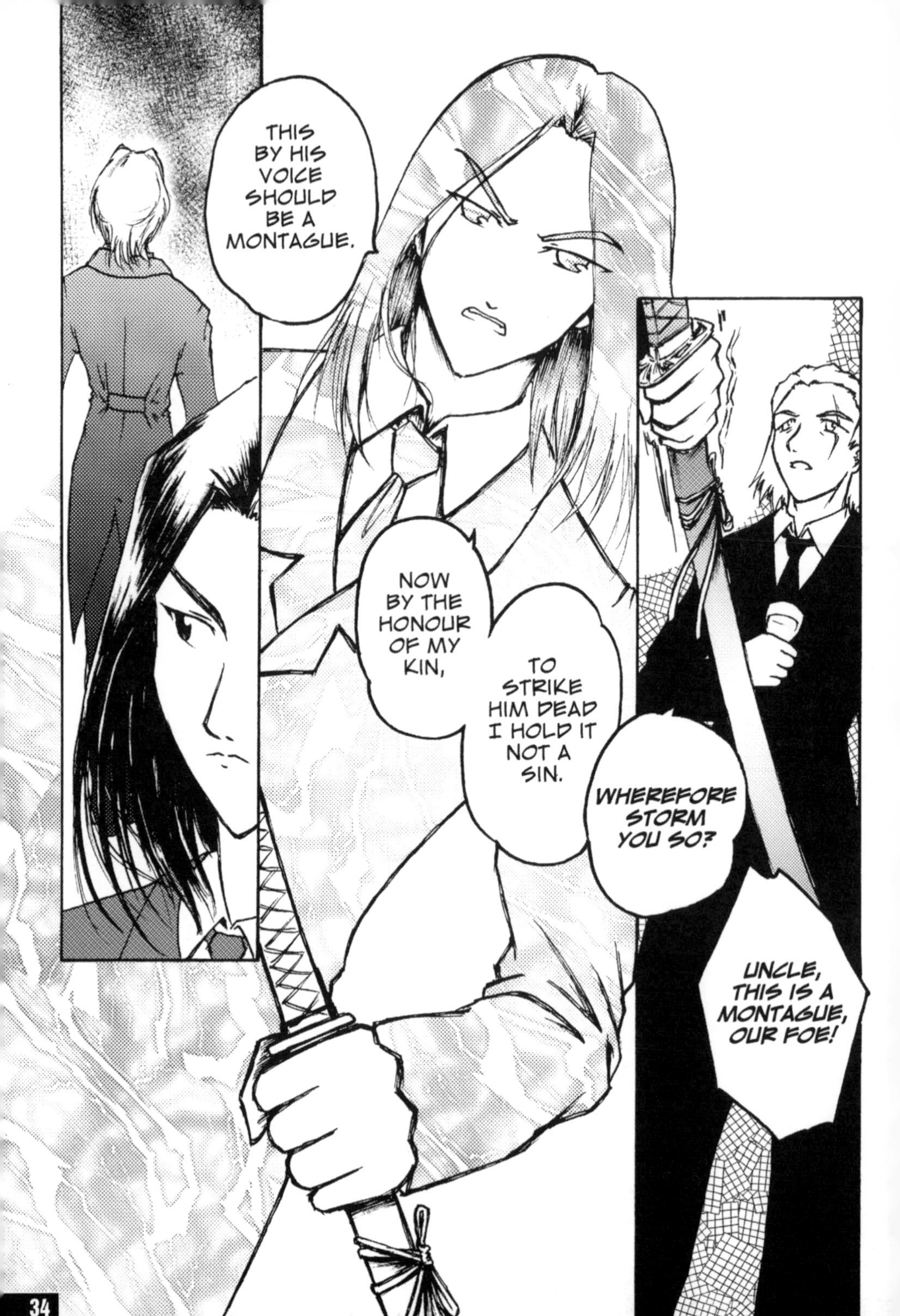
THIS BY HIS VOICE SHOULD BE A MONTAGUE.
NOW BY THE HONOUR OF MY KIN,
TO STRIKE HIM DEAD I HOLD IT NOT A SIN.
WHEREFORE STORM YOU SO?
UNCLE, THIS IS A MONTAGUE, OUR FOE!

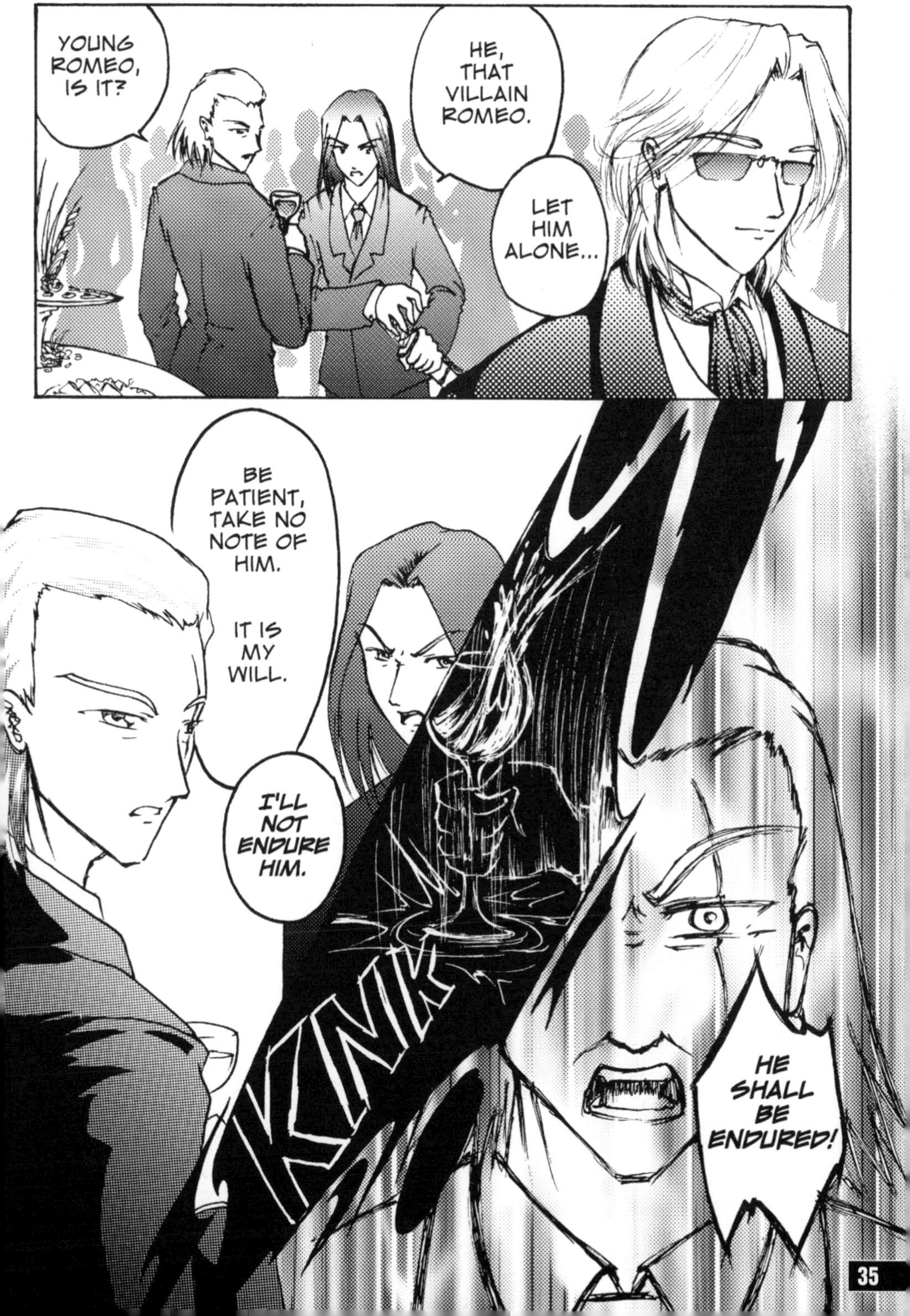
YOUNG ROMEO, IS IT?
HE, THAT VILLAIN ROMEO.
LET HIM ALONE...
BE PATIENT, TAKE NO NOTE OF HIM.
IT IS MY WILL.
I'LL NOT ENDURE HIM.
KLINK
HE SHALL BE ENDURED!

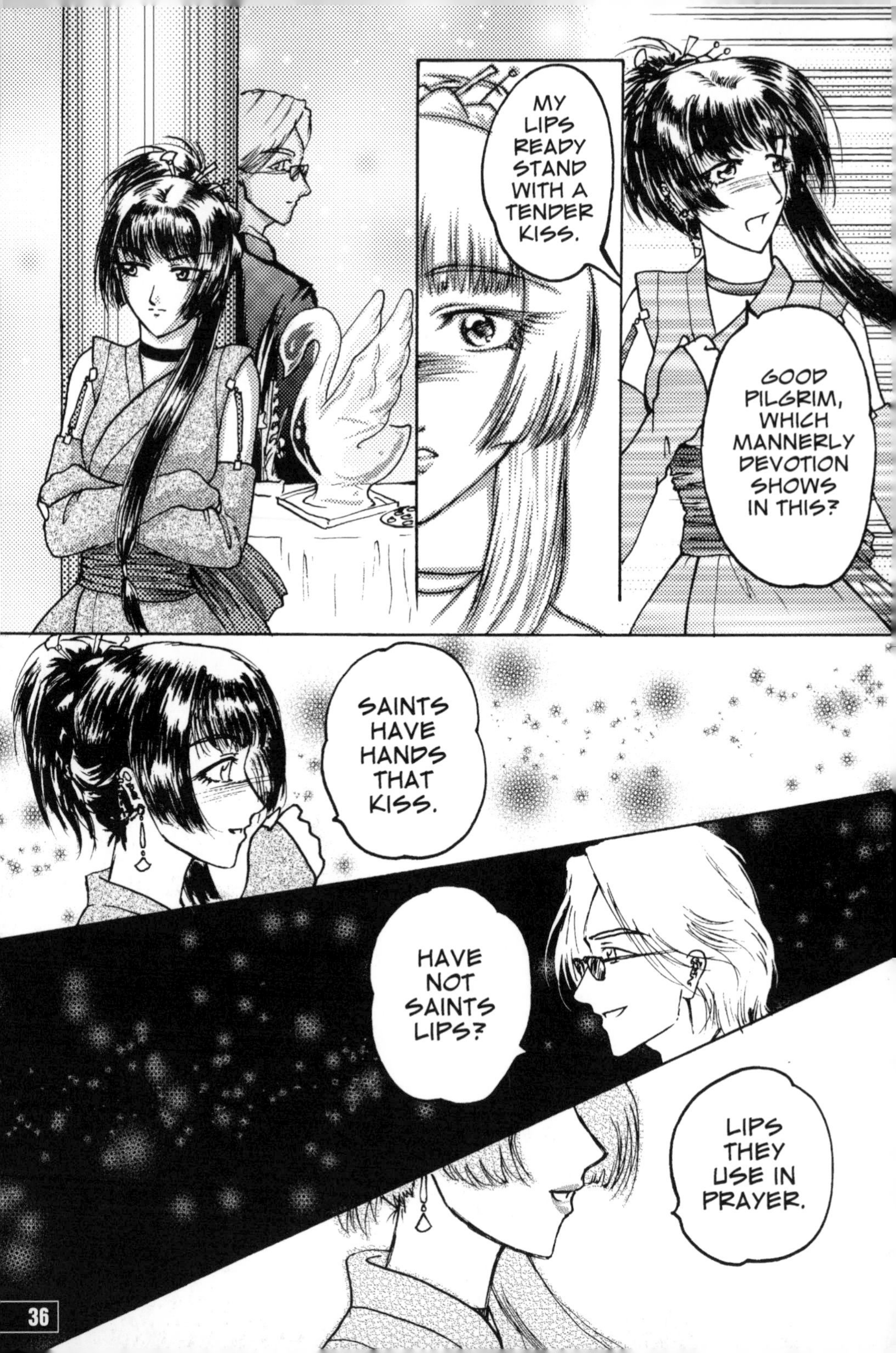
MY LIPS READY STAND WITH A TENDER KISS.
GOOD PILGRIM, WHICH MANNERLY DEVOTION SHOWS IN THIS?
SAINTS HAVE HANDS THAT KISS.
HAVE NOT SAINTS LIPS?
LIPS THEY USE IN PRAYER.

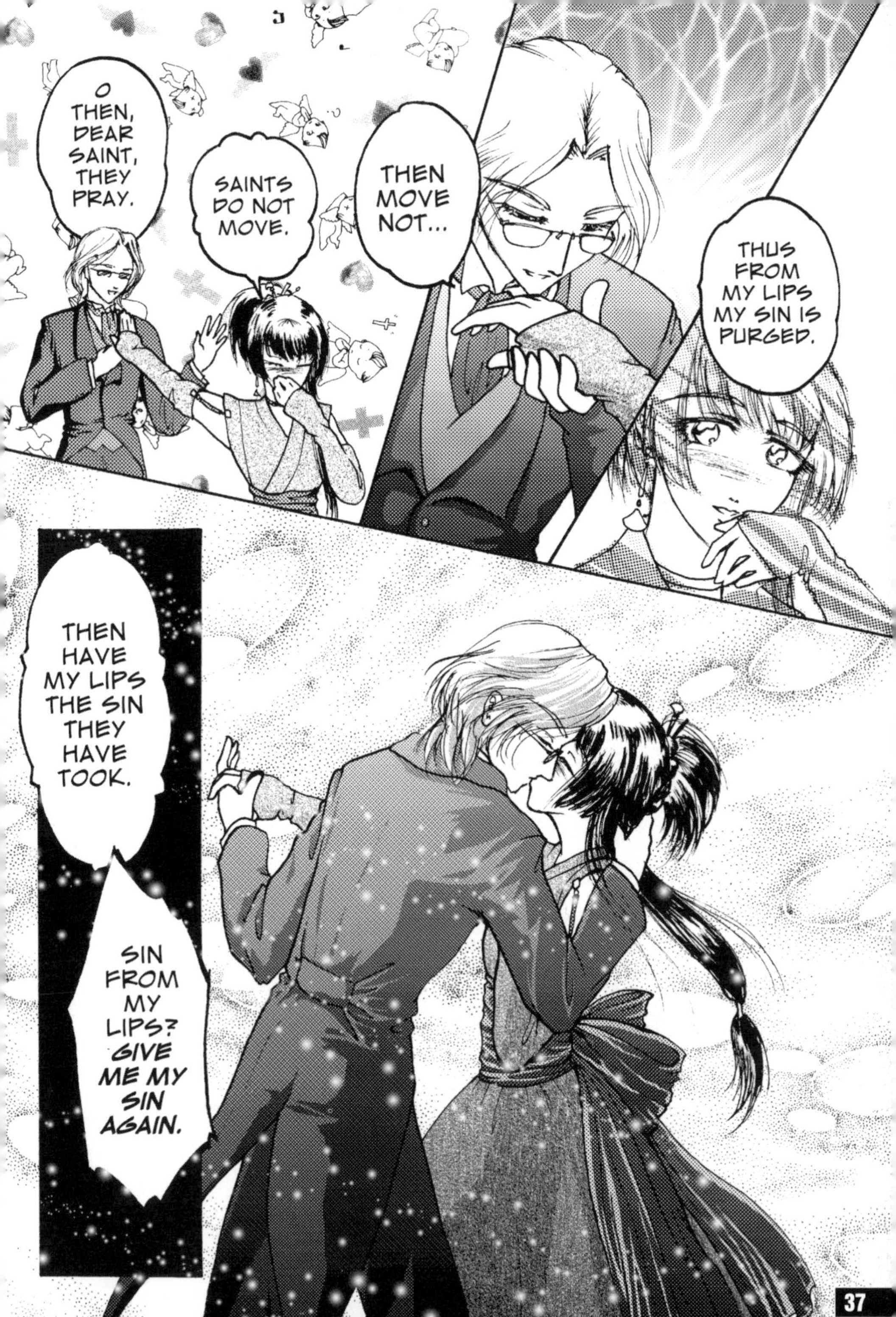
O THEN, DEAR SAINT, THEY PRAY.
SAINTS DO NOT MOVE.
THEN MOVE NOT...
THUS FROM MY LIPS MY SIN IS PURGED.
THEN HAVE MY LIPS THE SIN THEY HAVE TOOK.
SIN FROM MY LIPS? *GIVE ME MY SIN AGAIN.*

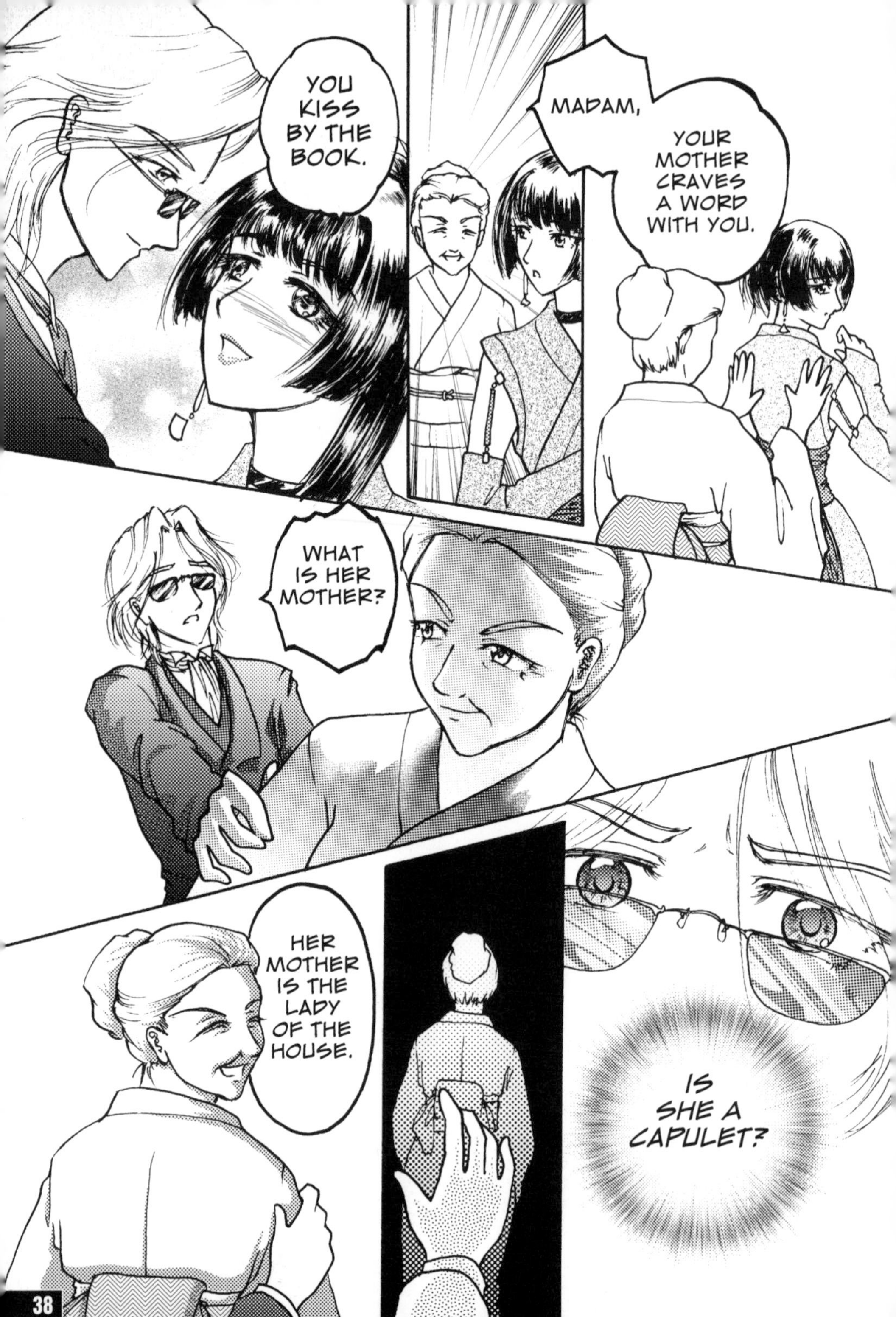

YOU KISS BY THE BOOK.
MADAM,
YOUR MOTHER CRAVES A WORD WITH YOU.
WHAT IS HER MOTHER?
HER MOTHER IS THE LADY OF THE HOUSE.
IS SHE A CAPULET?

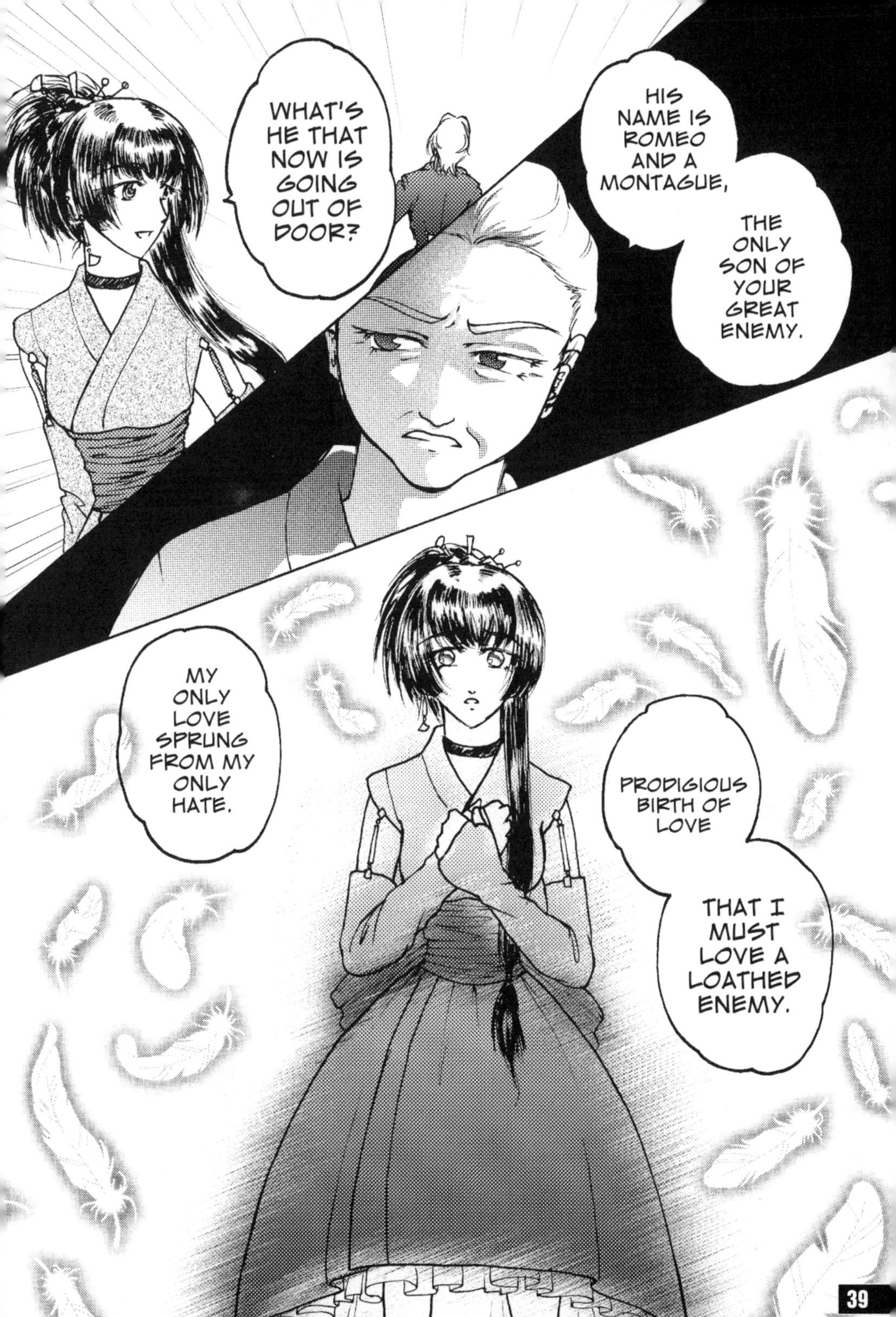
WHAT'S HE THAT NOW IS GOING OUT OF DOOR?
HIS NAME IS ROMEO AND A MONTAGUE,
THE ONLY SON OF YOUR GREAT ENEMY.
MY ONLY LOVE SPRUNG FROM MY ONLY HATE.
PRODIGIOUS BIRTH OF LOVE
THAT I MUST LOVE A LOATHED ENEMY.

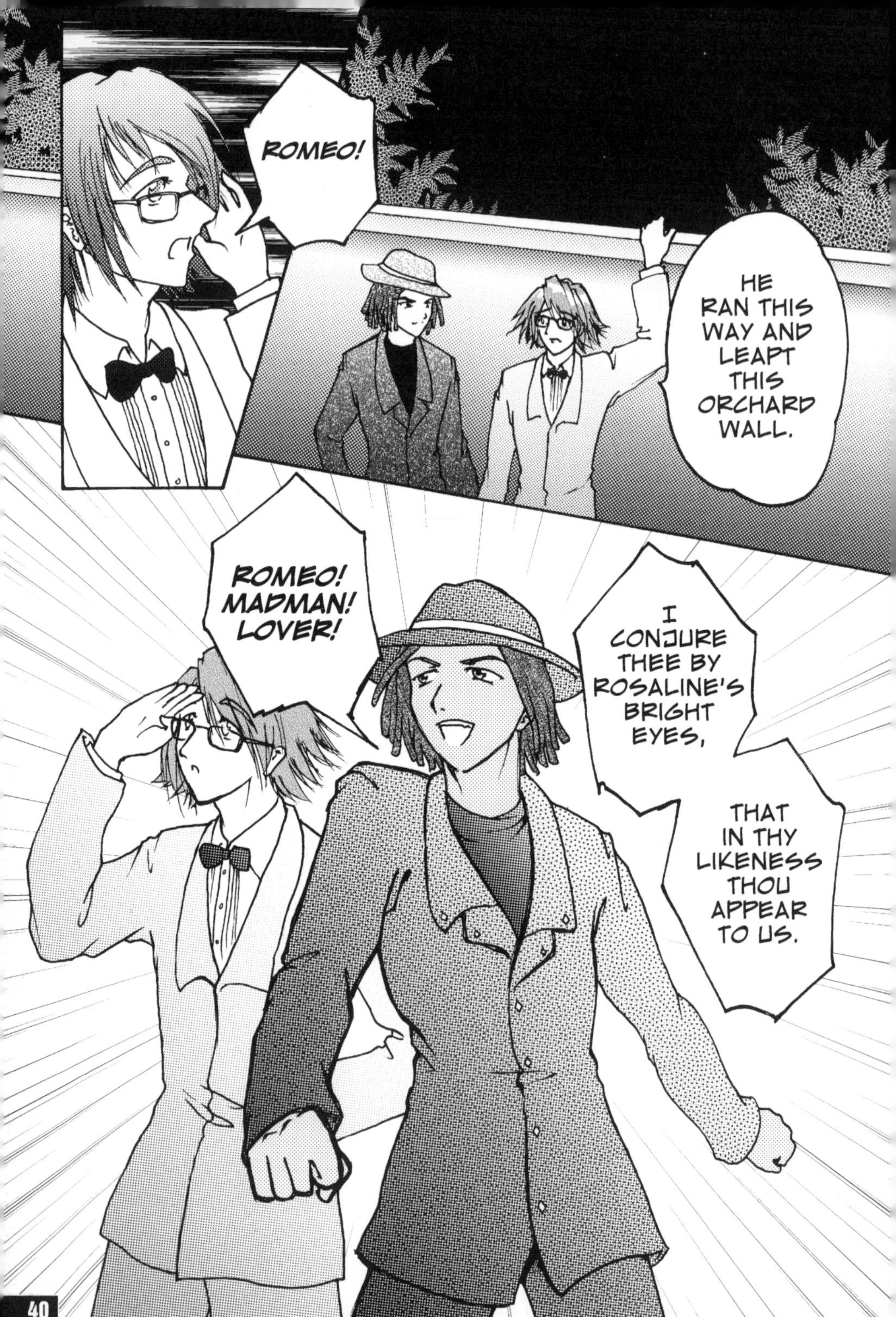

ROMEO!
HE RAN THIS WAY AND LEAPT THIS ORCHARD WALL.
ROMEO! MADMAN! LOVER!
I CONJURE THEE BY ROSALINE'S BRIGHT EYES,
THAT IN THY LIKENESS THOU APPEAR TO US.

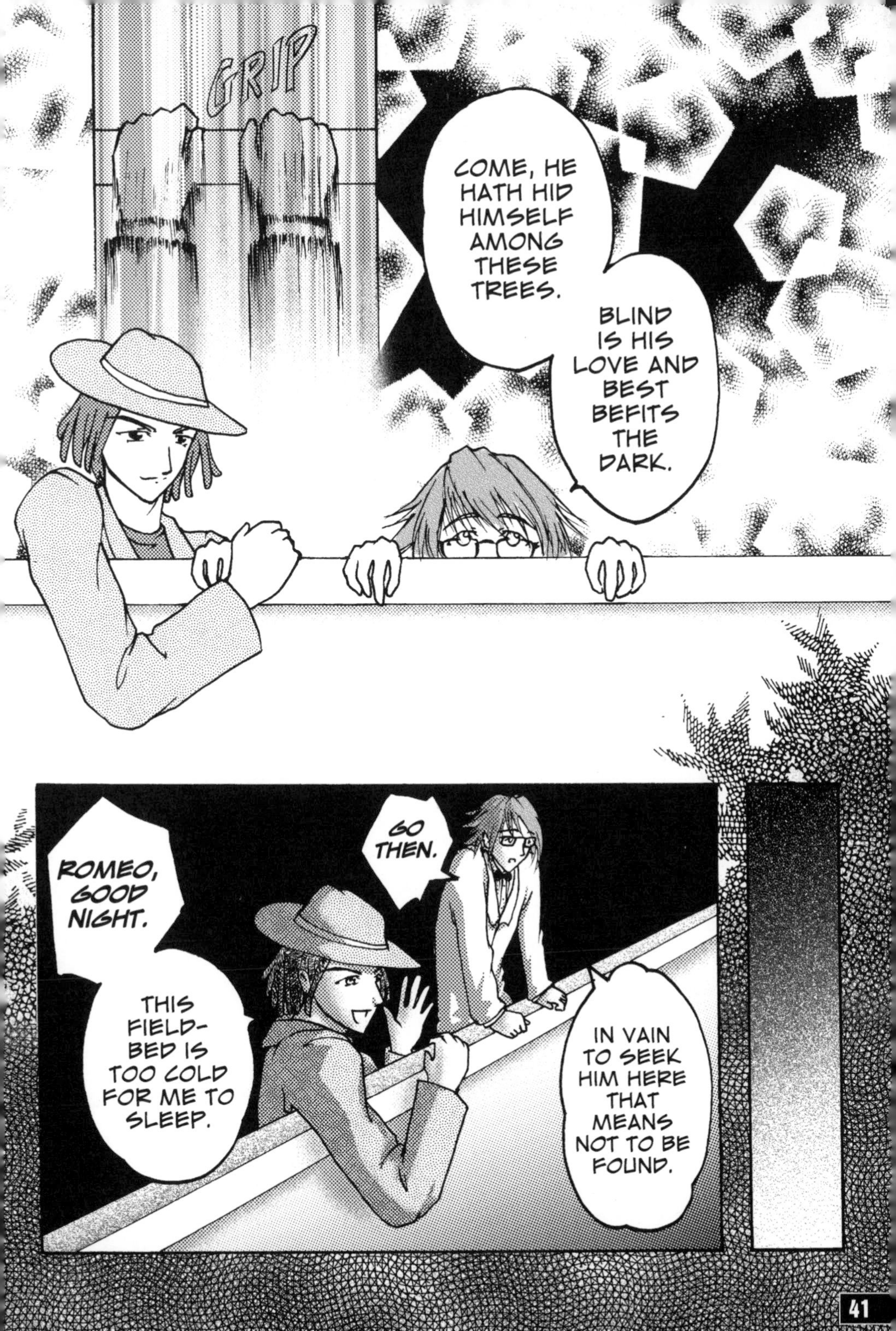
GRIP
COME, HE HATH HID HIMSELF AMONG THESE TREES.
BLIND IS HIS LOVE AND BEST BEFITS THE DARK.
ROMEO, GOOD NIGHT.
GO THEN.
THIS FIELD-BED IS TOO COLD FOR ME TO SLEEP.
IN VAIN TO SEEK HIM HERE THAT MEANS NOT TO BE FOUND.

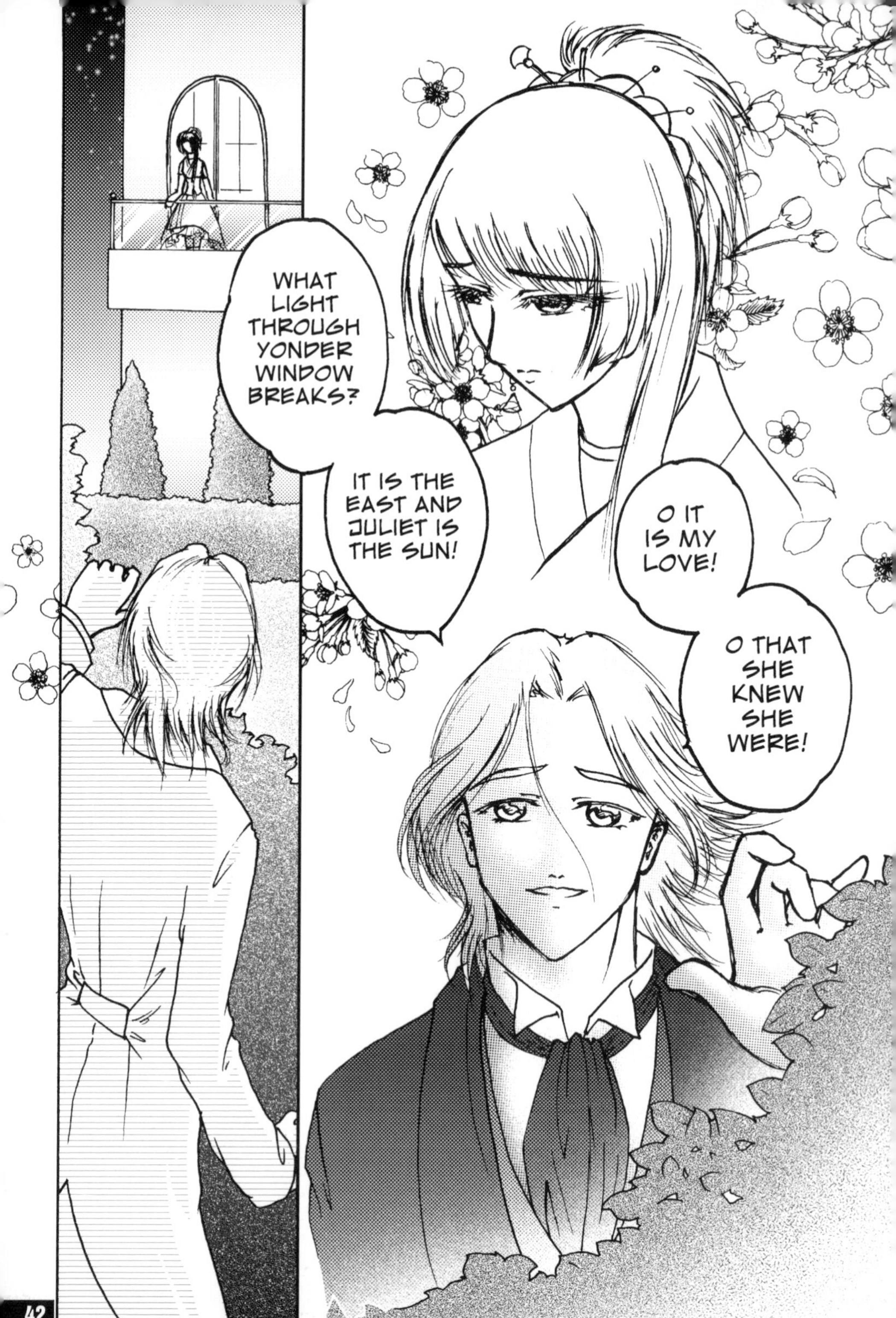
WHAT LIGHT THROUGH YONDER WINDOW BREAKS?
IT IS THE EAST AND JULIET IS THE SUN!
O IT IS MY LOVE!
O THAT SHE KNEW SHE WERE!

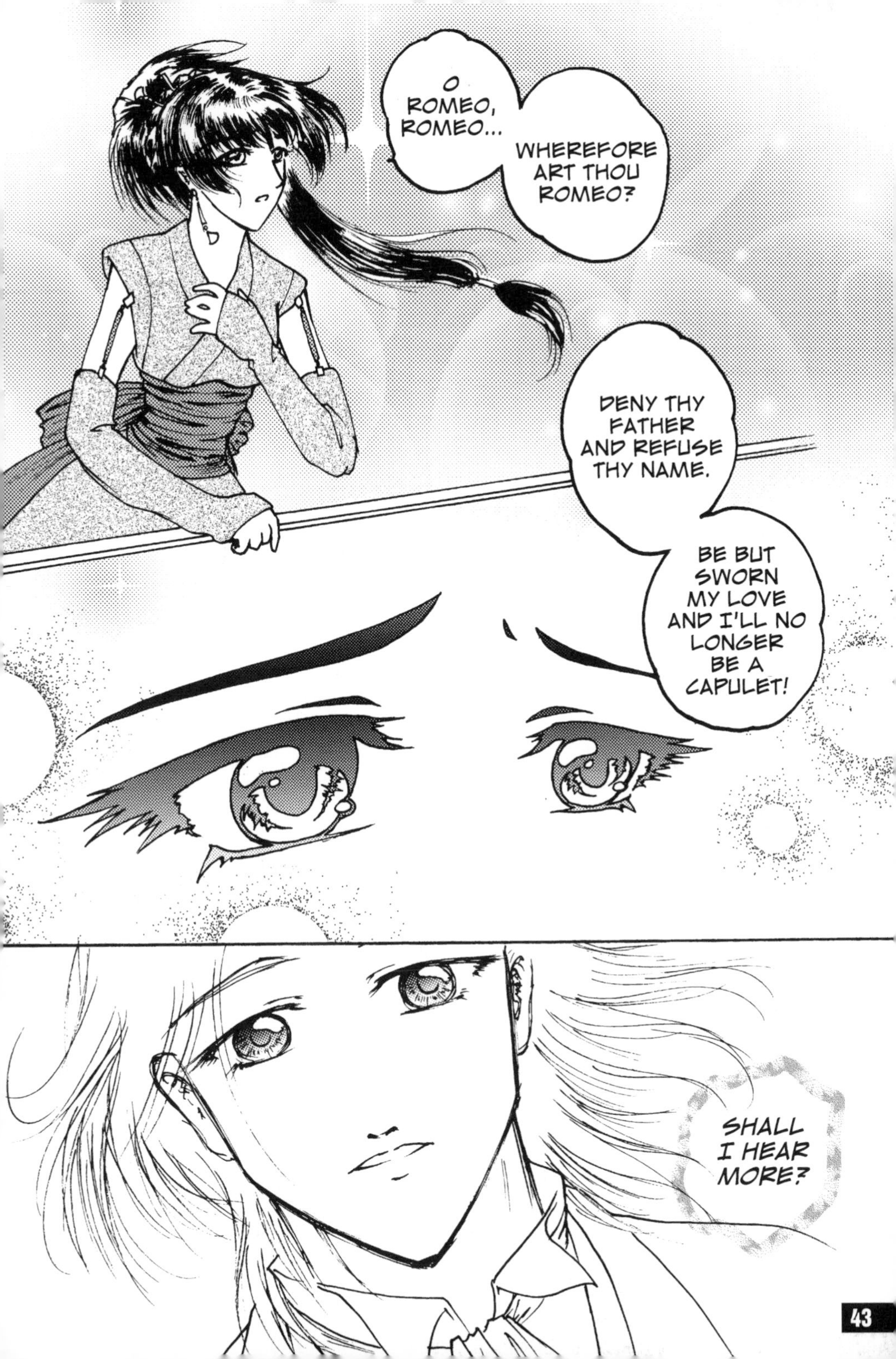
O ROMEO, ROMEO...
WHEREFORE ART THOU ROMEO?
DENY THY FATHER AND REFUSE THY NAME.
BE BUT SWORN MY LOVE AND I'LL NO LONGER BE A CAPULET!
SHALL I HEAR MORE?

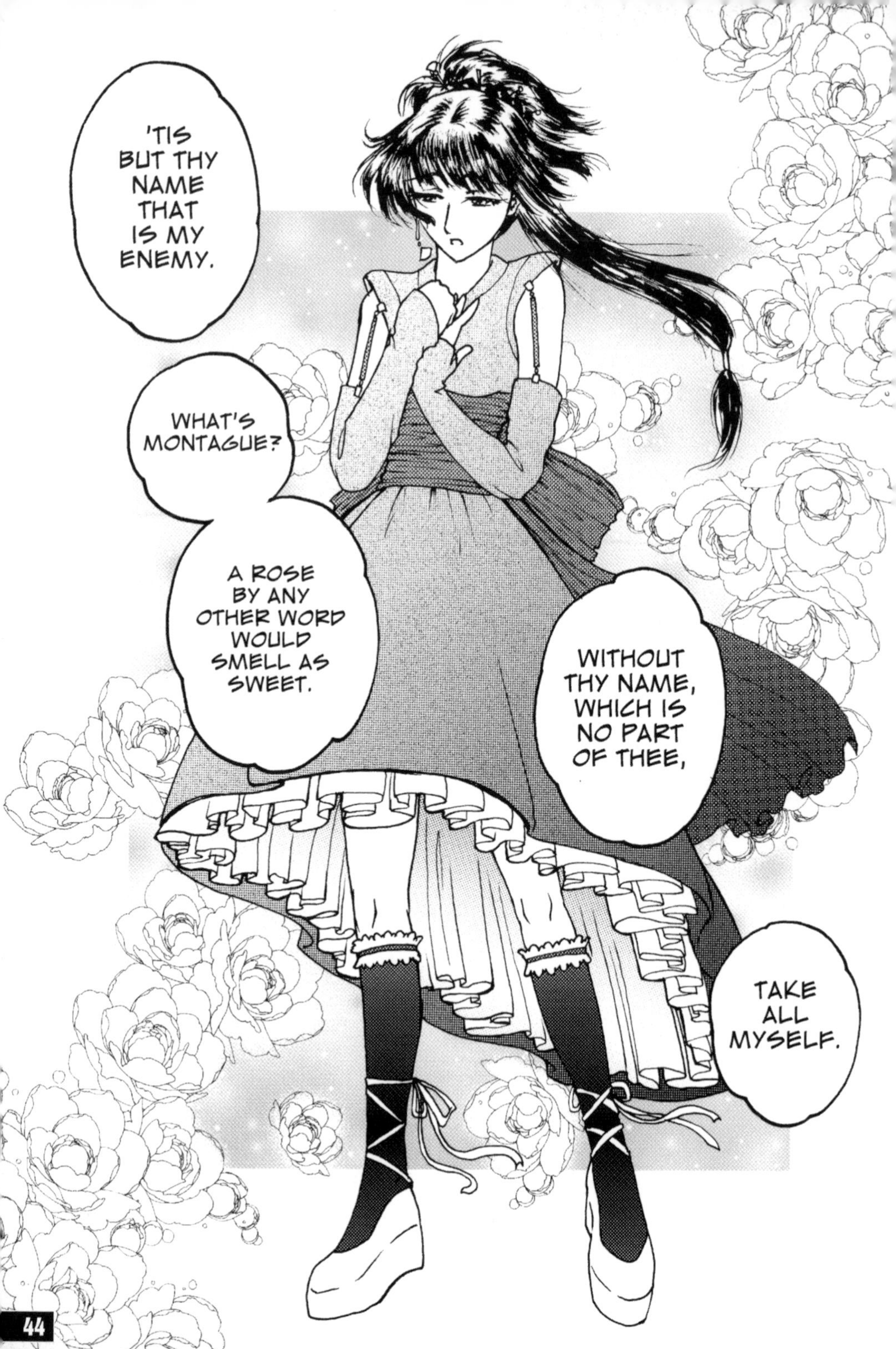
'TIS BUT THY NAME THAT IS MY ENEMY.
WHAT'S MONTAGUE?
A ROSE BY ANY OTHER WORD WOULD SMELL AS SWEET.
WITHOUT THY NAME, WHICH IS NO PART OF THEE,
TAKE ALL MYSELF.

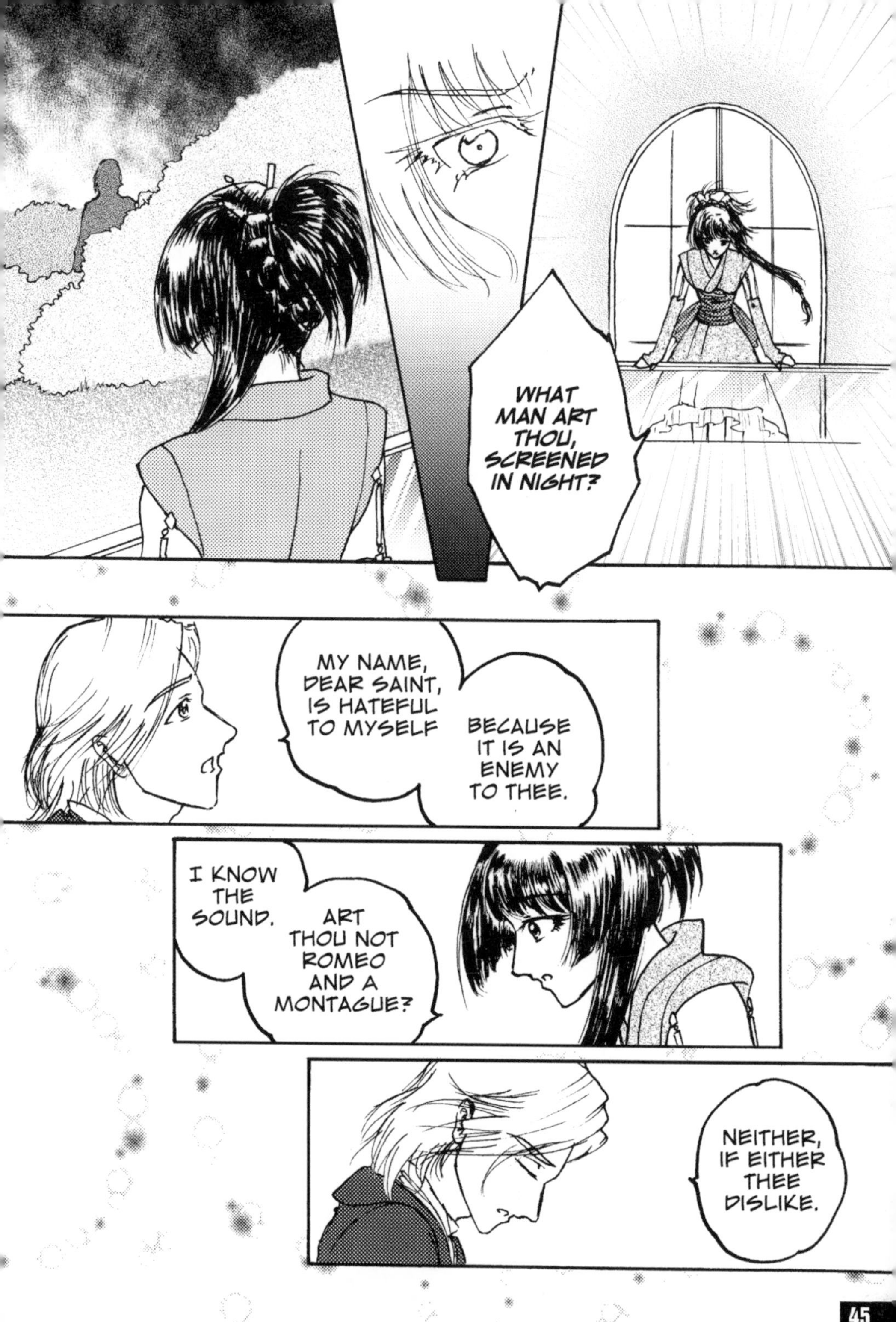
WHAT MAN ART THOU, SCREENED IN NIGHT?
MY NAME, DEAR SAINT, IS HATEFUL TO MYSELF
BECAUSE IT IS AN ENEMY TO THEE.
I KNOW THE SOUND.
ART THOU NOT ROMEO AND A MONTAGUE?
NEITHER, IF EITHER THEE DISLIKE.

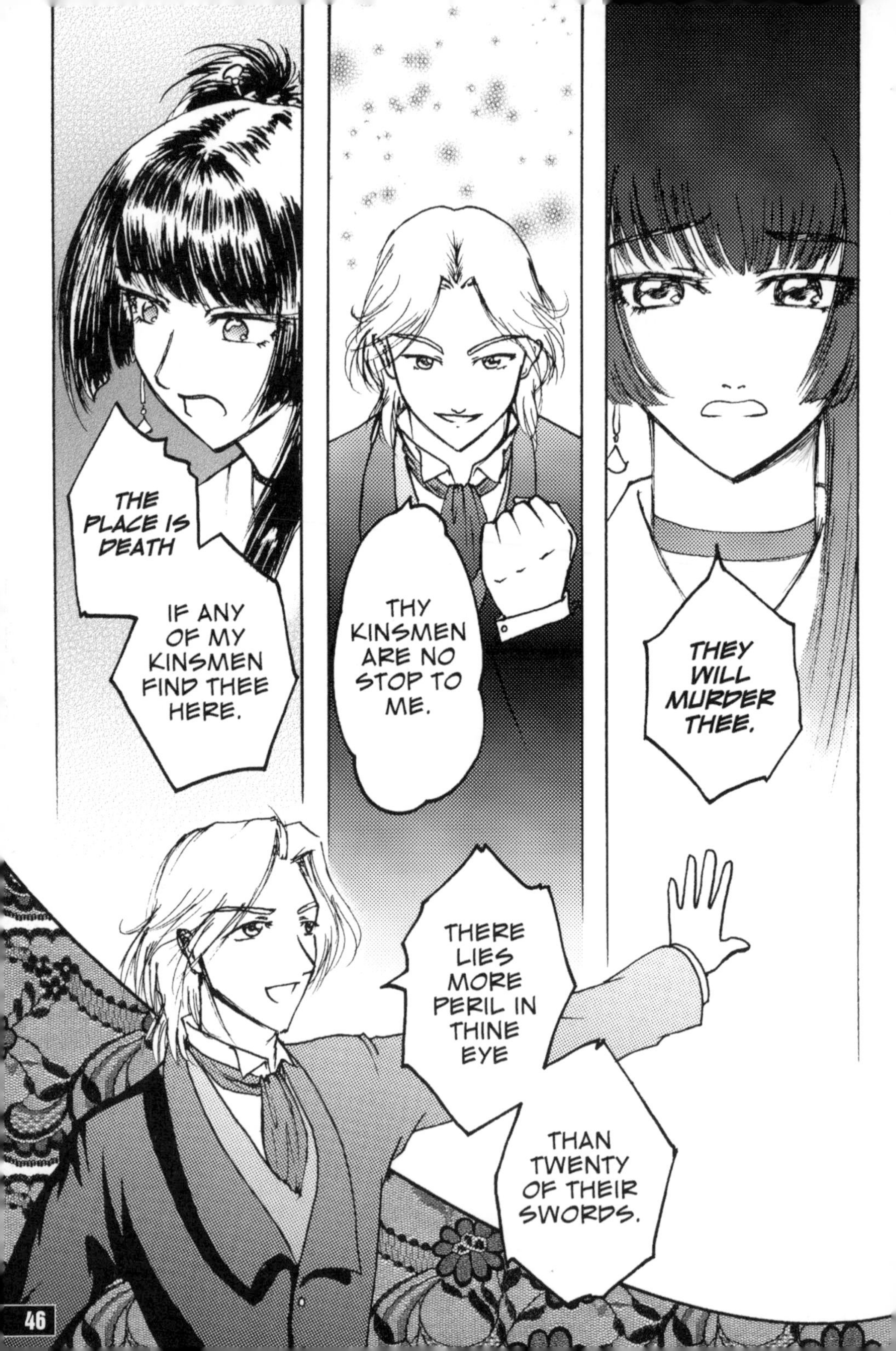
THE PLACE IS DEATH
IF ANY OF MY KINSMEN FIND THEE HERE.
THY KINSMEN ARE NO STOP TO ME.
THEY WILL MURDER THEE.
THERE LIES MORE PERIL IN THINE EYE
THAN TWENTY OF THEIR SWORDS.

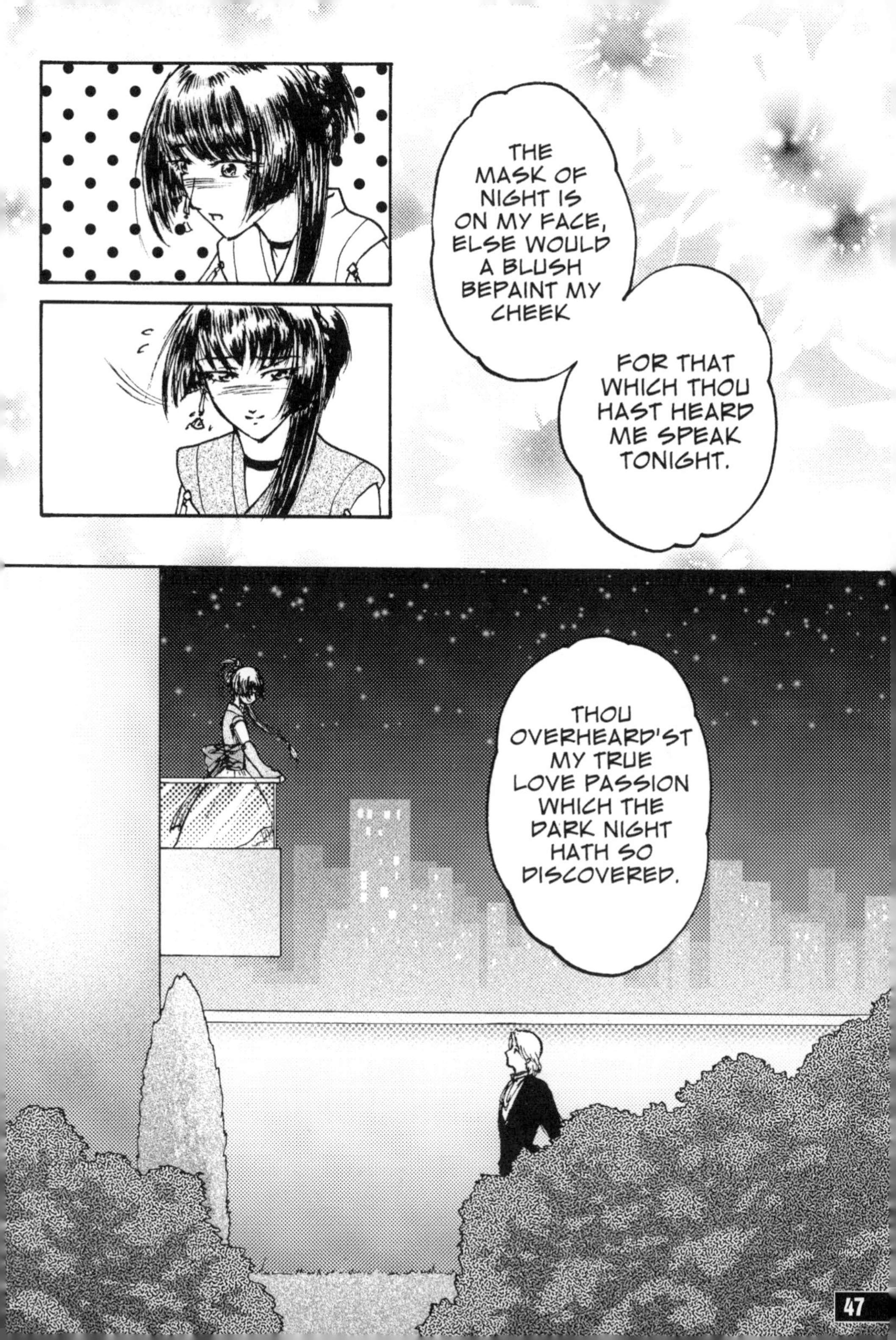
THE MASK OF NIGHT IS ON MY FACE, ELSE WOULD A BLUSH BEPAINT MY CHEEK
FOR THAT WHICH THOU HAST HEARD ME SPEAK TONIGHT.
THOU OVERHEARD'ST MY TRUE LOVE PASSION WHICH THE DARK NIGHT HATH SO DISCOVERED.

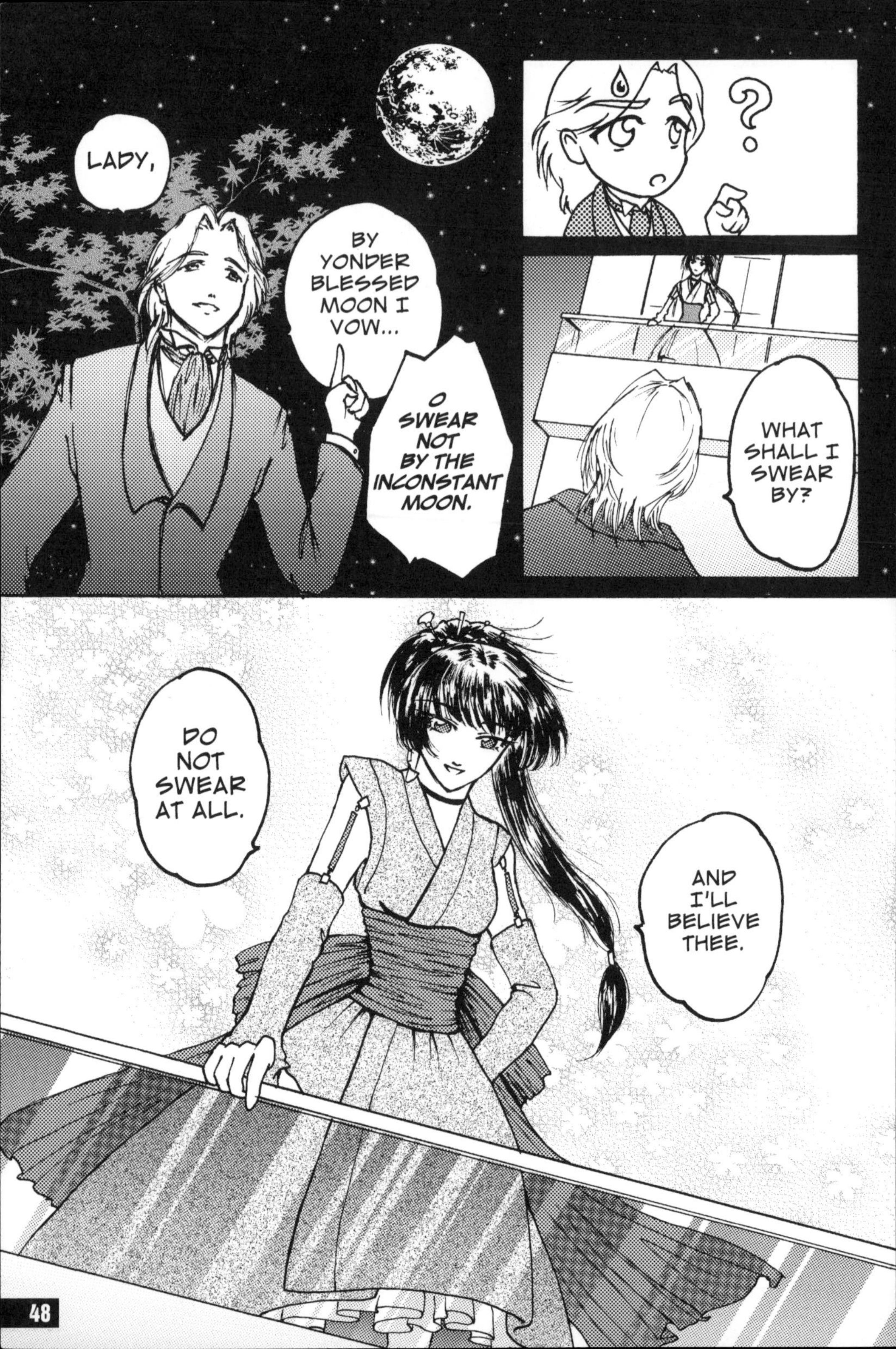
LADY,
BY YONDER BLESSED MOON I VOW...
O SWEAR NOT BY THE INCONSTANT MOON.
?
WHAT SHALL I SWEAR BY?
DO NOT SWEAR AT ALL.
AND I'LL BELIEVE THEE.

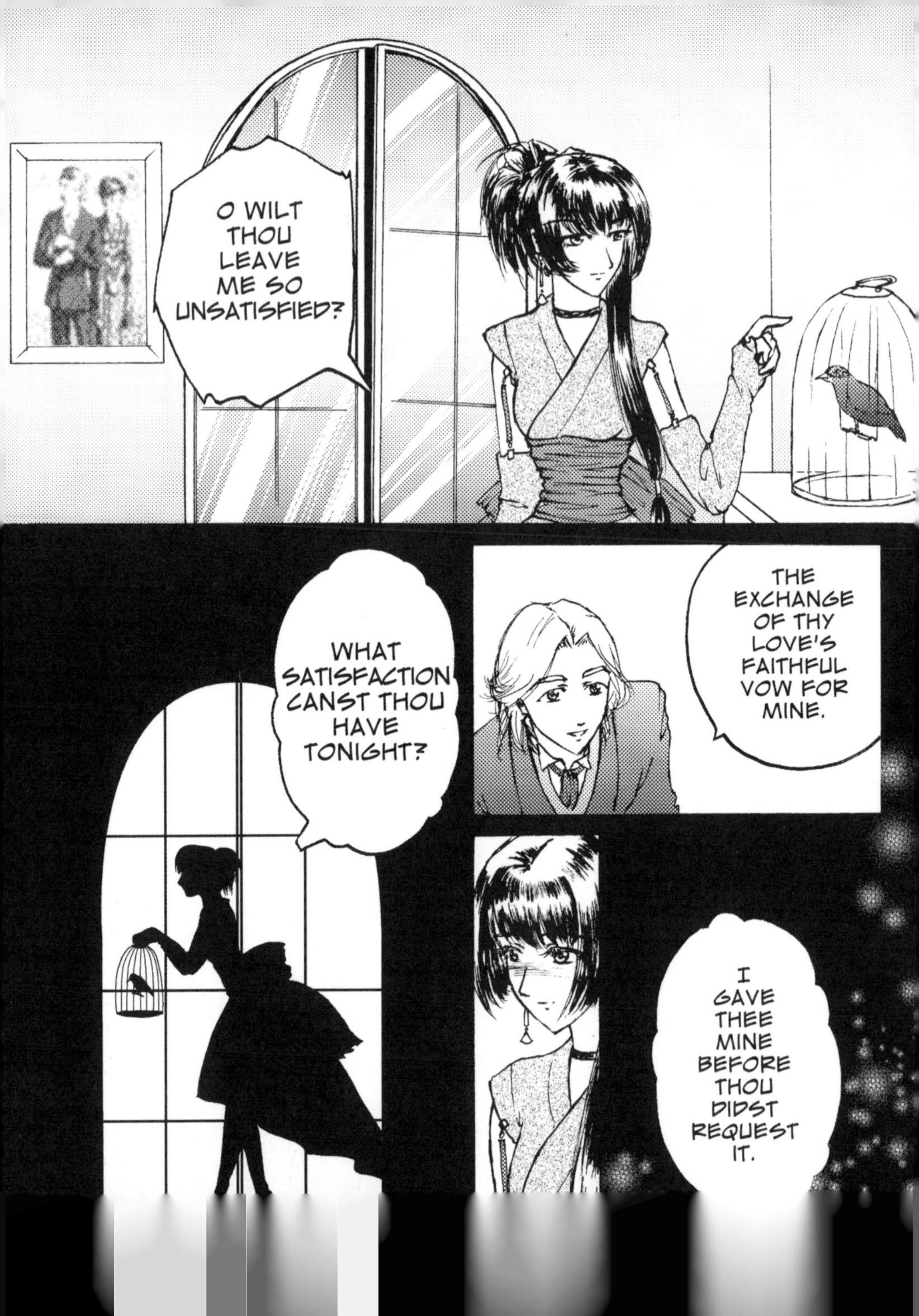
O WILT THOU LEAVE ME SO UNSATISFIED?
WHAT SATISFACTION CANST THOU HAVE TONIGHT?
THE EXCHANGE OF THY LOVE'S FAITHFUL VOW FOR MINE.
I GAVE THEE MINE BEFORE THOU DIDST REQUEST IT.

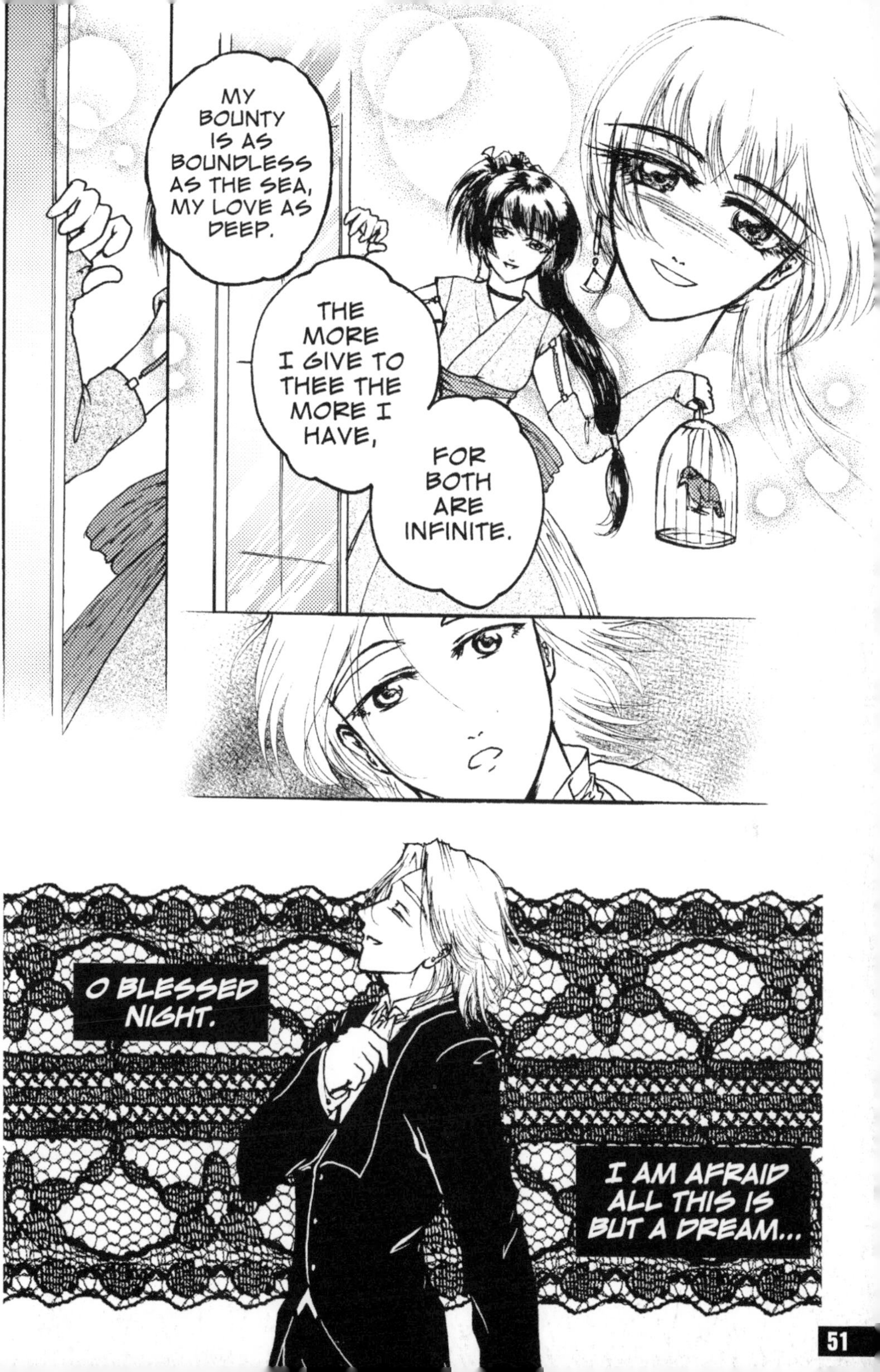
MY BOUNTY IS AS BOUNDLESS AS THE SEA, MY LOVE AS DEEP.
THE MORE I GIVE TO THEE THE MORE I HAVE,
FOR BOTH ARE INFINITE.
O BLESSED NIGHT.
I AM AFRAID ALL THIS IS BUT A DREAM...

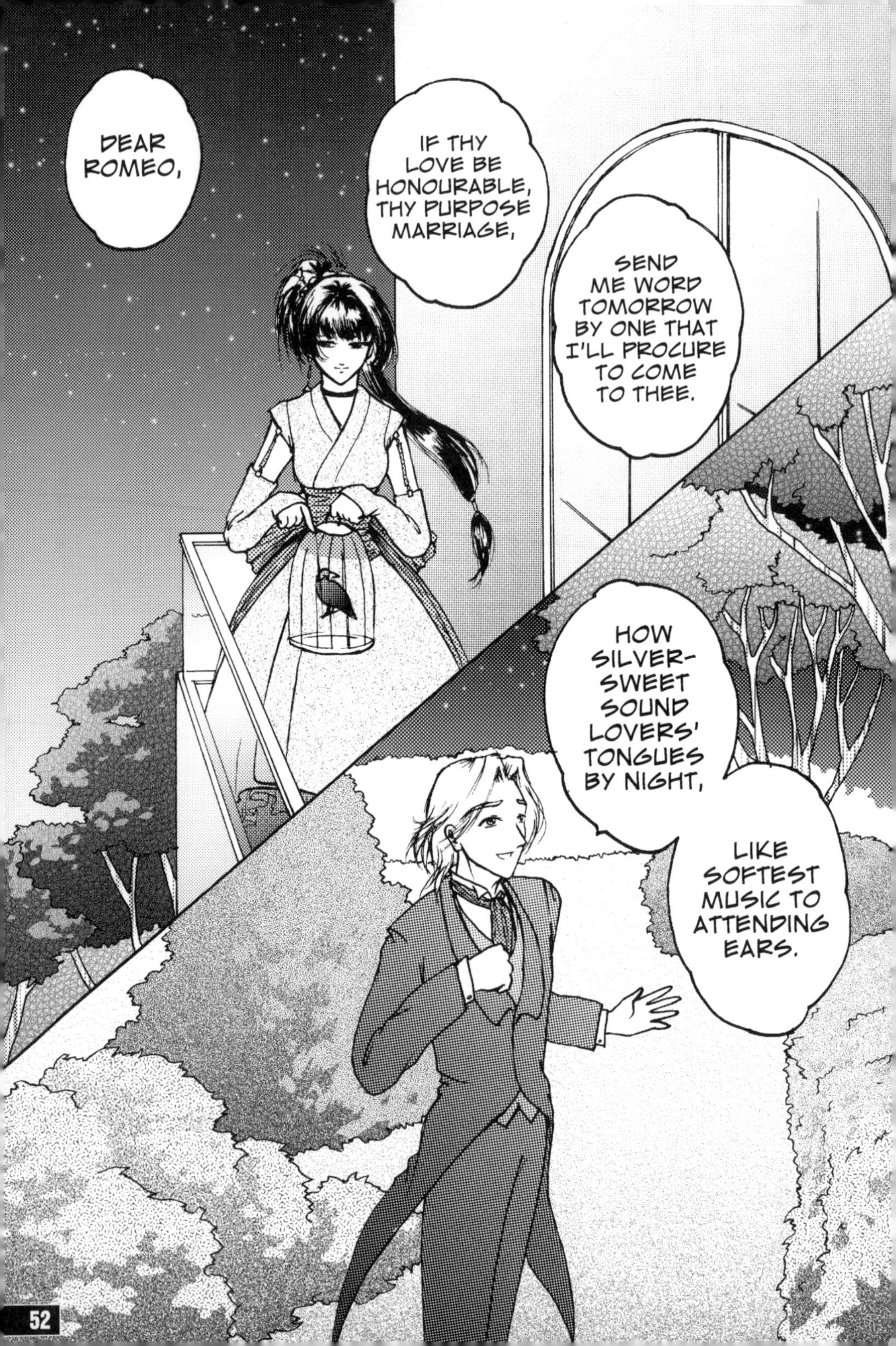
DEAR ROMEO,
IF THY LOVE BE HONOURABLE, THY PURPOSE MARRIAGE,
SEND ME WORD TOMORROW BY ONE THAT I'LL PROCURE TO COME TO THEE.
HOW SILVER-SWEET SOUND LOVERS' TONGUES BY NIGHT,
LIKE SOFTEST MUSIC TO ATTENDING EARS.

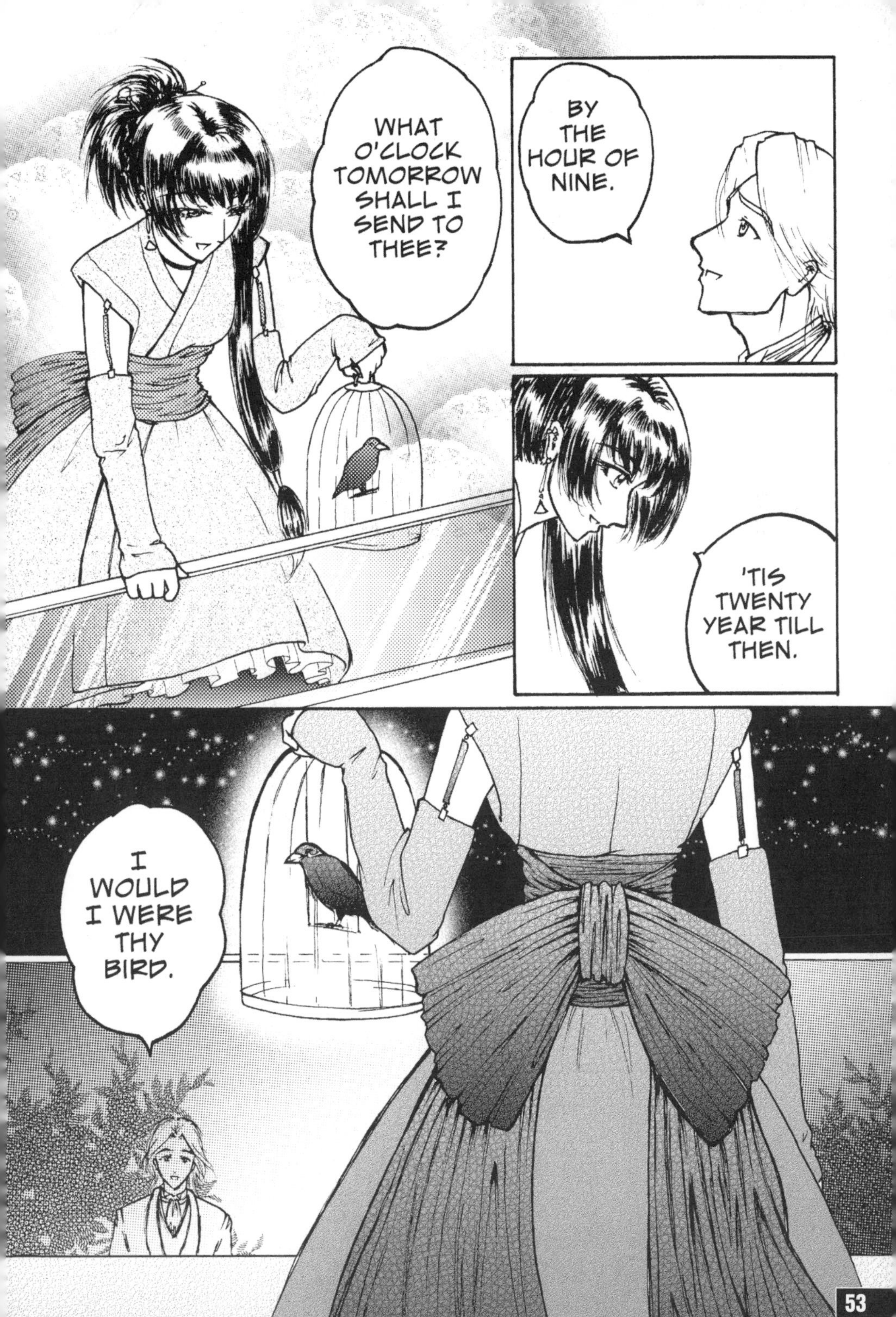
WHAT O'CLOCK TOMORROW SHALL I SEND TO THEE?
BY THE HOUR OF NINE.
'TIS TWENTY YEAR TILL THEN.
I WOULD I WERE THY BIRD.

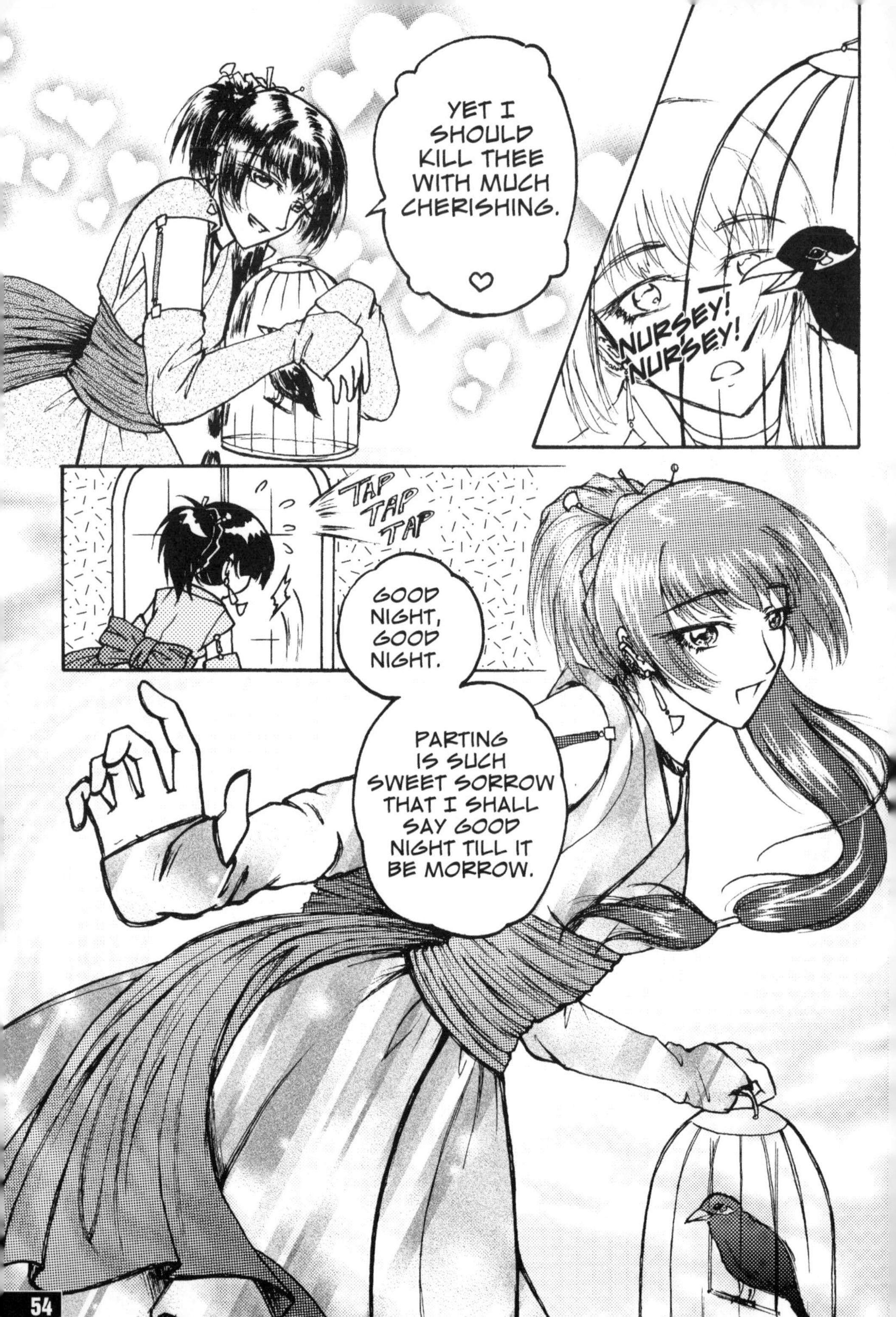

YET I SHOULD KILL THEE WITH MUCH CHERISHING. ♡
NURSEY! NURSEY!
TAP TAP TAP
GOOD NIGHT, GOOD NIGHT.
PARTING IS SUCH SWEET SORROW THAT I SHALL SAY GOOD NIGHT TILL IT BE MORROW.

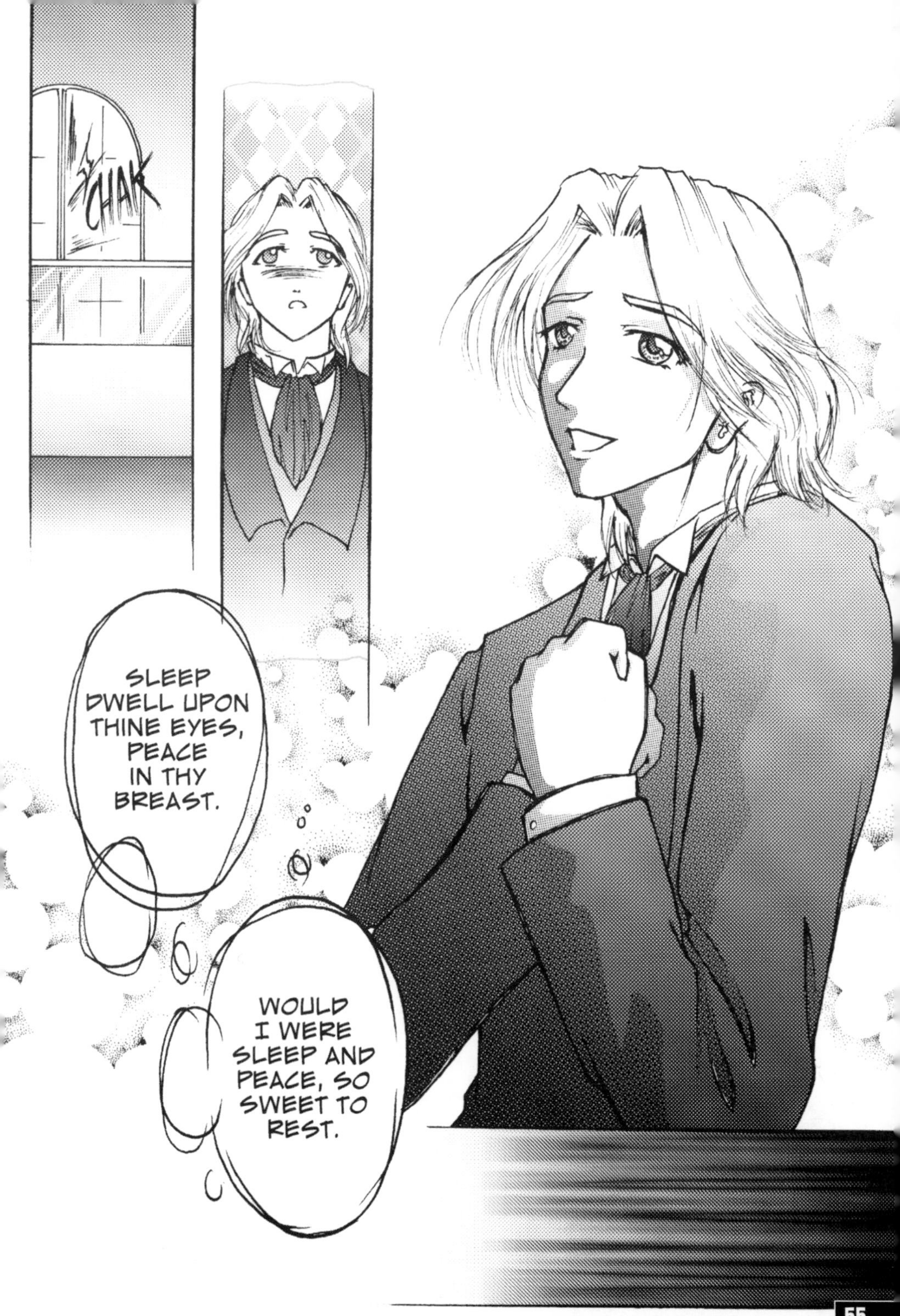
CHAK
SLEEP DWELL UPON THINE EYES, PEACE IN THY BREAST.
WOULD I WERE SLEEP AND PEACE, SO SWEET TO REST.

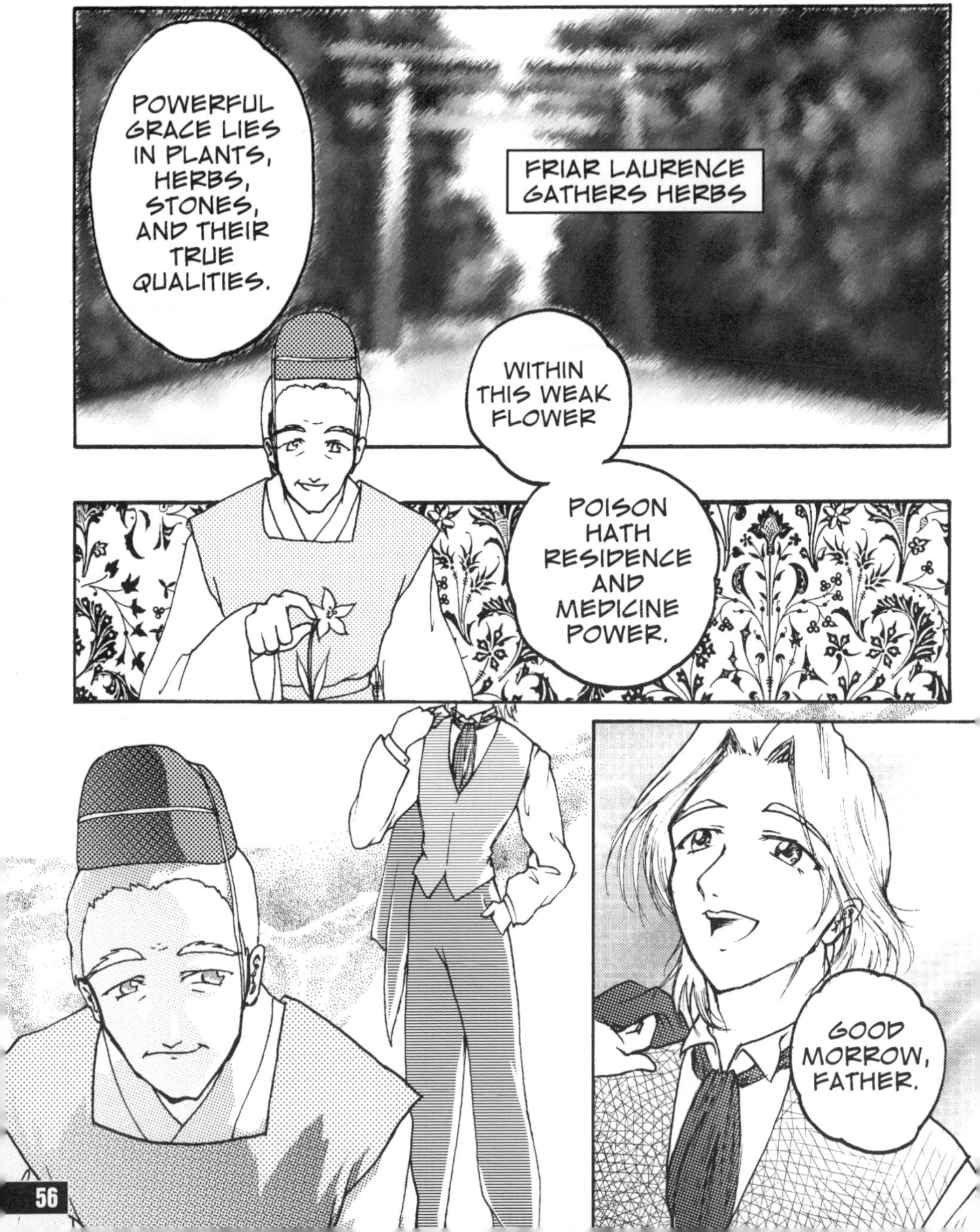
POWERFUL GRACE LIES IN PLANTS, HERBS, STONES, AND THEIR TRUE QUALITIES.
FRIAR LAURENCE GATHERS HERBS
WITHIN THIS WEAK FLOWER
POISON HATH RESIDENCE AND MEDICINE POWER.
GOOD MORROW, FATHER.

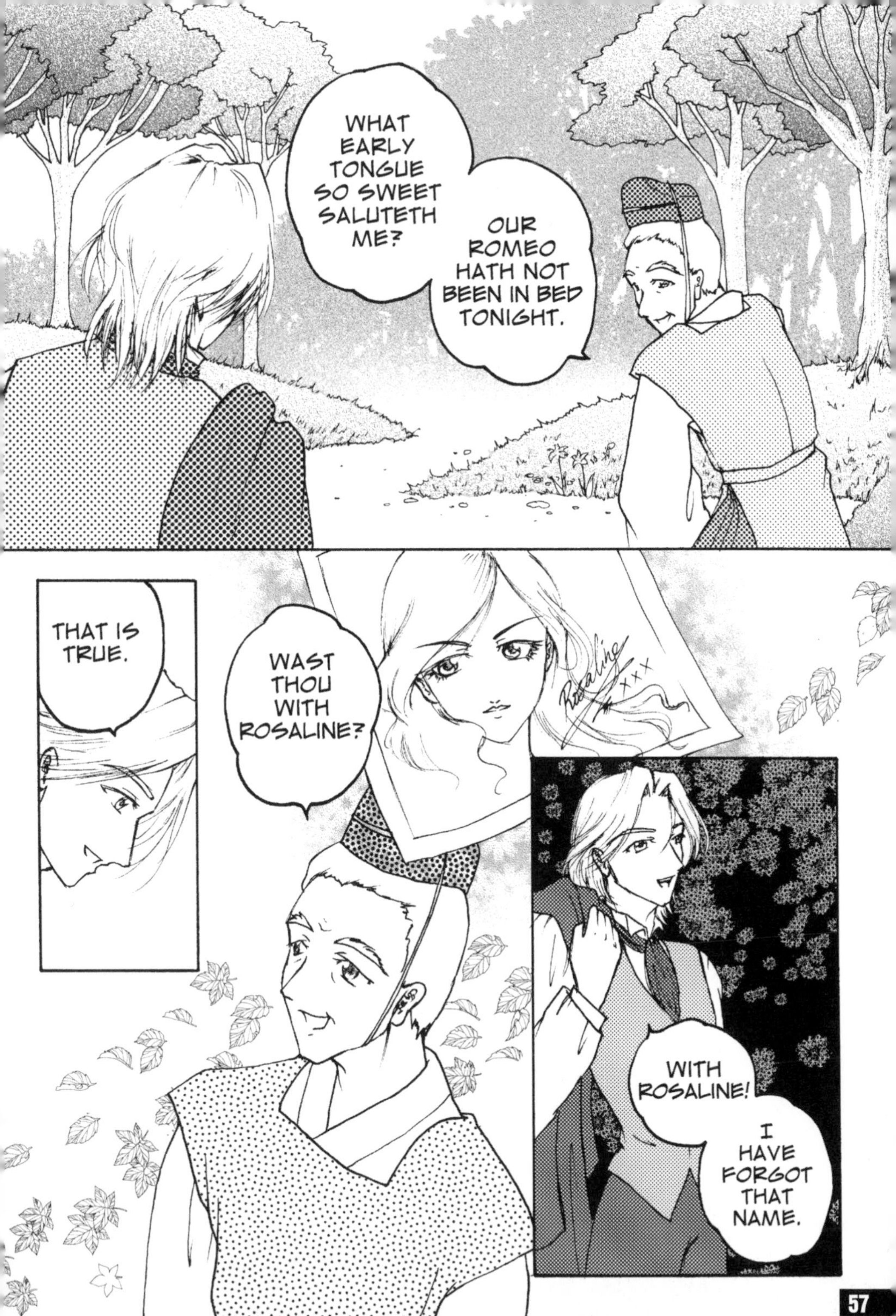
WHAT EARLY TONGUE SO SWEET SALUTETH ME?
OUR ROMEO HATH NOT BEEN IN BED TONIGHT.
THAT IS TRUE.
WAST THOU WITH ROSALINE?
Rosaline xxx
WITH ROSALINE!
I HAVE FORGOT THAT NAME.

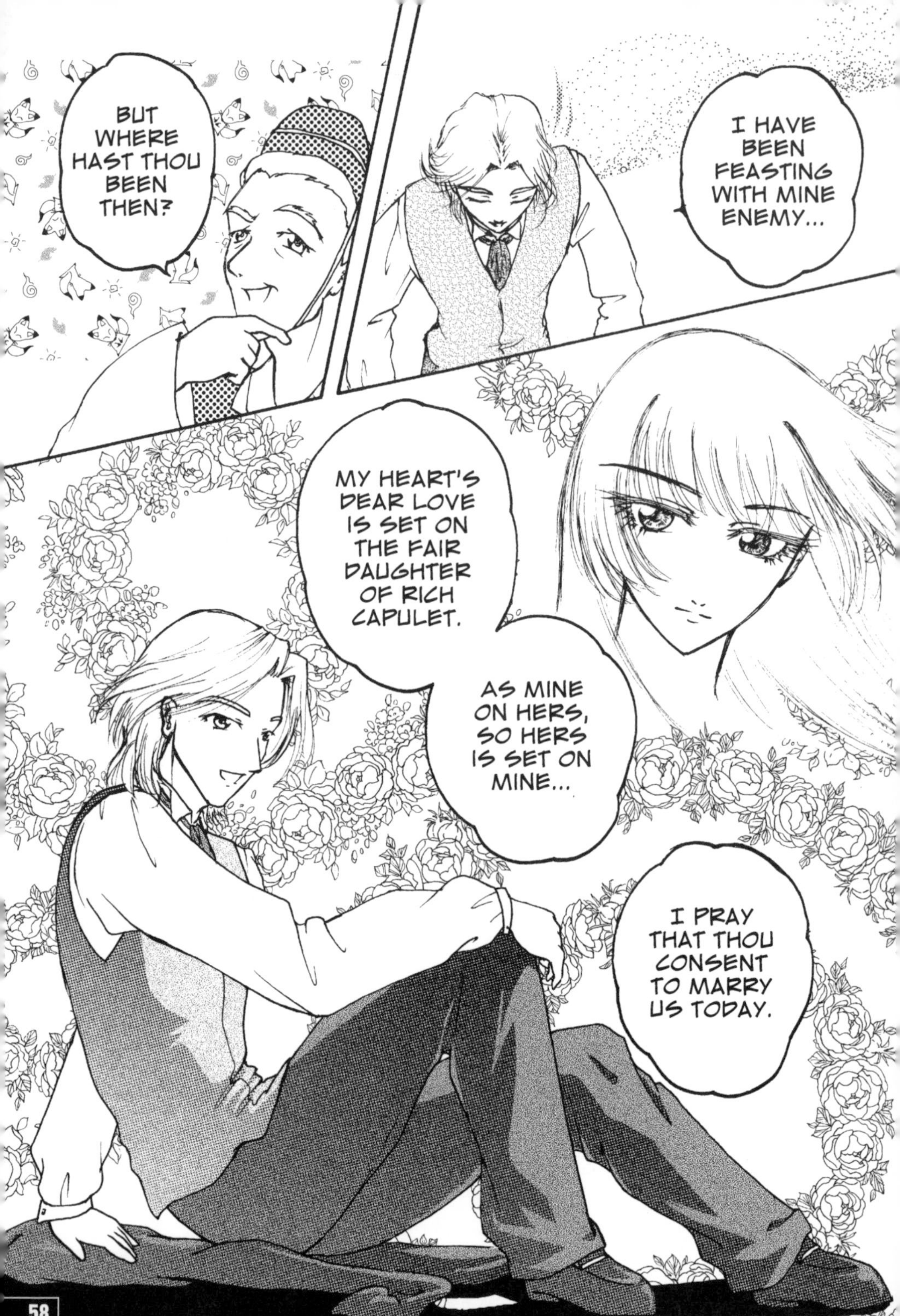
BUT WHERE HAST THOU BEEN THEN?
I HAVE BEEN FEASTING WITH MINE ENEMY...
MY HEART'S DEAR LOVE IS SET ON THE FAIR DAUGHTER OF RICH CAPULET.
AS MINE ON HERS, SO HERS IS SET ON MINE...
I PRAY THAT THOU CONSENT TO MARRY US TODAY.

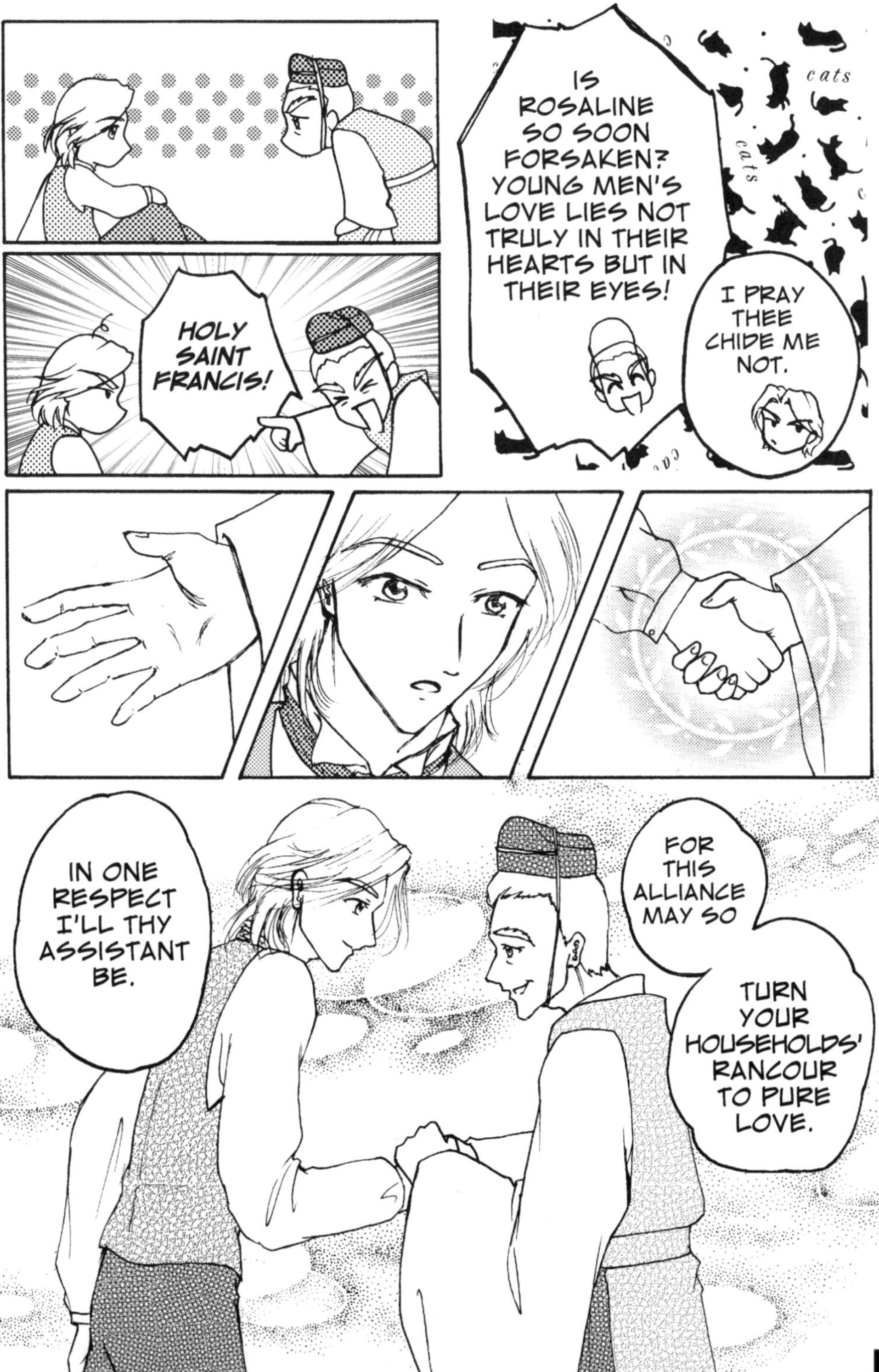
HOLY SAINT FRANCIS!
IS ROSALINE SO SOON FORSAKEN? YOUNG MEN'S LOVE LIES NOT TRULY IN THEIR HEARTS BUT IN THEIR EYES!
I PRAY THEE CHIDE ME NOT.
IN ONE RESPECT I'LL THY ASSISTANT BE.
FOR THIS ALLIANCE MAY SO
TURN YOUR HOUSEHOLDS' RANCOUR TO PURE LOVE.

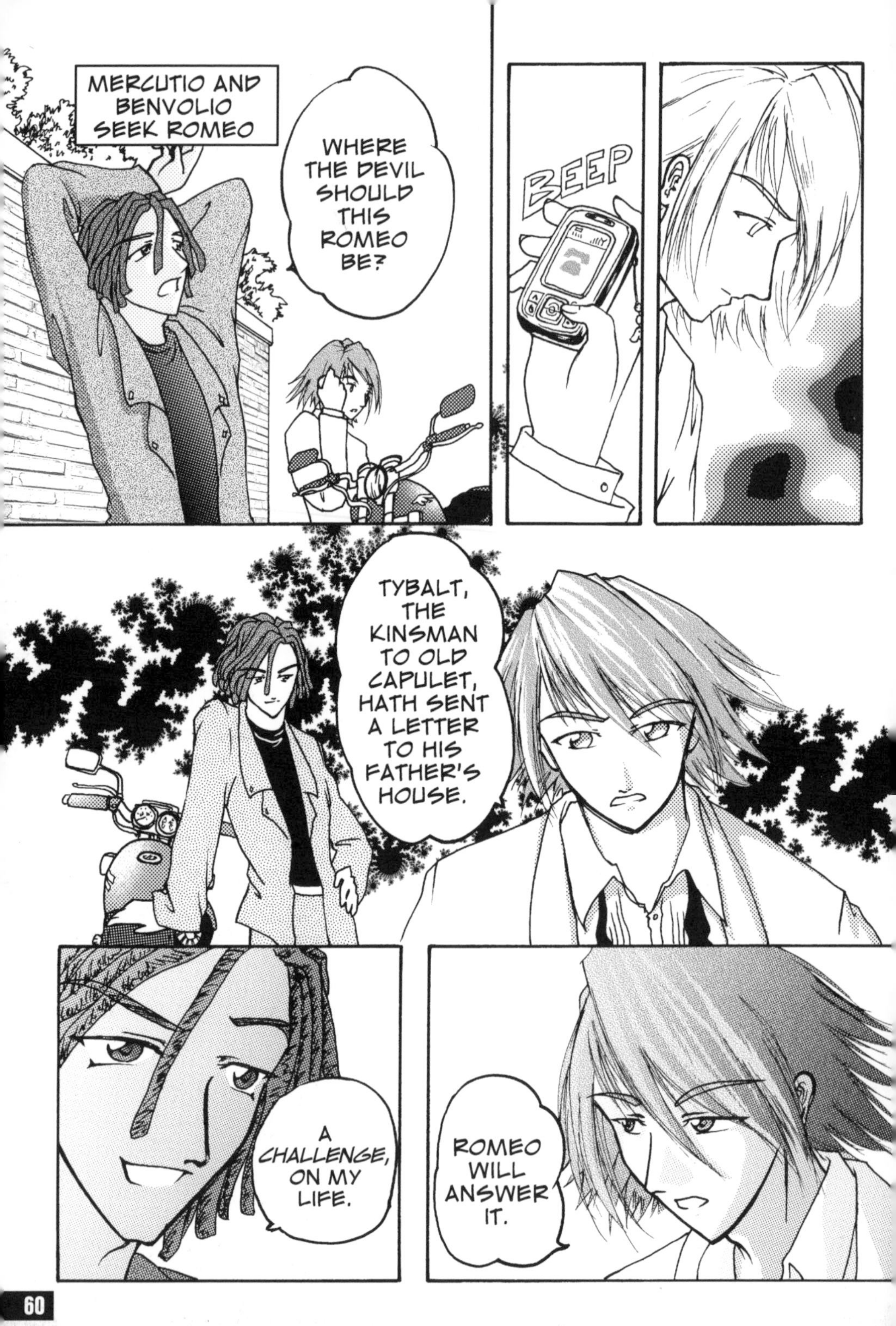
MERCUTIO AND BENVOLIO SEEK ROMEO
WHERE THE DEVIL SHOULD THIS ROMEO BE?
BEEP
TYBALT, THE KINSMAN TO OLD CAPULET, HATH SENT A LETTER TO HIS FATHER'S HOUSE.
A CHALLENGE, ON MY LIFE.
ROMEO WILL ANSWER IT.

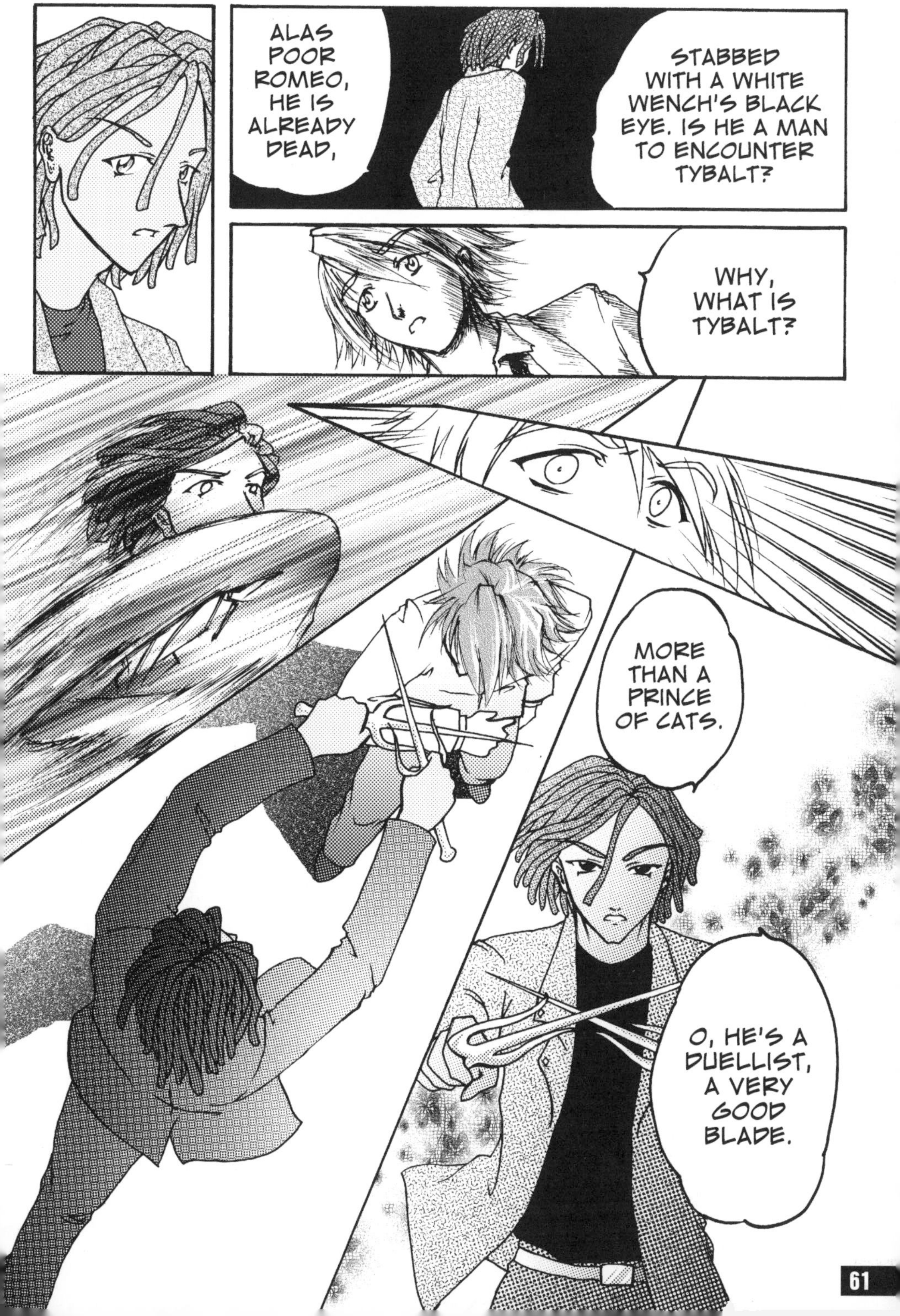
ALAS POOR ROMEO, HE IS ALREADY DEAD,
STABBED WITH A WHITE WENCH'S BLACK EYE. IS HE A MAN TO ENCOUNTER TYBALT?
WHY, WHAT IS TYBALT?
MORE THAN A PRINCE OF CATS.
O, HE'S A DUELLIST, A VERY GOOD BLADE.

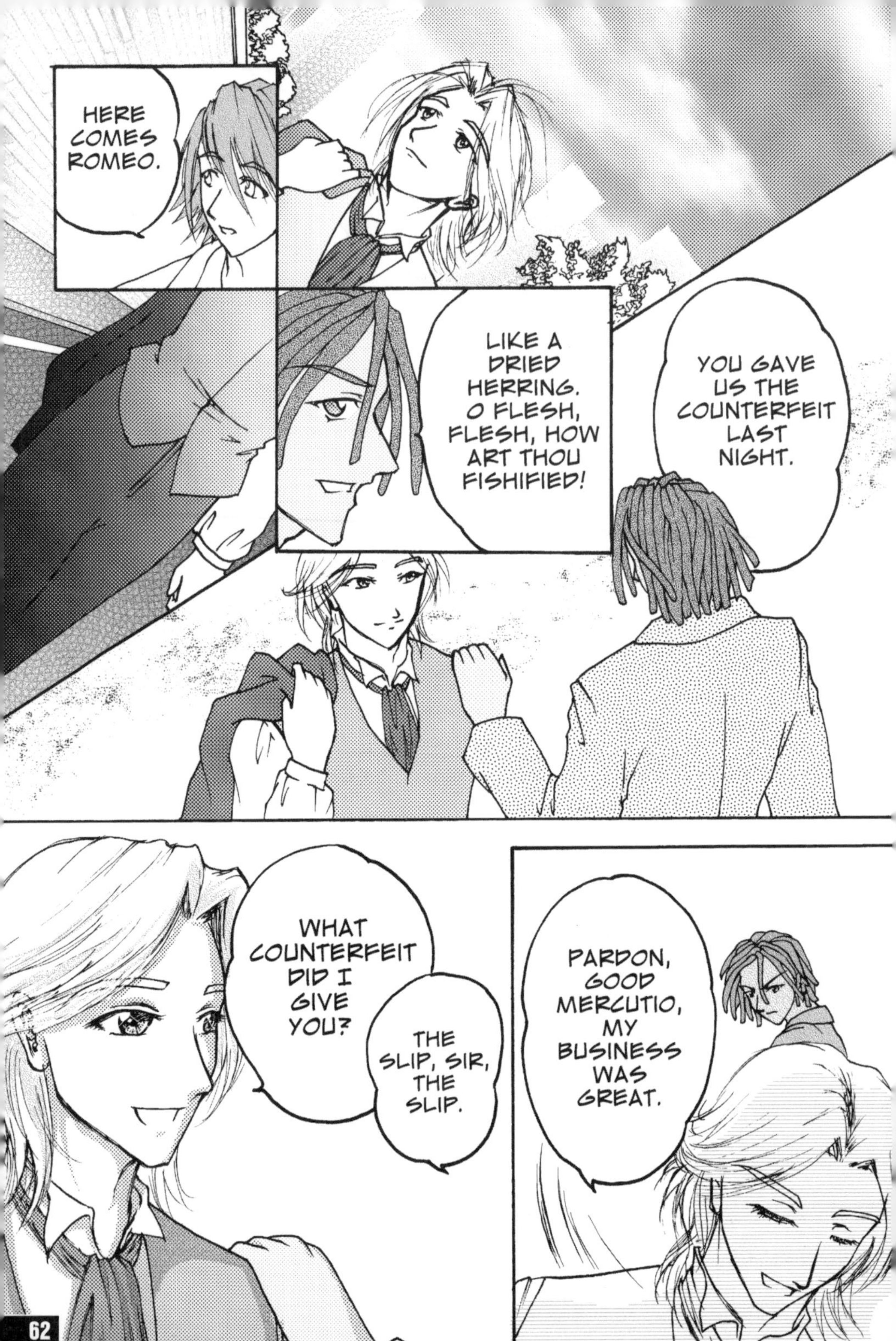

HERE COMES ROMEO.
LIKE A DRIED HERRING. O FLESH, FLESH, HOW ART THOU FISHIFIED!
YOU GAVE US THE COUNTERFEIT LAST NIGHT.
WHAT COUNTERFEIT DID I GIVE YOU?
THE SLIP, SIR, THE SLIP.
PARDON, GOOD MERCUTIO, MY BUSINESS WAS GREAT.

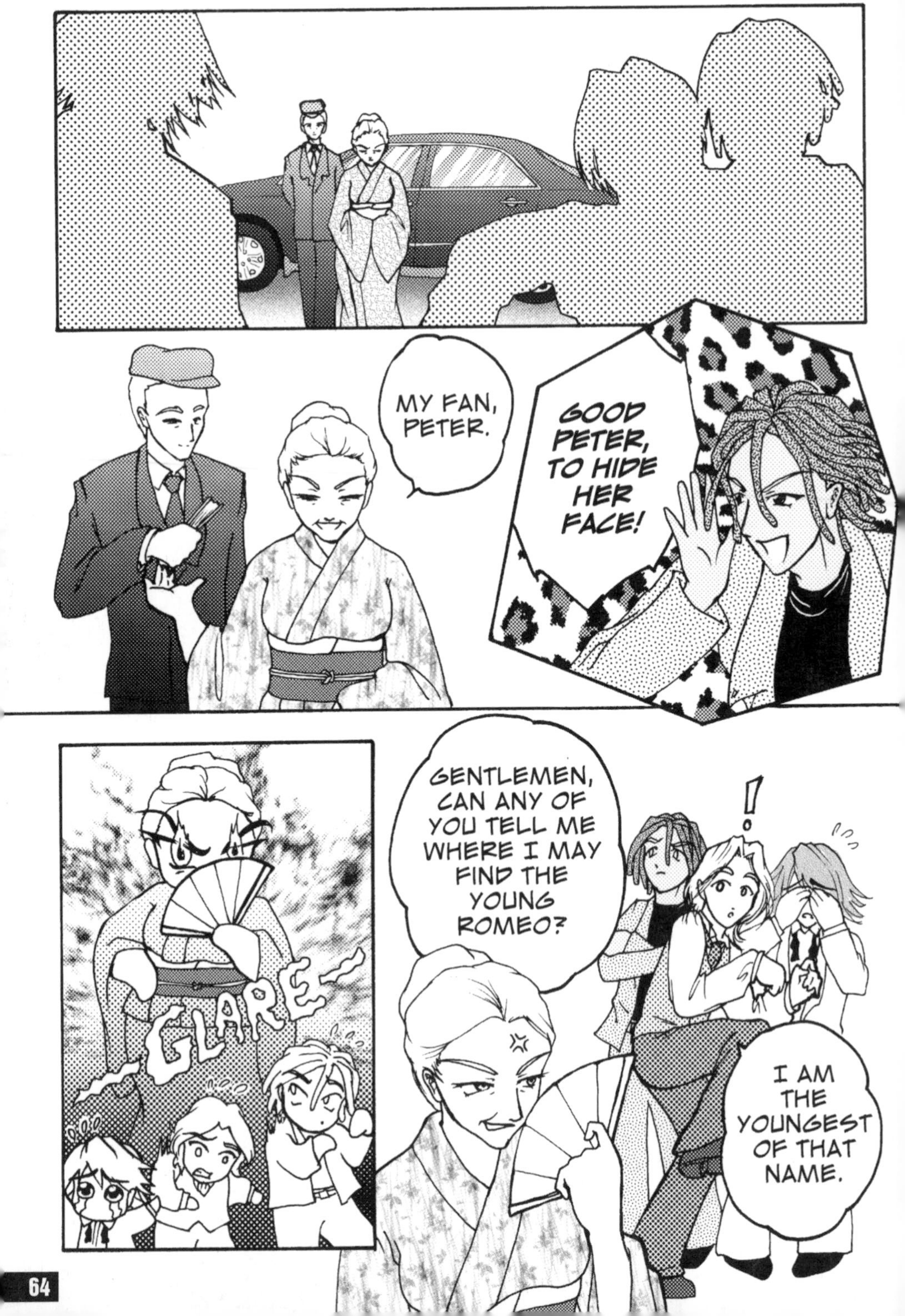
MY FAN, PETER.
GOOD PETER, TO HIDE HER FACE!
GLARE
GENTLEMEN, CAN ANY OF YOU TELL ME WHERE I MAY FIND THE YOUNG ROMEO?
!
I AM THE YOUNGEST OF THAT NAME.

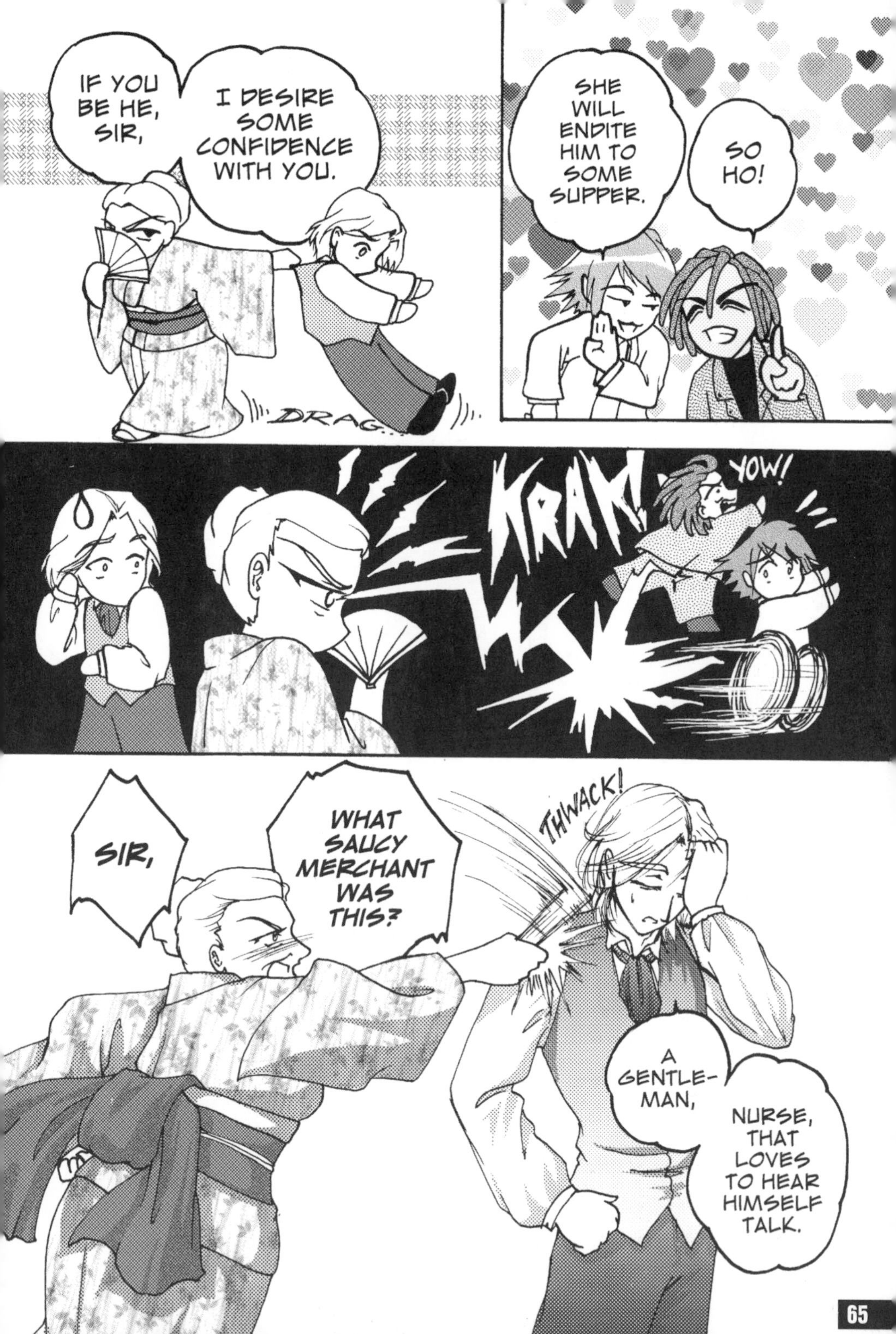
IF YOU BE HE, SIR,
I DESIRE SOME CONFIDENCE WITH YOU.
DRAG...
SHE WILL ENDITE HIM TO SOME SUPPER.
SO HO!
KRAK!
YOW!
SIR,
WHAT SAUCY MERCHANT WAS THIS?
THWACK!
A GENTLE-MAN,
NURSE, THAT LOVES TO HEAR HIMSELF TALK.

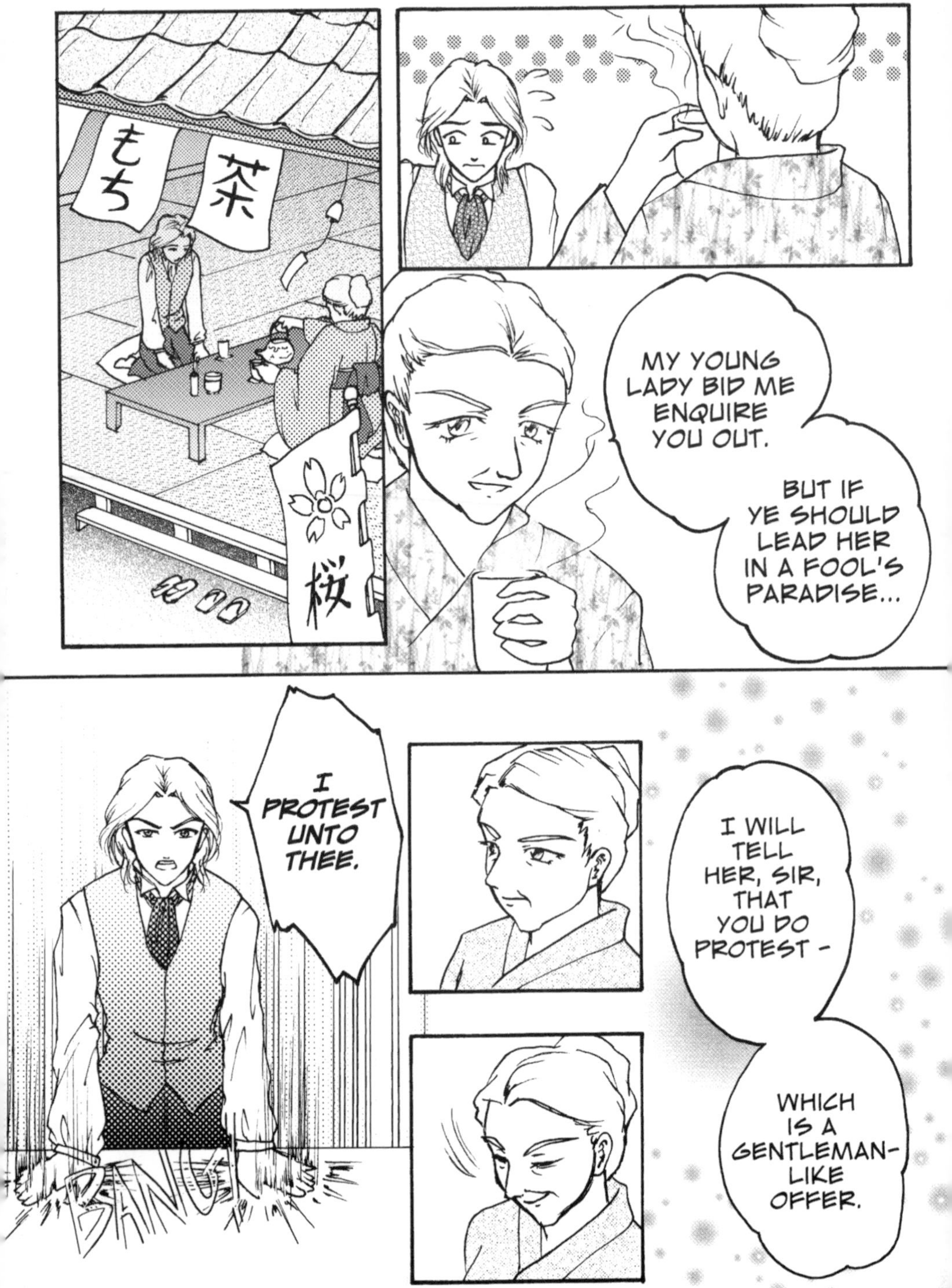

もち
茶
桜
MY YOUNG LADY BID ME ENQUIRE YOU OUT.
BUT IF YE SHOULD LEAD HER IN A FOOL'S PARADISE...
I PROTEST UNTO THEE.
BANG!
I WILL TELL HER, SIR, THAT YOU DO PROTEST -
WHICH IS A GENTLEMAN-LIKE OFFER.

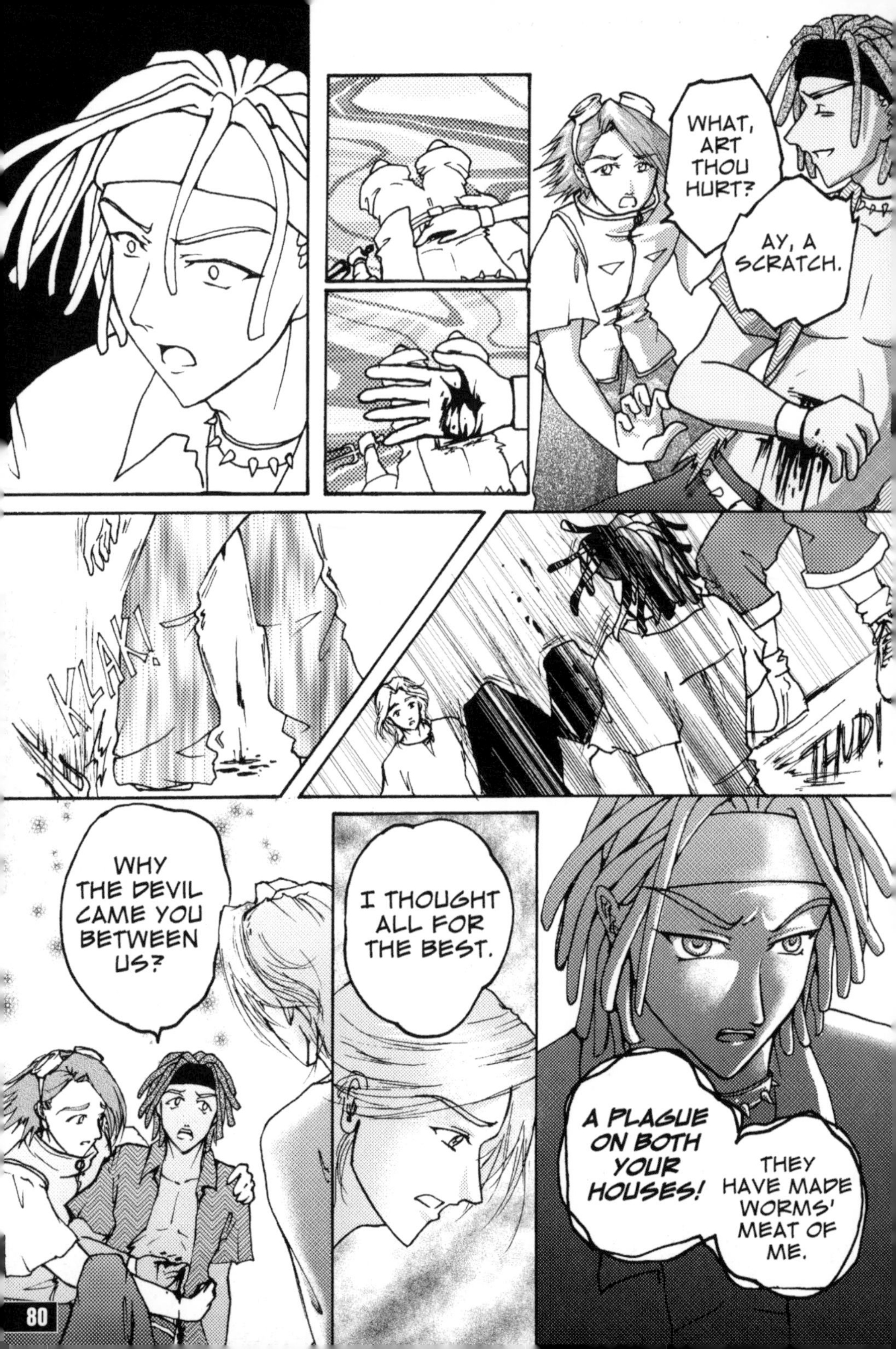

WHAT, ART THOU HURT?
AY, A SCRATCH.
KLAK!
THUD!
WHY THE DEVIL CAME YOU BETWEEN US?
I THOUGHT ALL FOR THE BEST.
A PLAGUE ON BOTH YOUR HOUSES!
THEY HAVE MADE WORMS' MEAT OF ME.

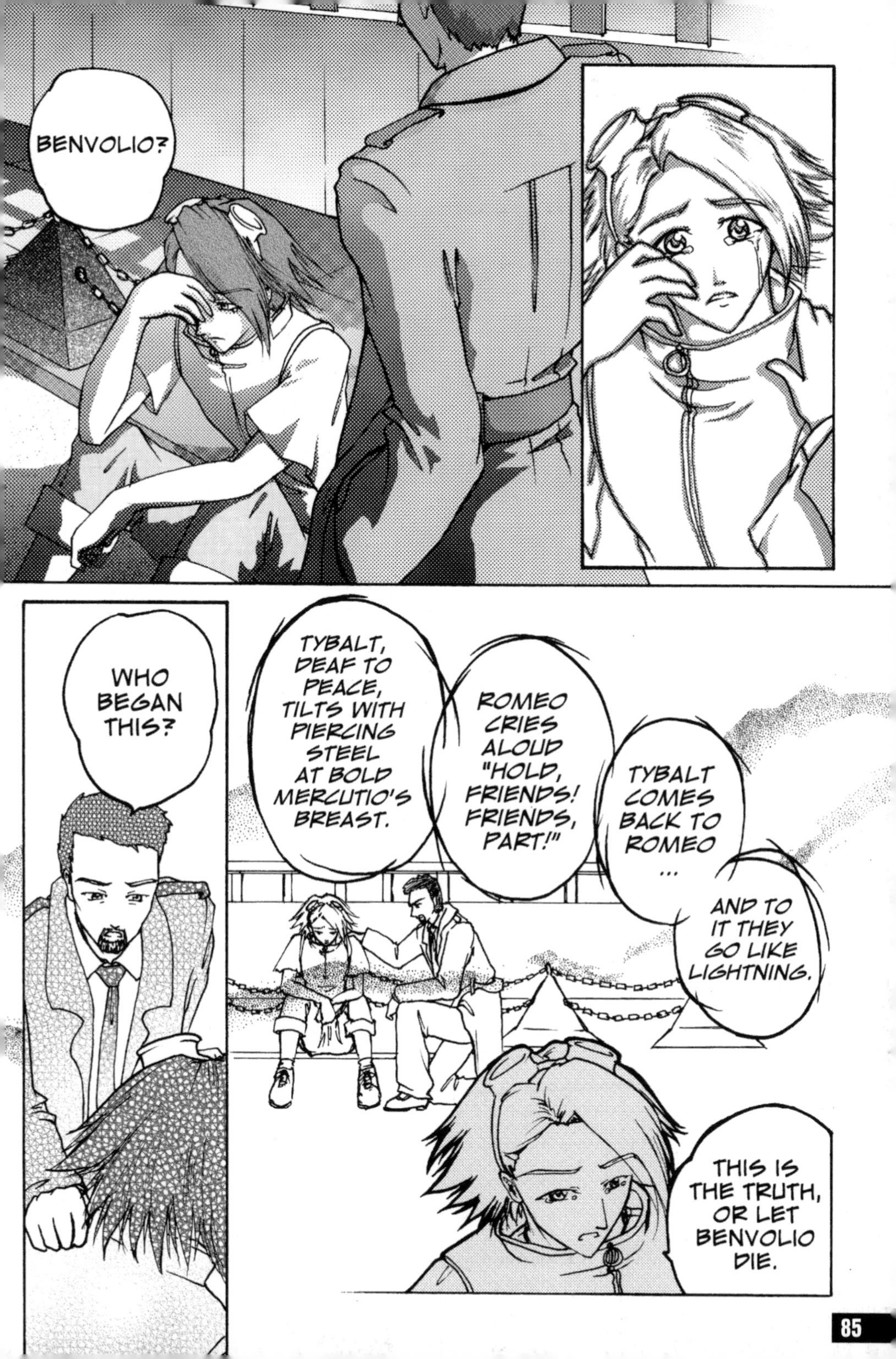

BENVOLIO?
WHO BEGAN THIS?
TYBALT, DEAF TO PEACE, TILTS WITH PIERCING STEEL AT BOLD MERCUTIO'S BREAST.
ROMEO CRIES ALOUD "HOLD, FRIENDS! FRIENDS, PART!"
TYBALT COMES BACK TO ROMEO ...
AND TO IT THEY GO LIKE LIGHTNING.
THIS IS THE TRUTH, OR LET BENVOLIO DIE.

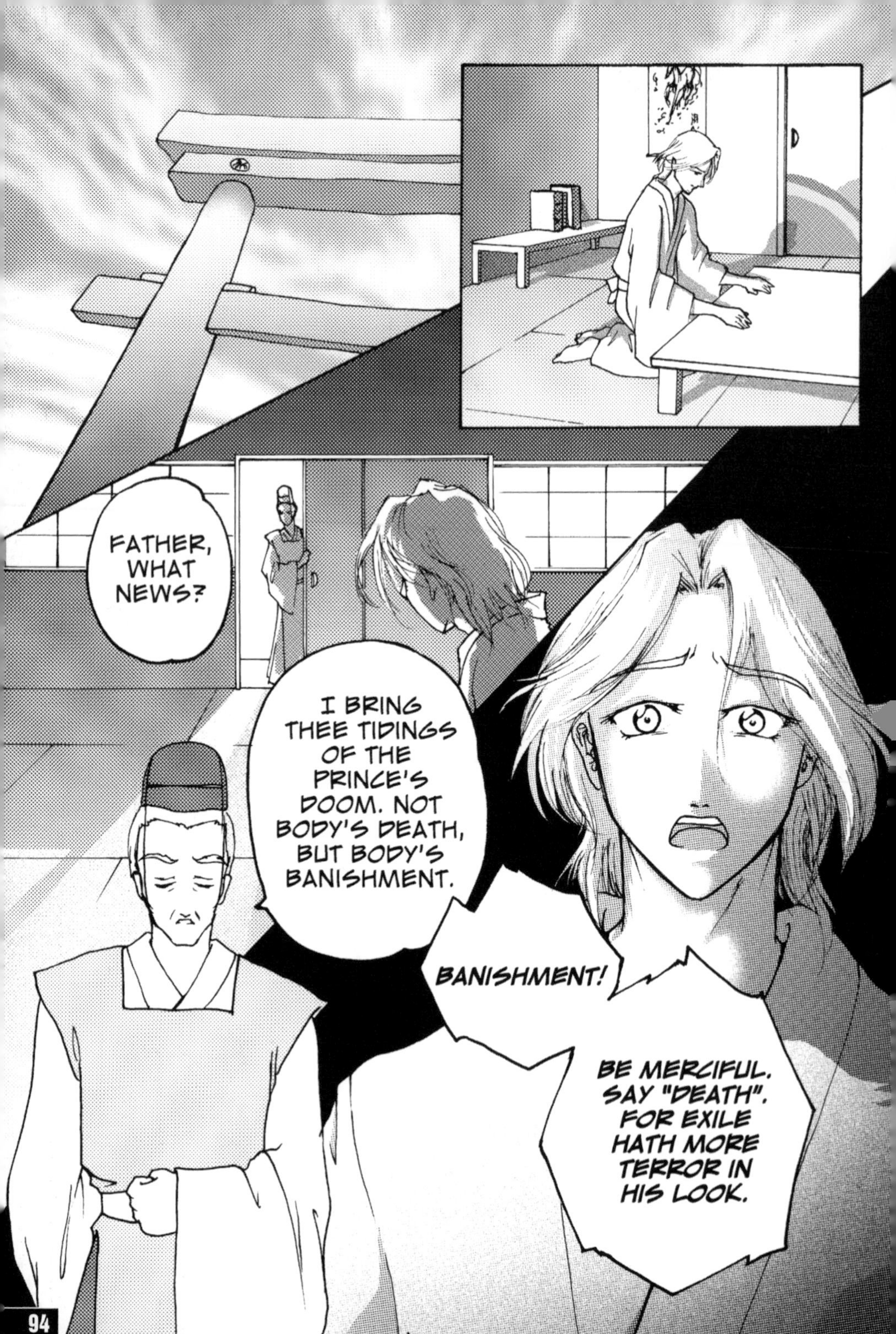
FATHER, WHAT NEWS?
I BRING THEE TIDINGS OF THE PRINCE'S DOOM. NOT BODY'S DEATH, BUT BODY'S BANISHMENT.
BANISHMENT!
BE MERCIFUL. SAY "DEATH". FOR EXILE HATH MORE TERROR IN HIS LOOK.

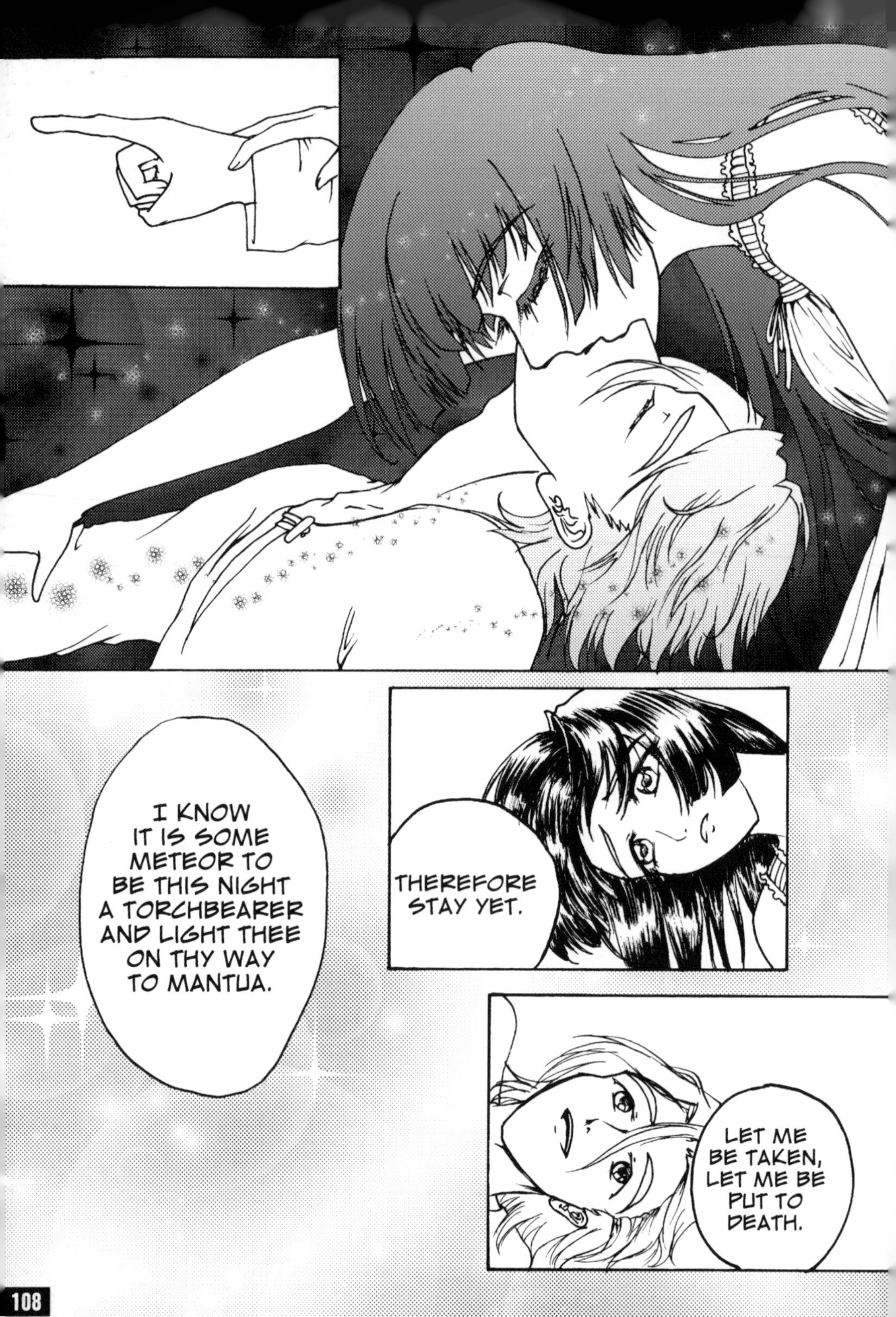
I KNOW IT IS SOME METEOR TO BE THIS NIGHT A TORCHBEARER AND LIGHT THEE ON THY WAY TO MANTUA.
THEREFORE STAY YET.
LET ME BE TAKEN, LET ME BE PUT TO DEATH.

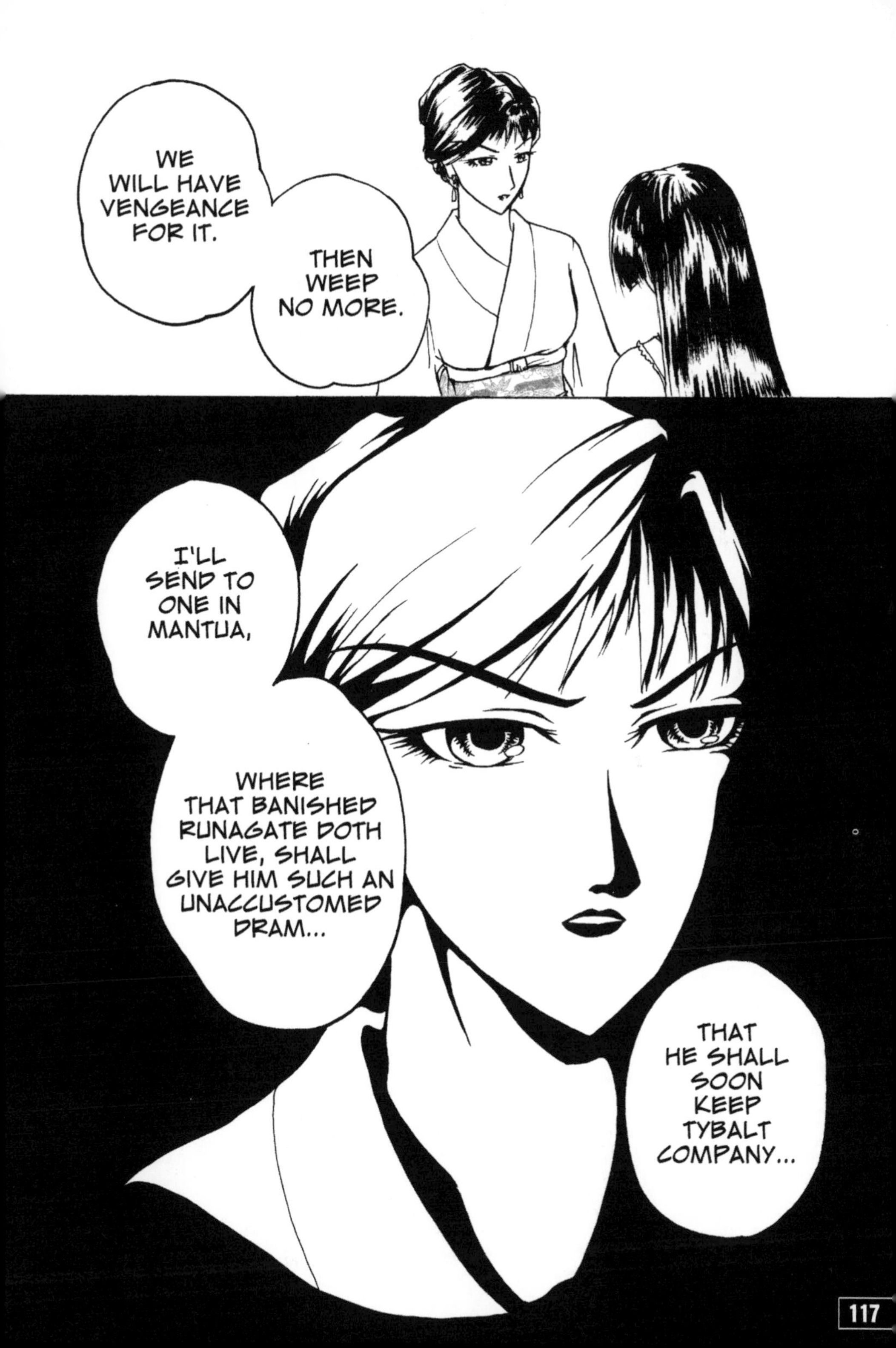
WE WILL HAVE VENGEANCE FOR IT.
THEN WEEP NO MORE.
I'LL SEND TO ONE IN MANTUA,
WHERE THAT BANISHED RUNAGATE DOTH LIVE, SHALL GIVE HIM SUCH AN UNACCUSTOMED DRAM...
THAT HE SHALL SOON KEEP TYBALT COMPANY...

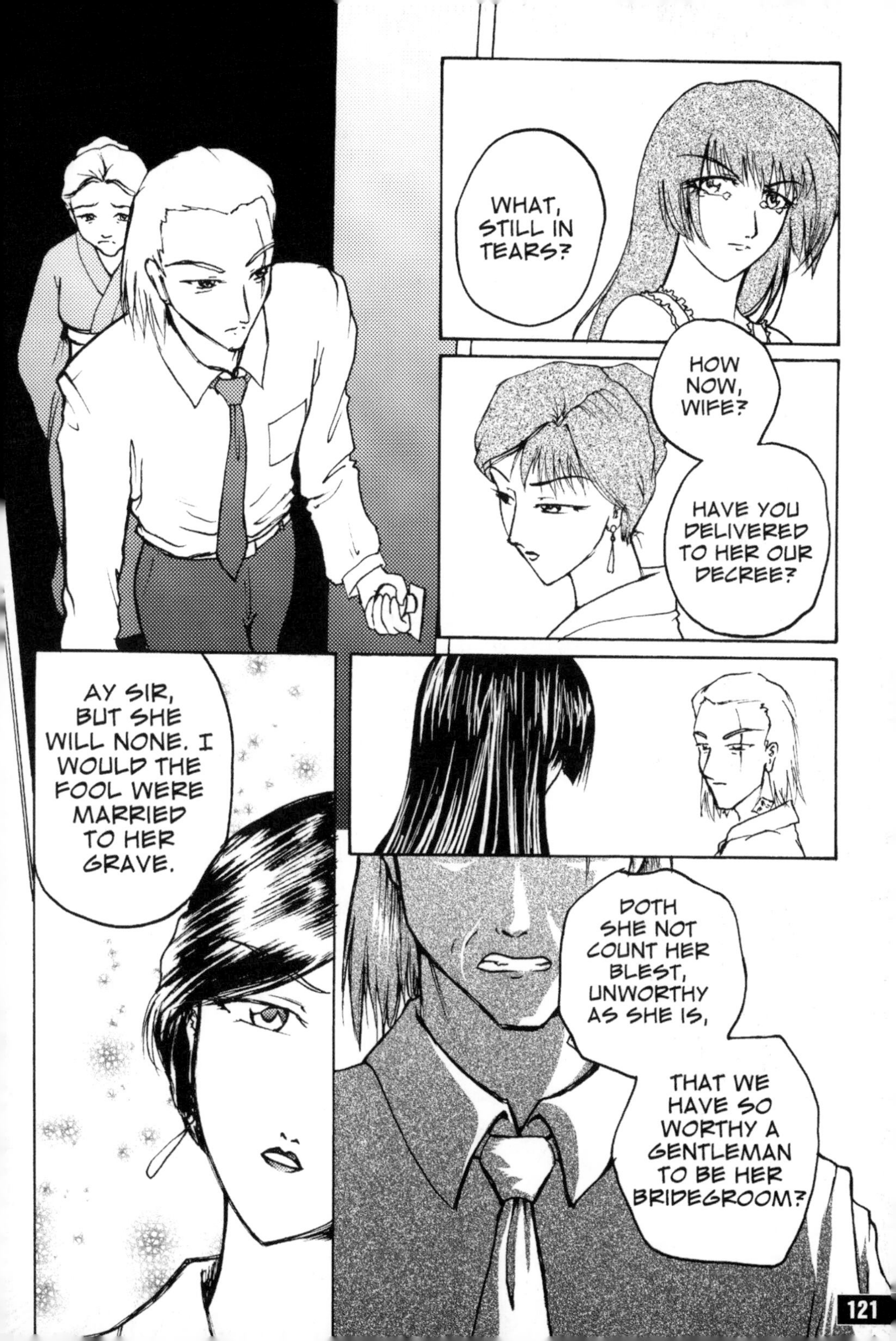
WHAT, STILL IN TEARS?
HOW NOW, WIFE?
HAVE YOU DELIVERED TO HER OUR DECREE?
AY SIR, BUT SHE WILL NONE. I WOULD THE FOOL WERE MARRIED TO HER GRAVE.
DOTH SHE NOT COUNT HER BLEST, UNWORTHY AS SHE IS,
THAT WE HAVE SO WORTHY A GENTLEMAN TO BE HER BRIDEGROOM?

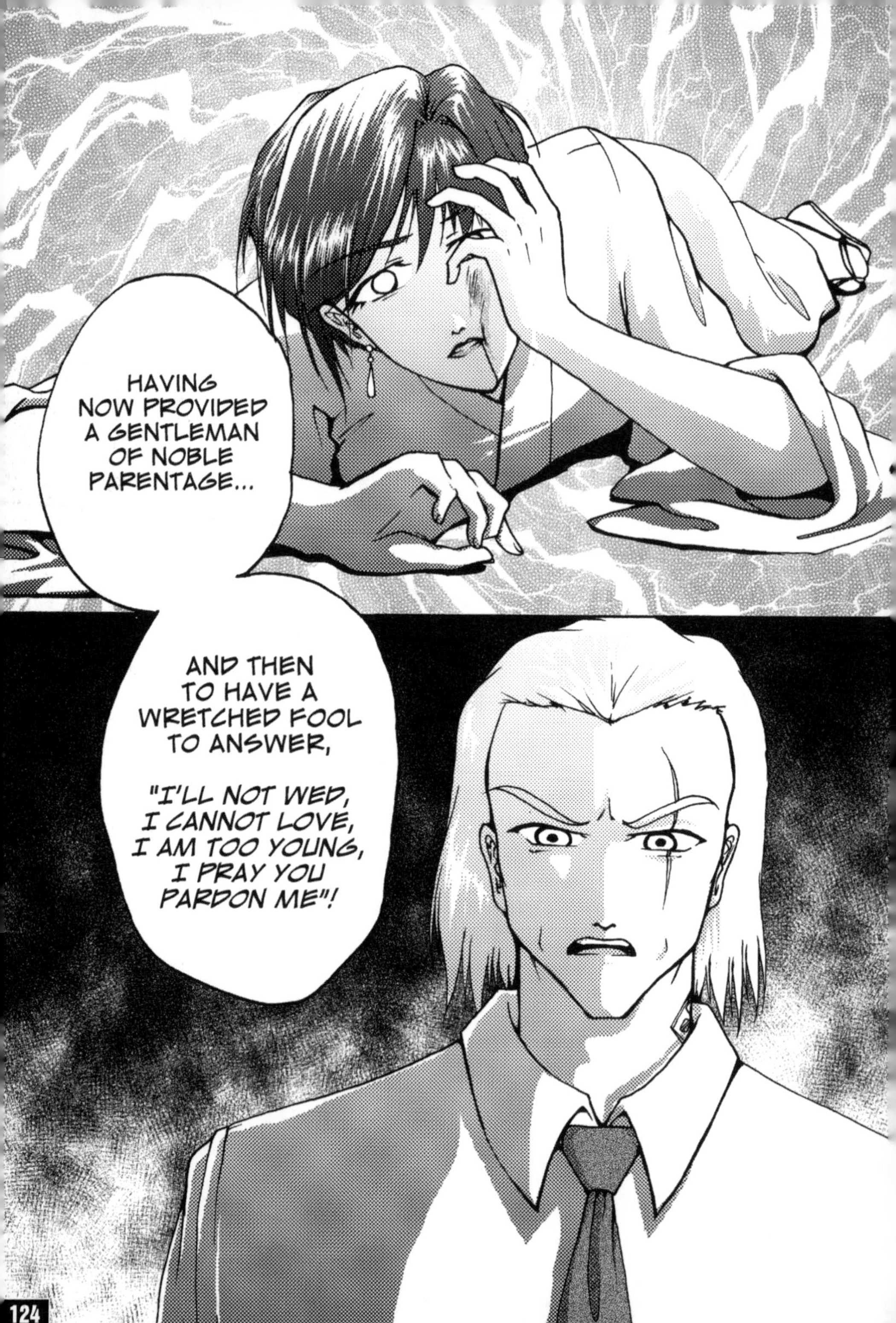
HAVING NOW PROVIDED A GENTLEMAN OF NOBLE PARENTAGE...
AND THEN TO HAVE A WRETCHED FOOL TO ANSWER,
"I'LL NOT WED, I CANNOT LOVE, I AM TOO YOUNG, I PRAY YOU PARDON ME"!

125

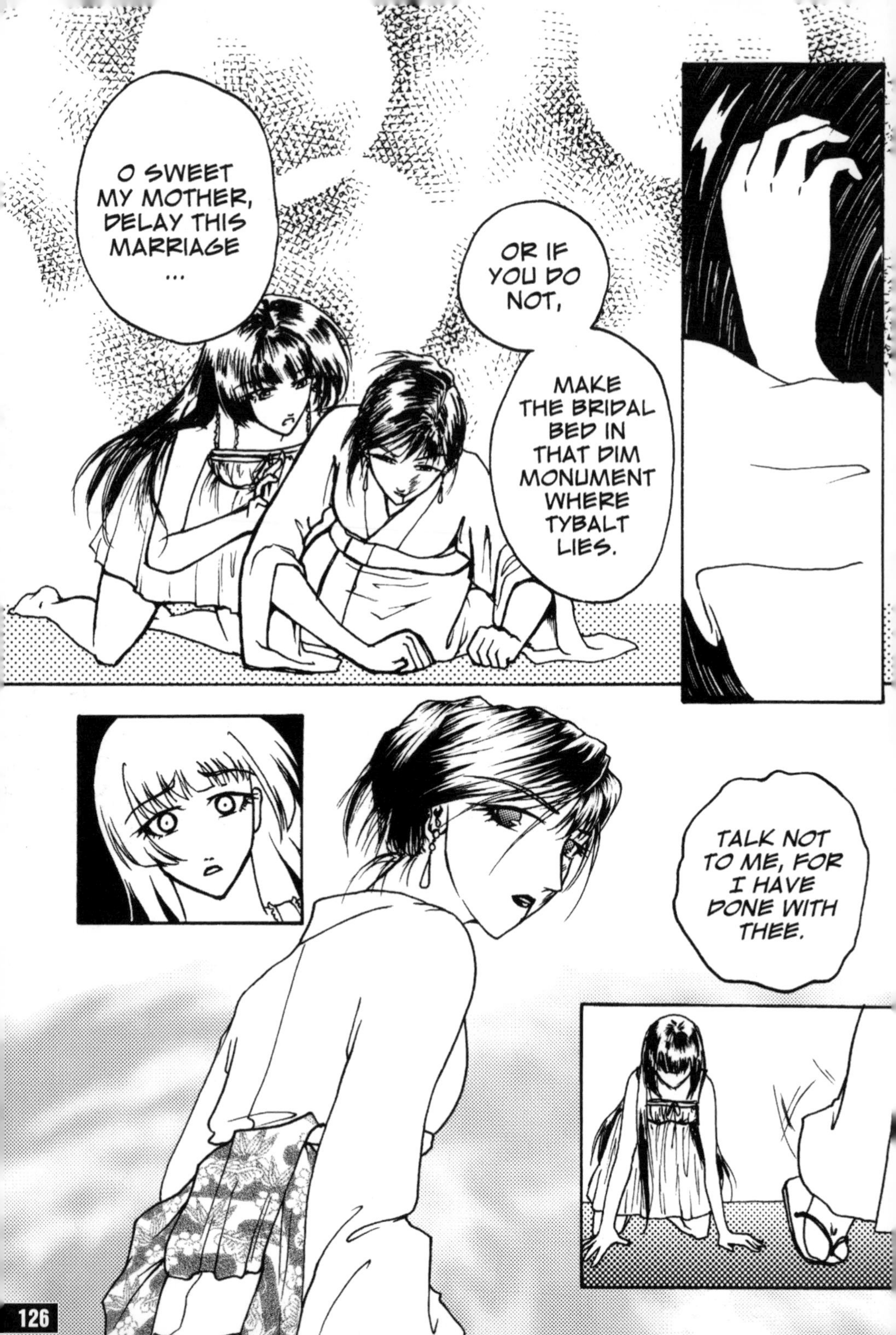
O SWEET MY MOTHER, DELAY THIS MARRIAGE ...
OR IF YOU DO NOT,
MAKE THE BRIDAL BED IN THAT DIM MONUMENT WHERE TYBALT LIES.
TALK NOT TO ME, FOR I HAVE DONE WITH THEE.

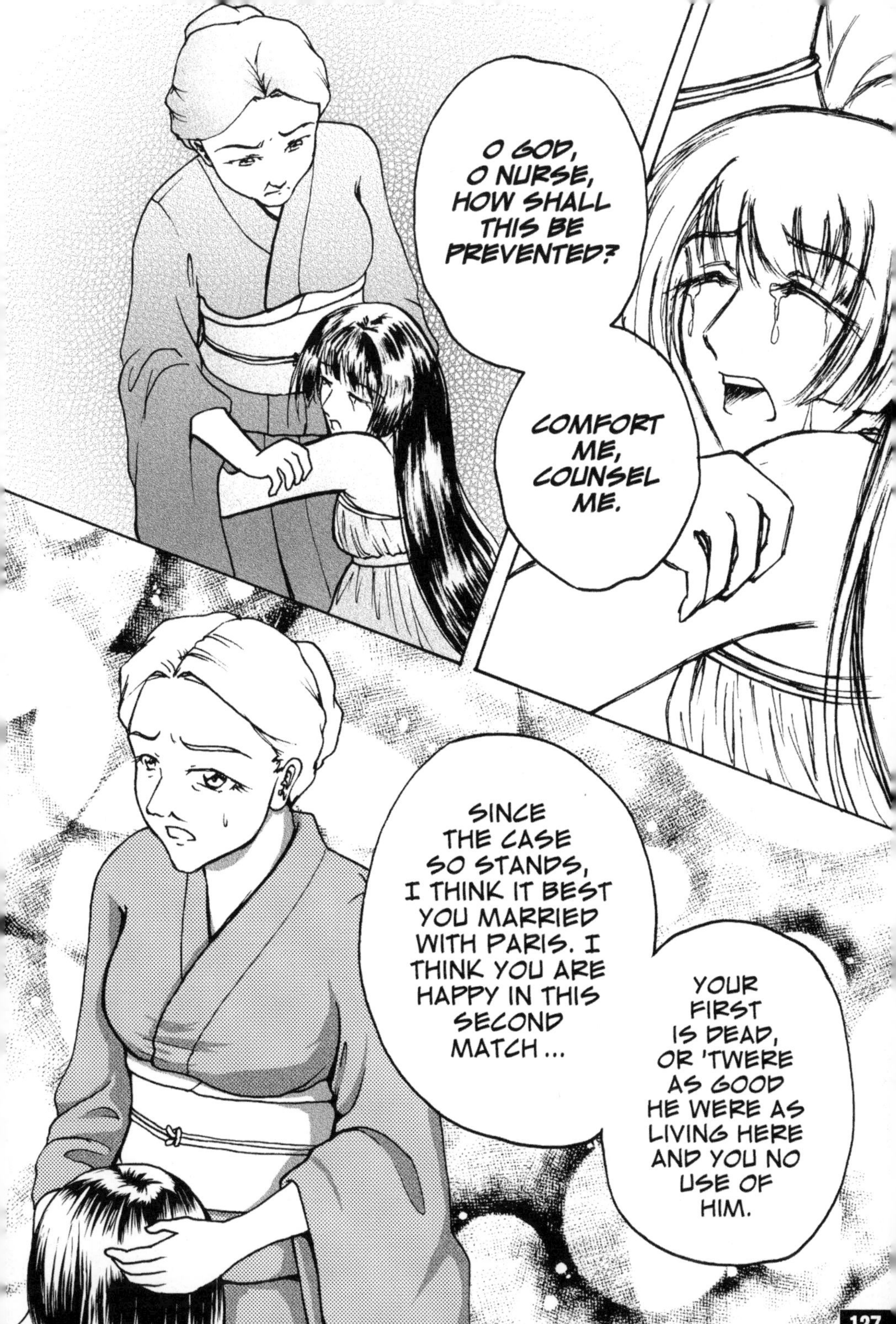
O GOD, O NURSE, HOW SHALL THIS BE PREVENTED?
COMFORT ME, COUNSEL ME.
SINCE THE CASE SO STANDS, I THINK IT BEST YOU MARRIED WITH PARIS. I THINK YOU ARE HAPPY IN THIS SECOND MATCH ...
YOUR FIRST IS DEAD, OR 'TWERE AS GOOD HE WERE AS LIVING HERE AND YOU NO USE OF HIM.

131

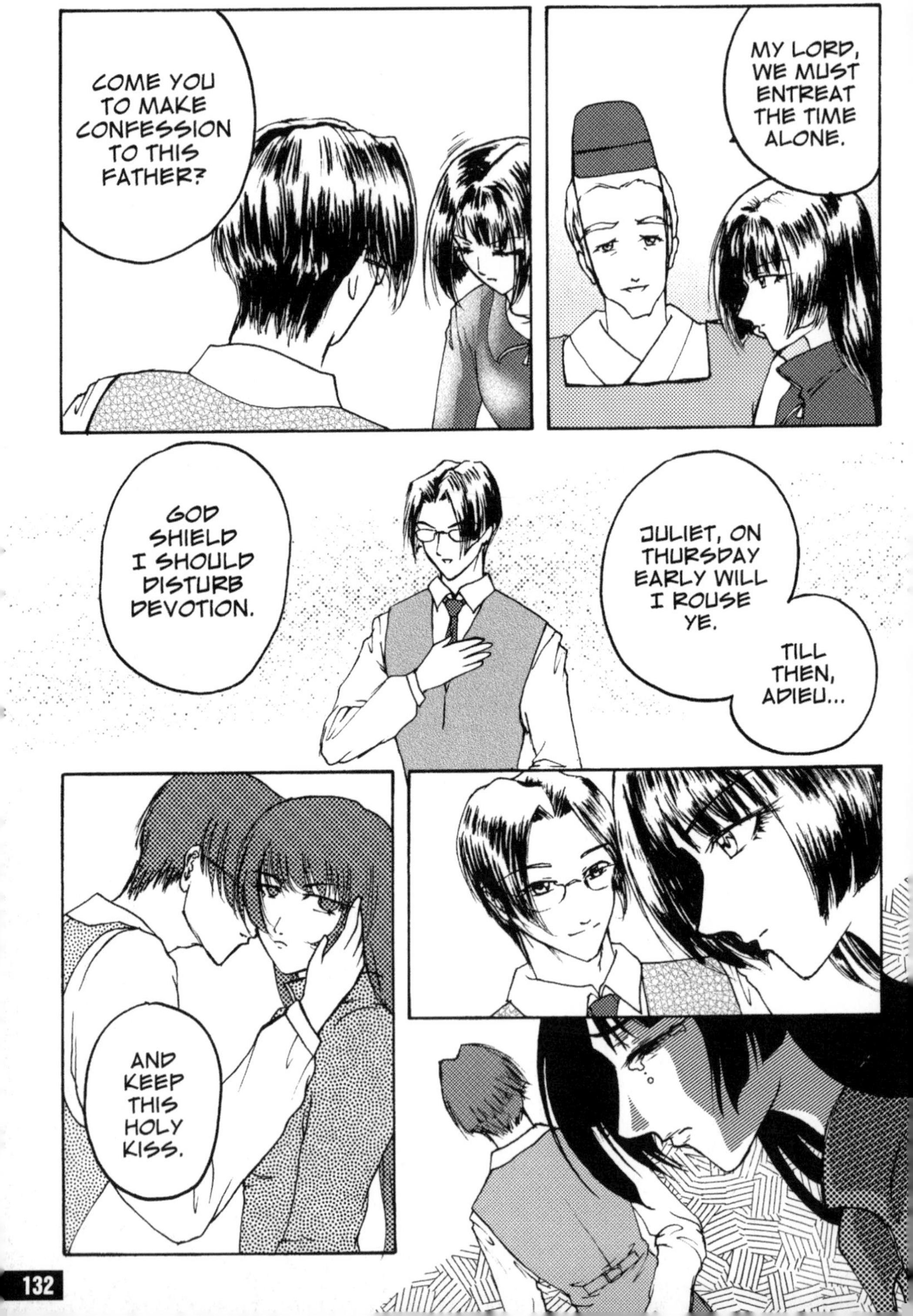
COME YOU TO MAKE CONFESSION TO THIS FATHER?
MY LORD, WE MUST ENTREAT THE TIME ALONE.
GOD SHIELD I SHOULD DISTURB DEVOTION.
JULIET, ON THURSDAY EARLY WILL I ROUSE YE.
TILL THEN, ADIEU...
AND KEEP THIS HOLY KISS.

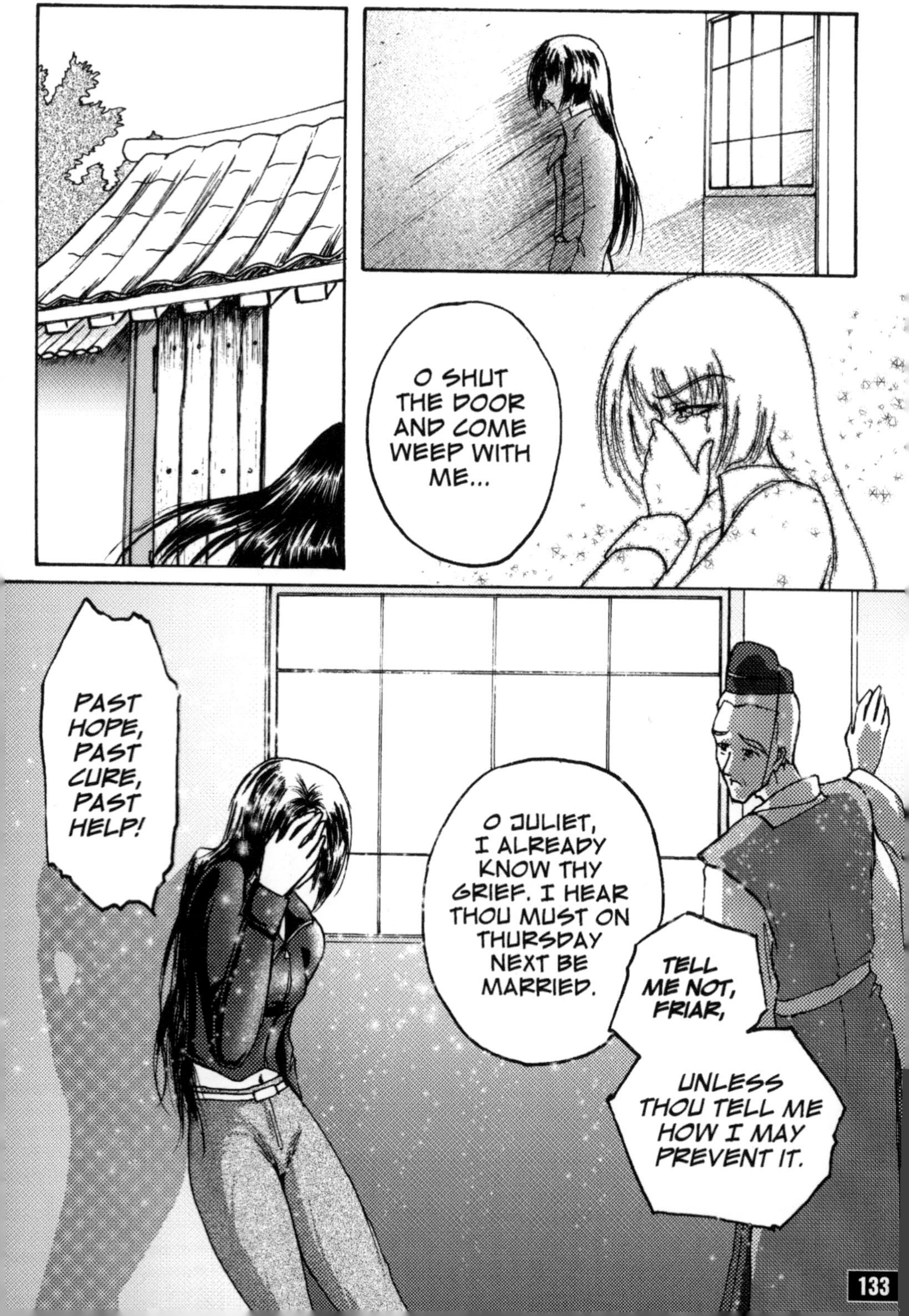
O SHUT THE DOOR AND COME WEEP WITH ME...
PAST HOPE, PAST CURE, PAST HELP!
O JULIET, I ALREADY KNOW THY GRIEF. I HEAR THOU MUST ON THURSDAY NEXT BE MARRIED.
TELL ME NOT, FRIAR,
UNLESS THOU TELL ME HOW I MAY PREVENT IT.

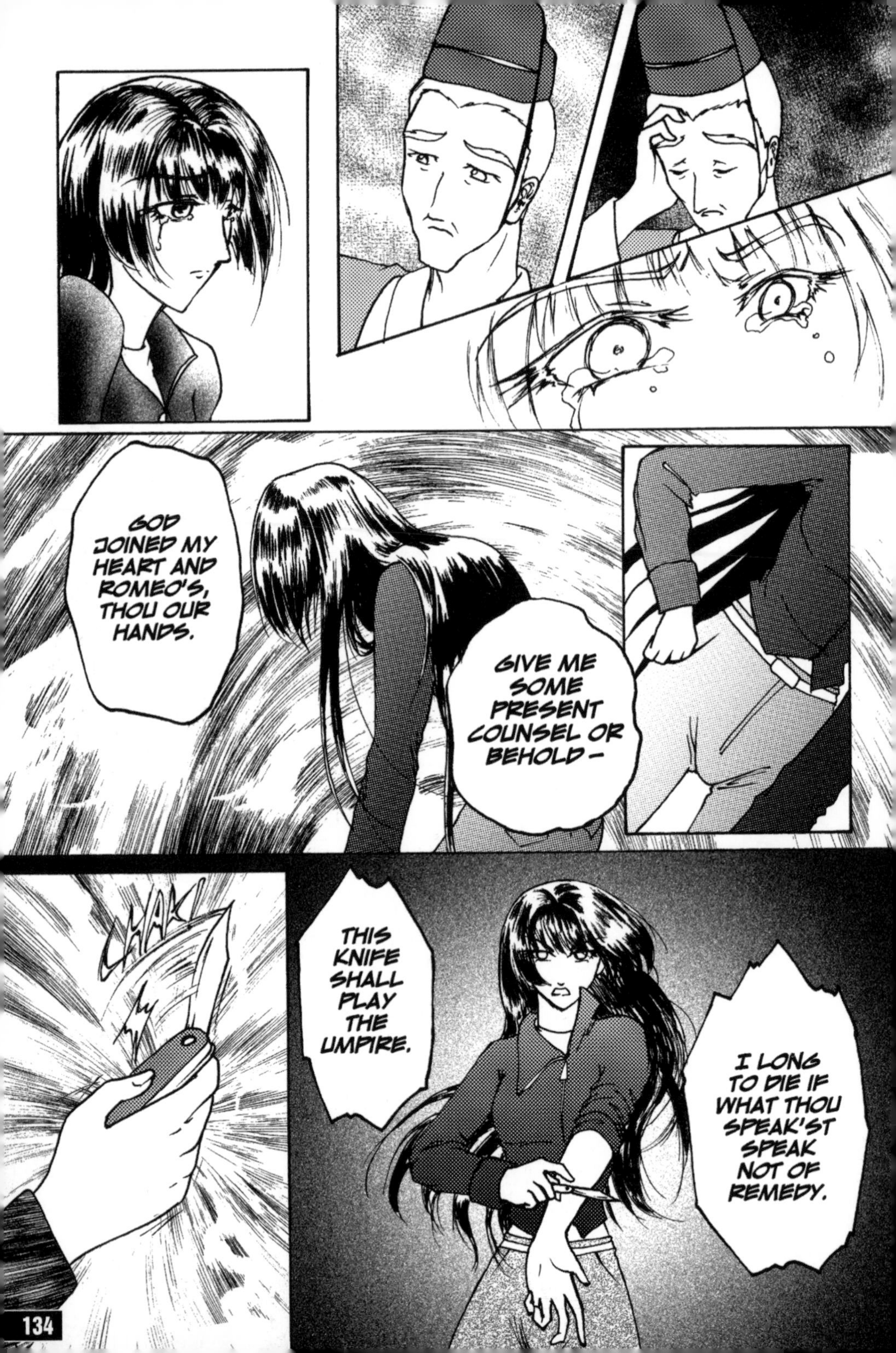
GOD JOINED MY HEART AND ROMEO'S, THOU OUR HANDS.
GIVE ME SOME PRESENT COUNSEL OR BEHOLD –
CHAK!
THIS KNIFE SHALL PLAY THE UMPIRE.
I LONG TO DIE IF WHAT THOU SPEAK'ST SPEAK NOT OF REMEDY.

137

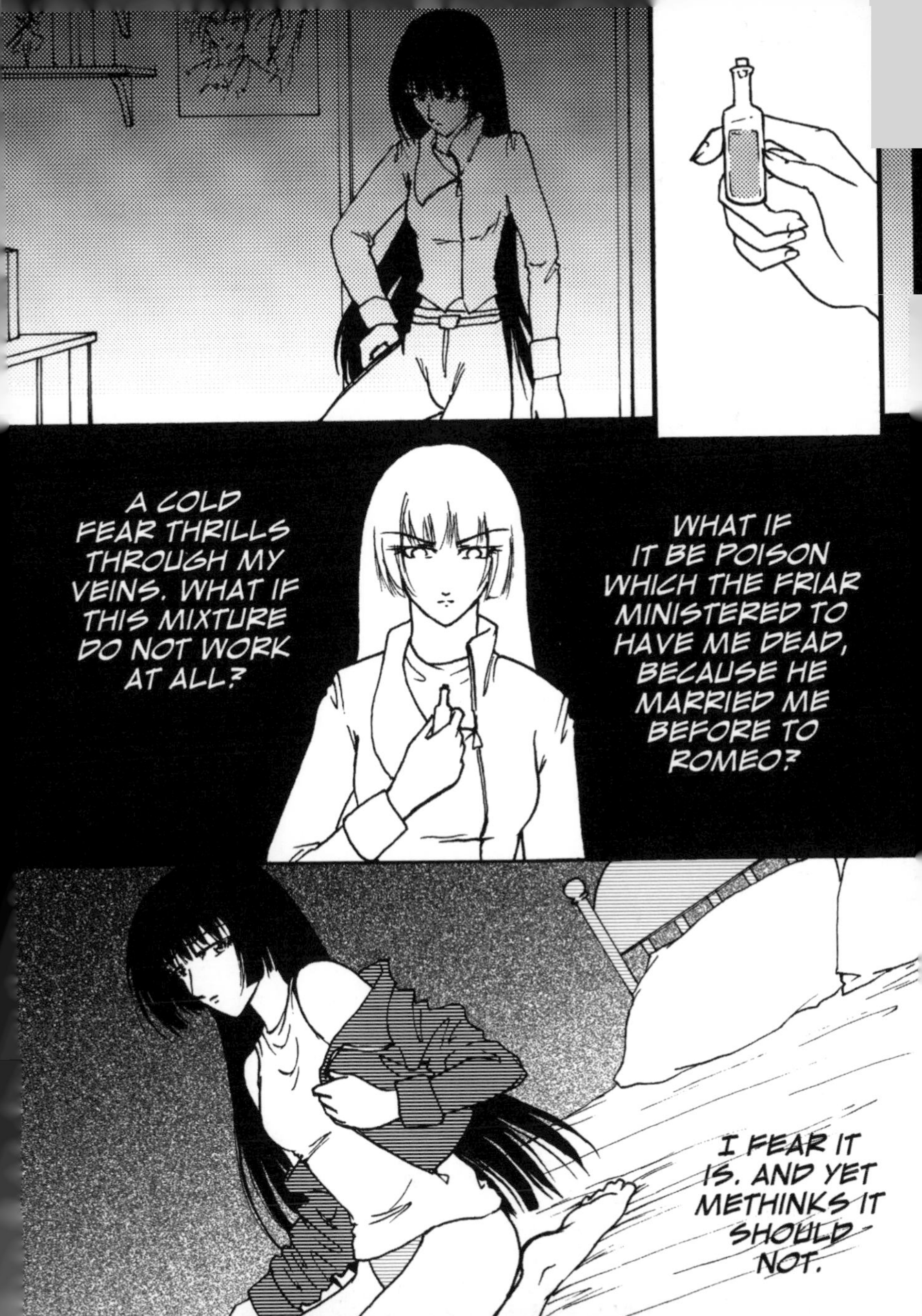
A COLD FEAR THRILLS THROUGH MY VEINS. WHAT IF THIS MIXTURE DO NOT WORK AT ALL?
WHAT IF IT BE POISON WHICH THE FRIAR MINISTERED TO HAVE ME DEAD, BECAUSE HE MARRIED ME BEFORE TO ROMEO?
I FEAR IT IS. AND YET METHINKS IT SHOULD NOT.

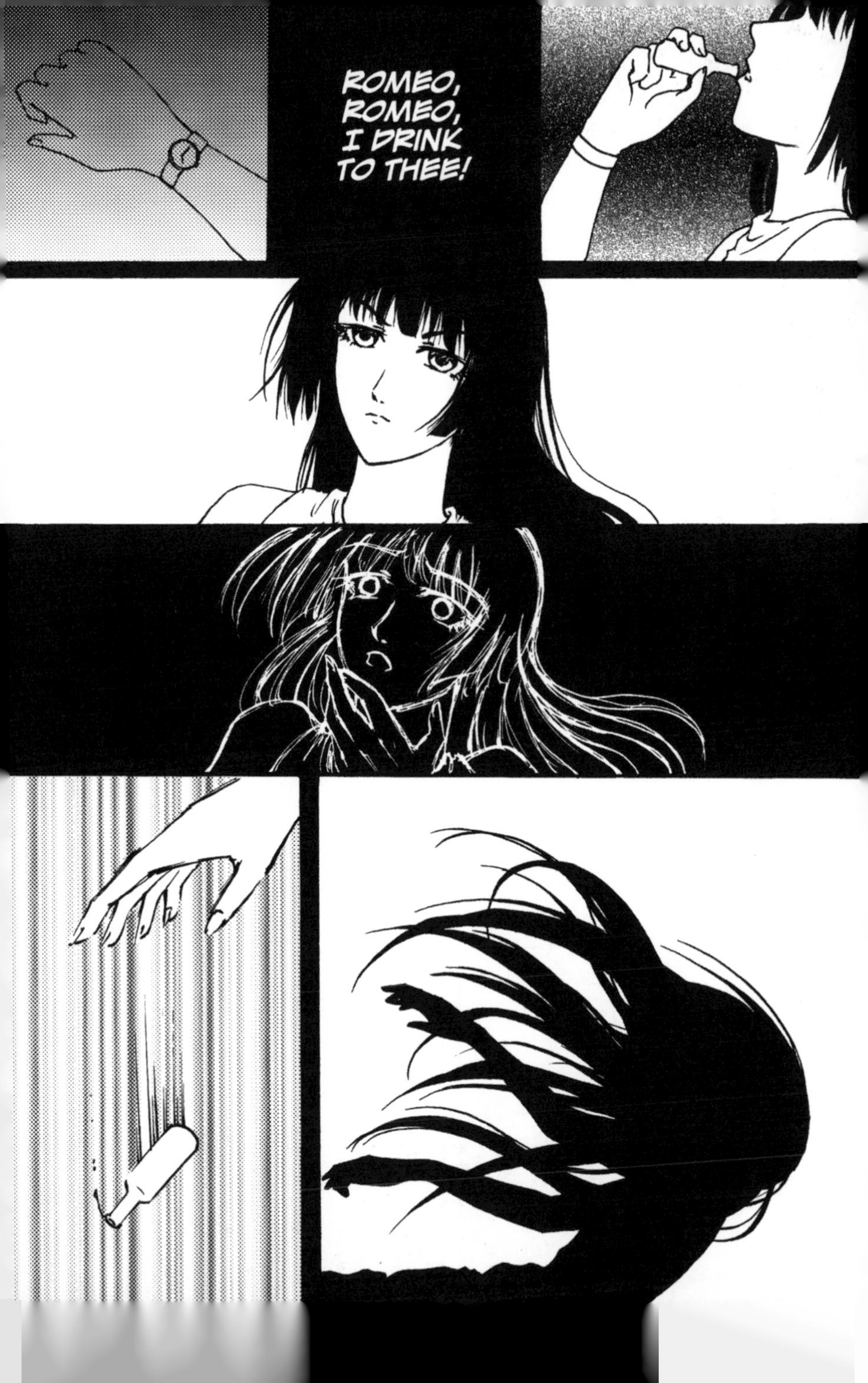
ROMEO, ROMEO, I DRINK TO THEE!

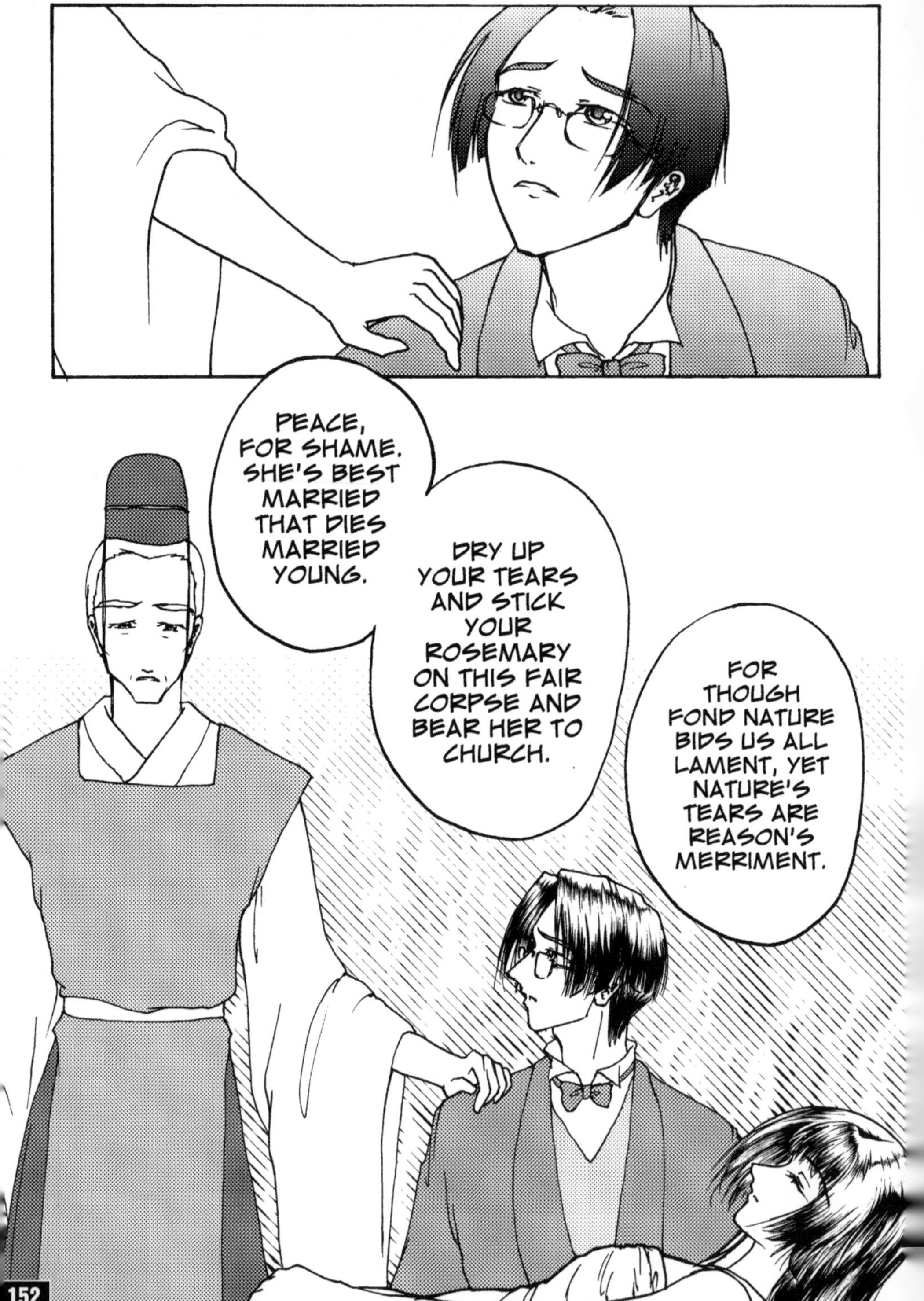
PEACE, FOR SHAME. SHE'S BEST MARRIED THAT DIES MARRIED YOUNG.
DRY UP YOUR TEARS AND STICK YOUR ROSEMARY ON THIS FAIR CORPSE AND BEAR HER TO CHURCH.
FOR THOUGH FOND NATURE BIDS US ALL LAMENT, YET NATURE'S TEARS ARE REASON'S MERRIMENT.

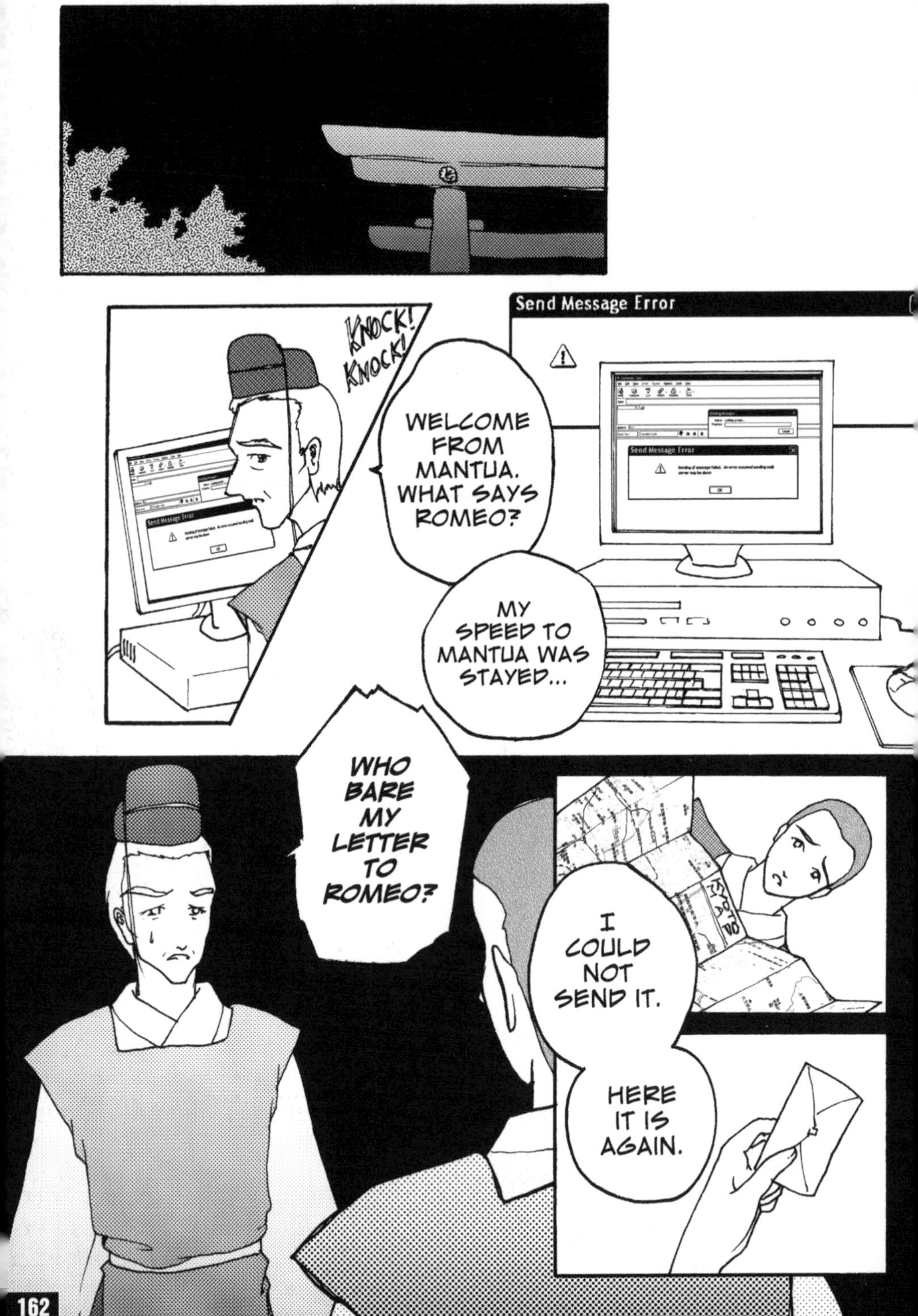
KNOCK! KNOCK!
WELCOME FROM MANTUA. WHAT SAYS ROMEO?
Send Message Error
Send Message Error
MY SPEED TO MANTUA WAS STAYED...
WHO BARE MY LETTER TO ROMEO?
KYOTO MAP
I COULD NOT SEND IT.
HERE IT IS AGAIN.

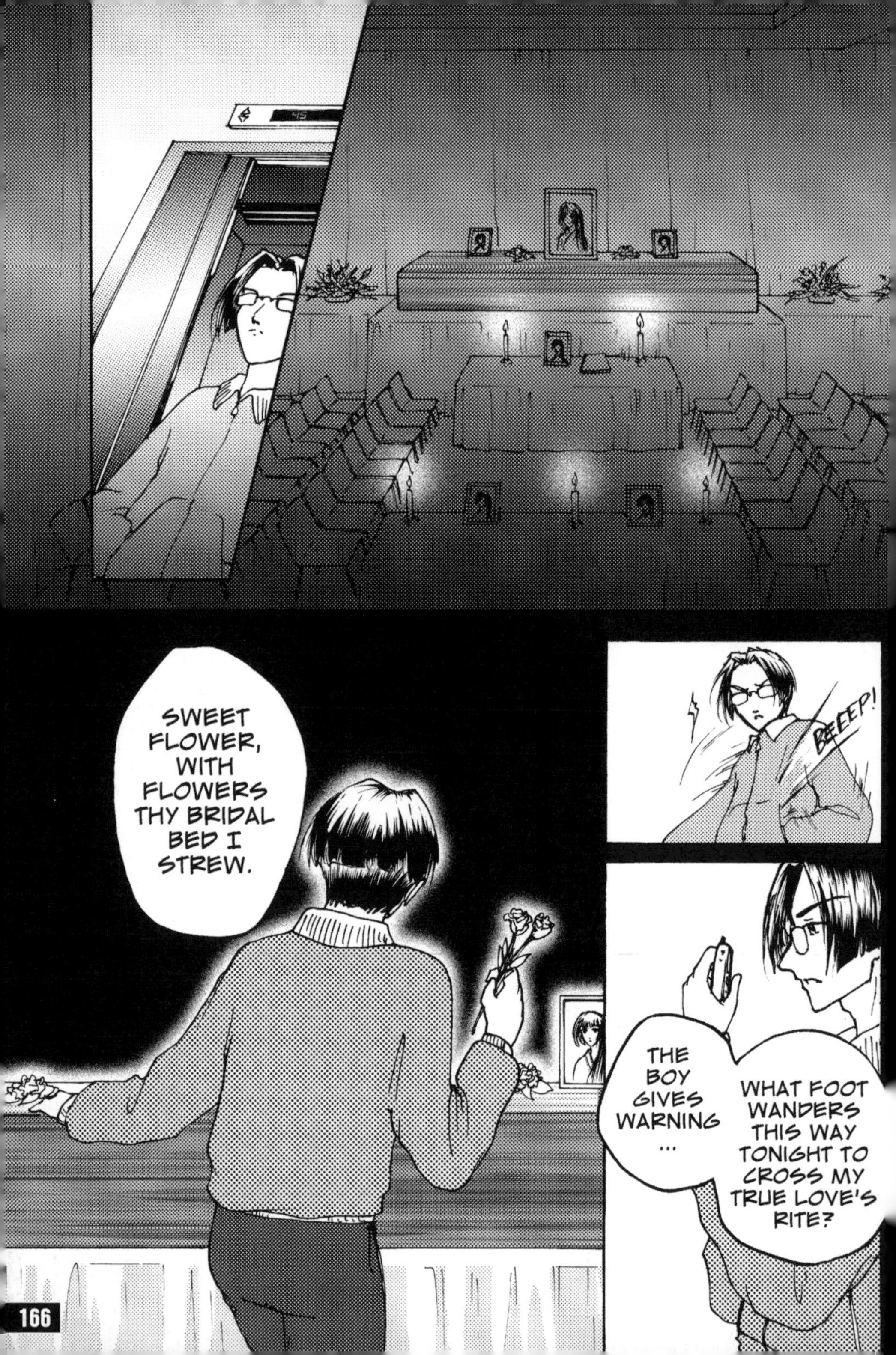
SWEET FLOWER, WITH FLOWERS THY BRIDAL BED I STREW.
BEEEP!
THE BOY GIVES WARNING ...
WHAT FOOT WANDERS THIS WAY TONIGHT TO CROSS MY TRUE LOVE'S RITE?

I DESCEND INTO THIS BED OF DEATH...

PARTLY TO BEHOLD MY LADY'S FACE...

BUT CHIEFLY TO TAKE THENCE FROM HER DEAD FINGER A PRECIOUS RING...

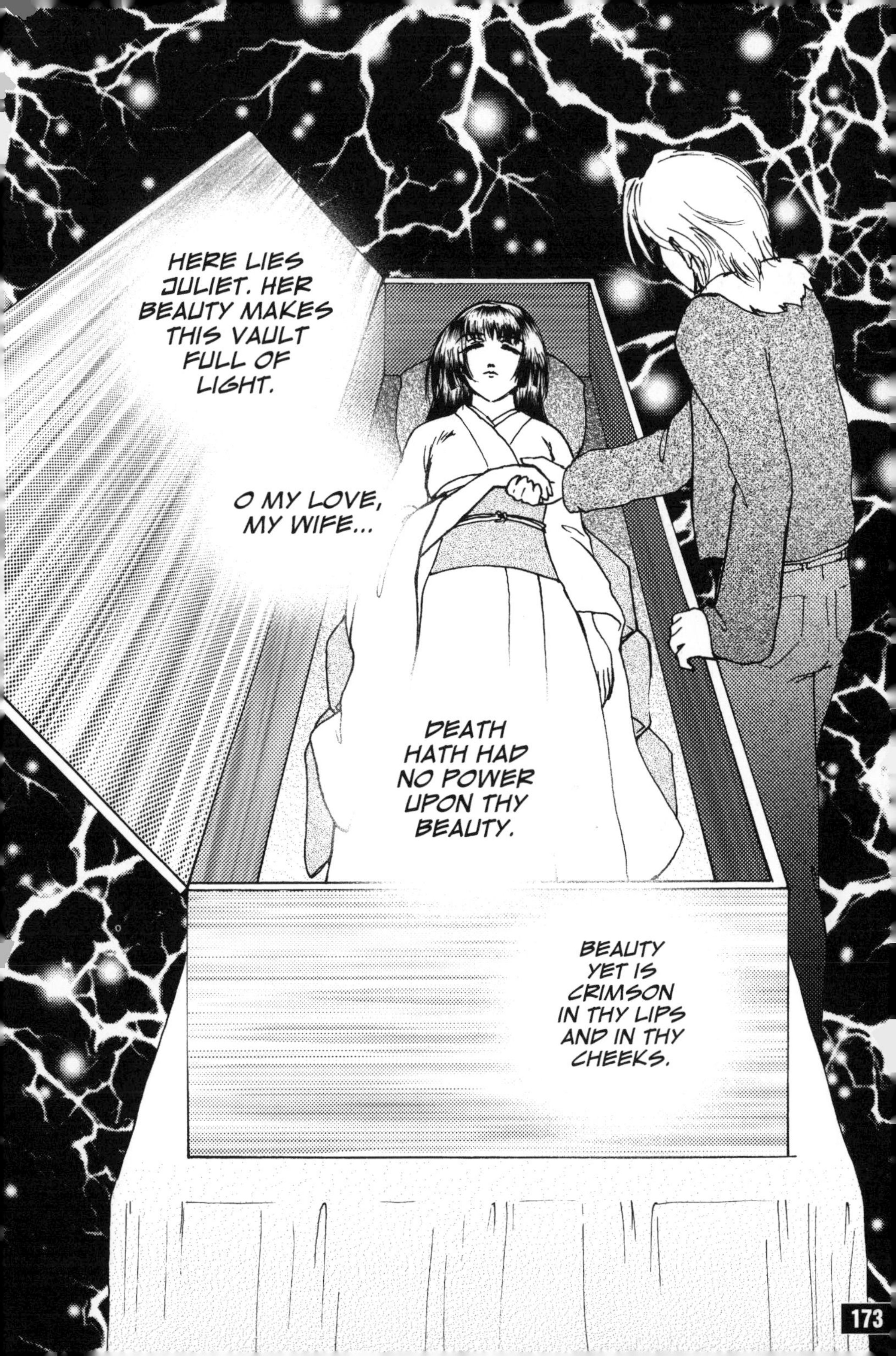
HERE LIES JULIET. HER BEAUTY MAKES THIS VAULT FULL OF LIGHT.
O MY LOVE, MY WIFE...
DEATH HATH HAD NO POWER UPON THY BEAUTY.
BEAUTY YET IS CRIMSON IN THY LIPS AND IN THY CHEEKS.

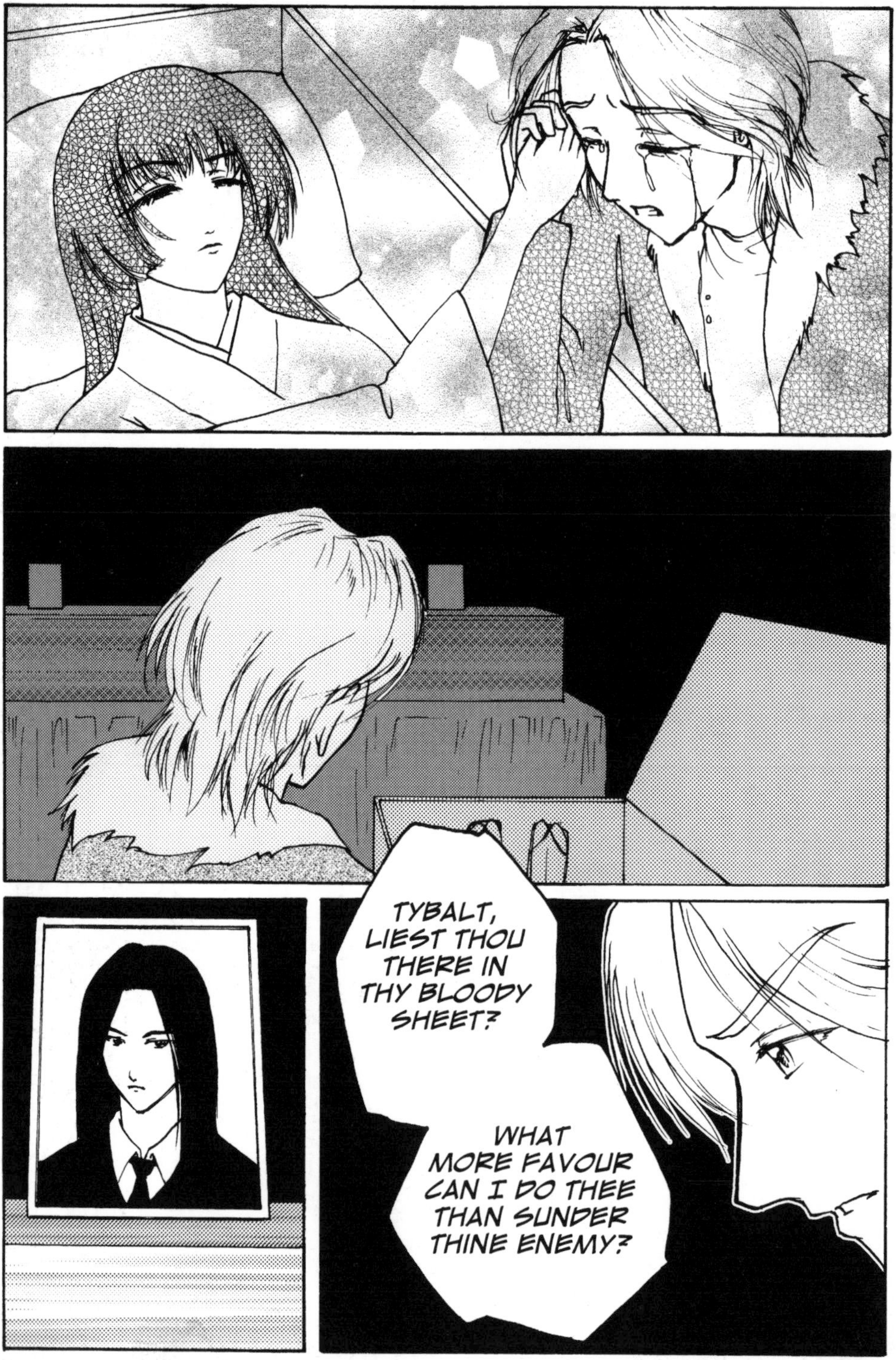
TYBALT, LIEST THOU THERE IN THY BLOODY SHEET?
WHAT MORE FAVOUR CAN I DO THEE THAN SUNDER THINE ENEMY?

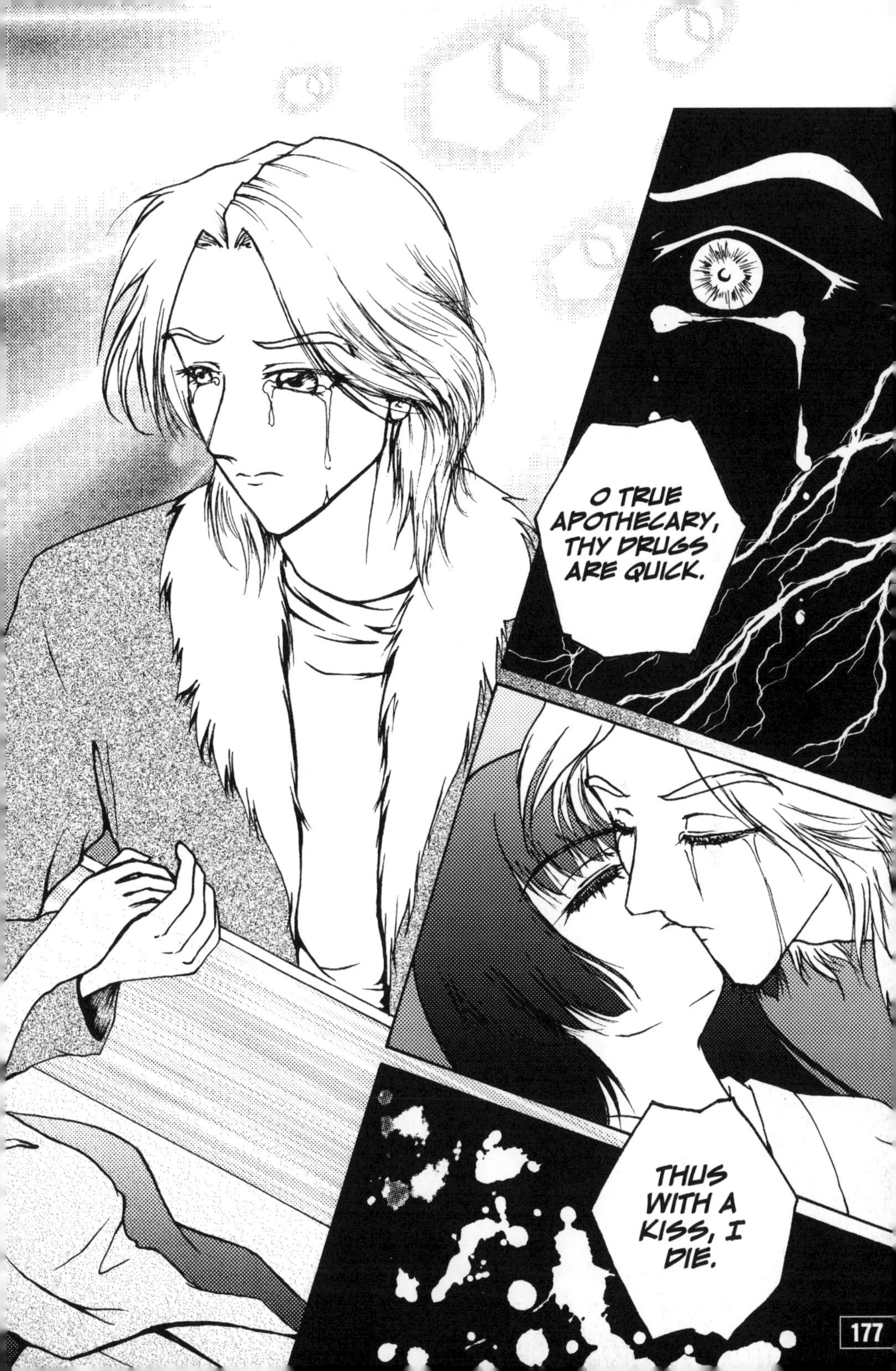
O TRUE APOTHECARY, THY DRUGS ARE QUICK.
THUS WITH A KISS, I DIE.

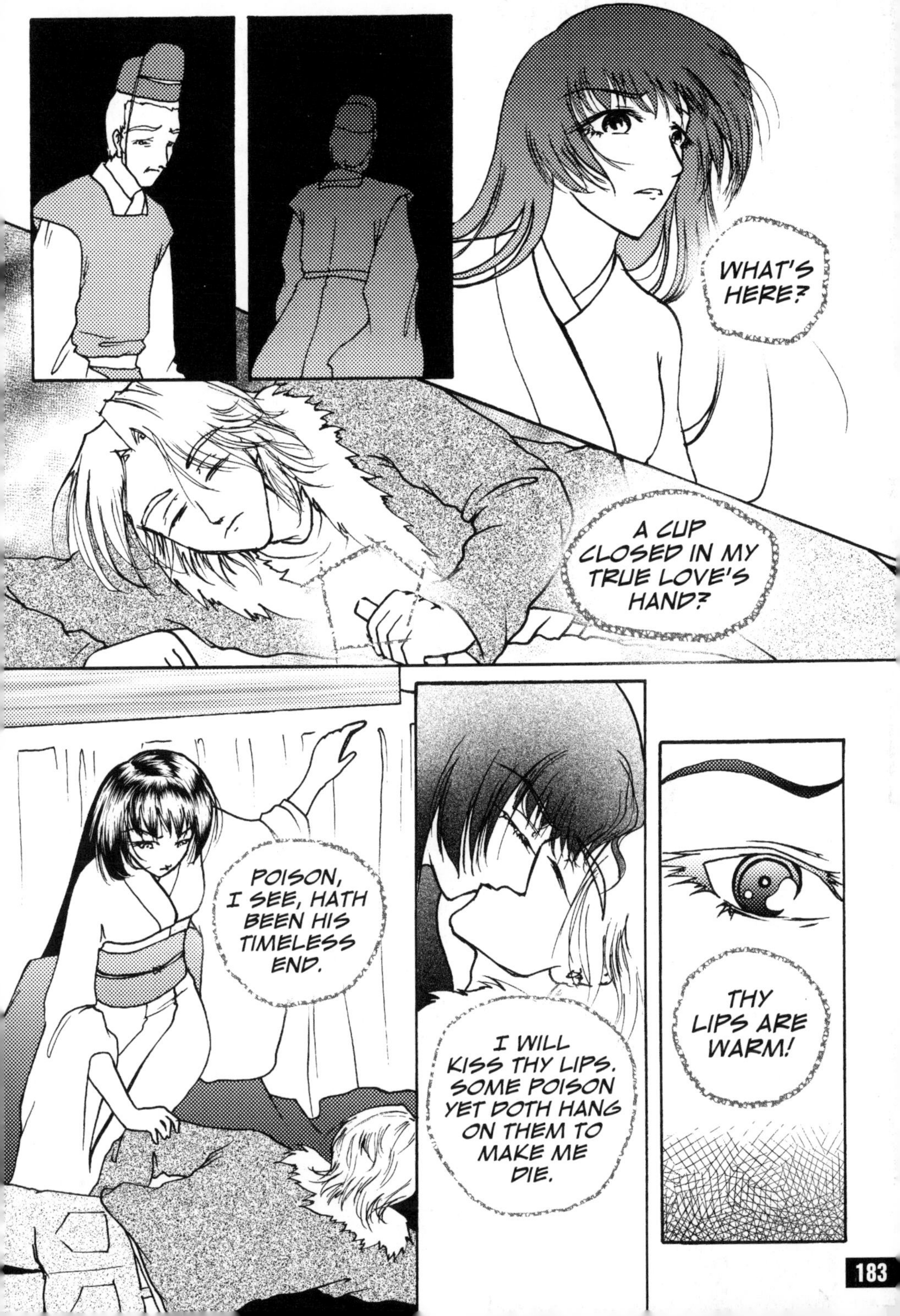
WHAT'S HERE?
A CUP CLOSED IN MY TRUE LOVE'S HAND?
POISON, I SEE, HATH BEEN HIS TIMELESS END.
I WILL KISS THY LIPS. SOME POISON YET DOTH HANG ON THEM TO MAKE ME DIE.
THY LIPS ARE WARM!

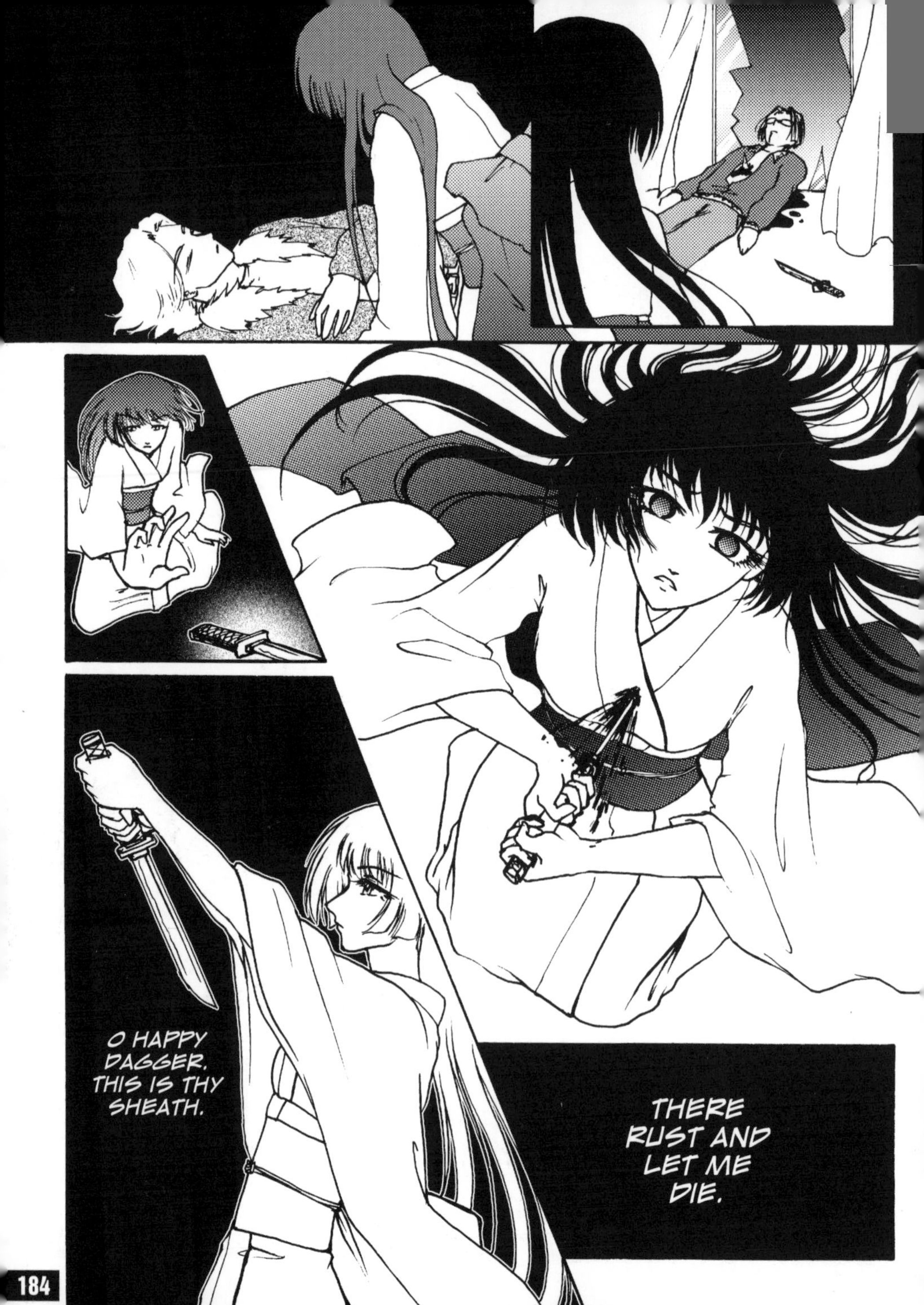
O HAPPY DAGGER. THIS IS THY SHEATH.
THERE RUST AND LET ME DIE.

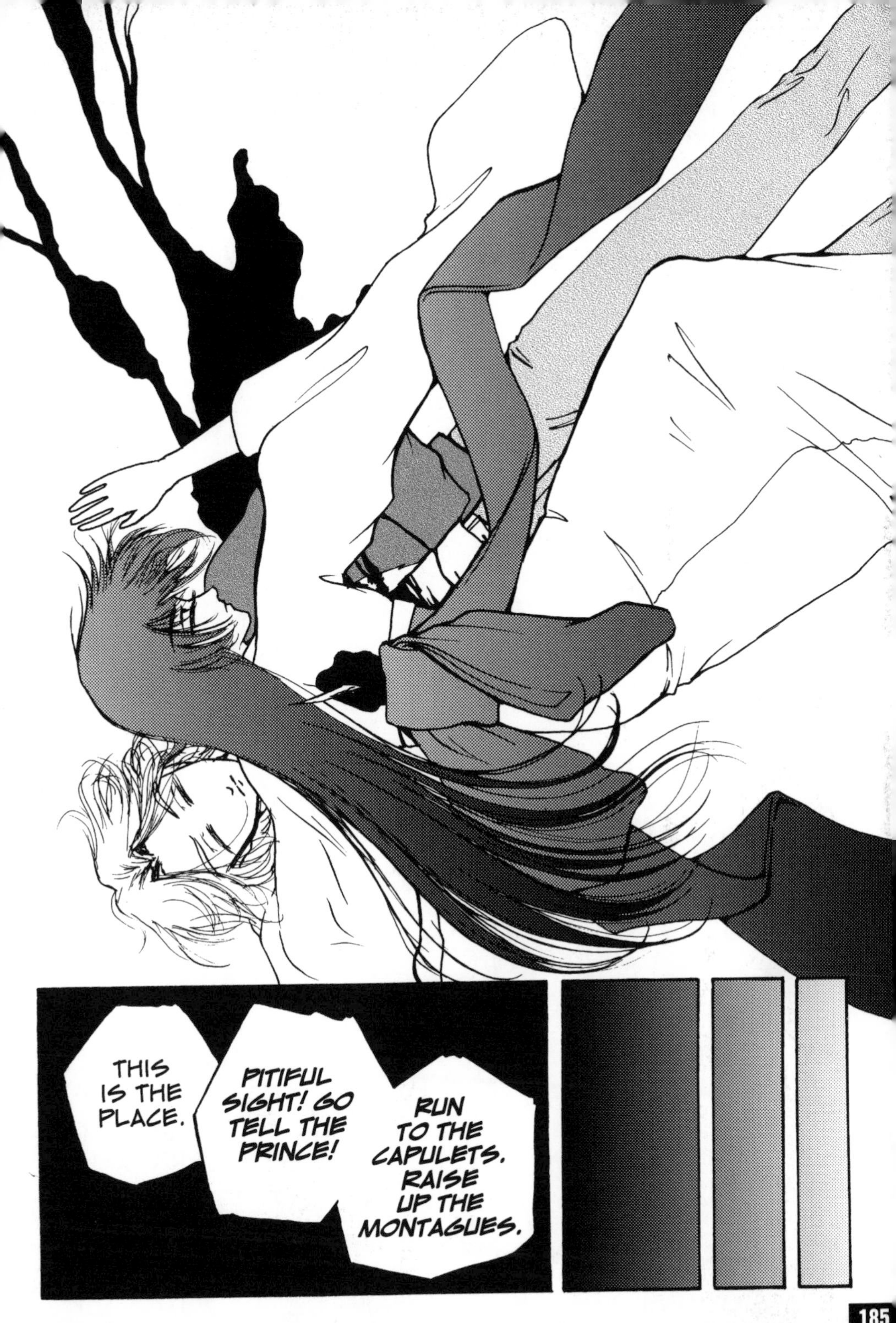
THIS IS THE PLACE.
PITIFUL SIGHT! GO TELL THE PRINCE!
RUN TO THE CAPULETS. RAISE UP THE MONTAGUES.

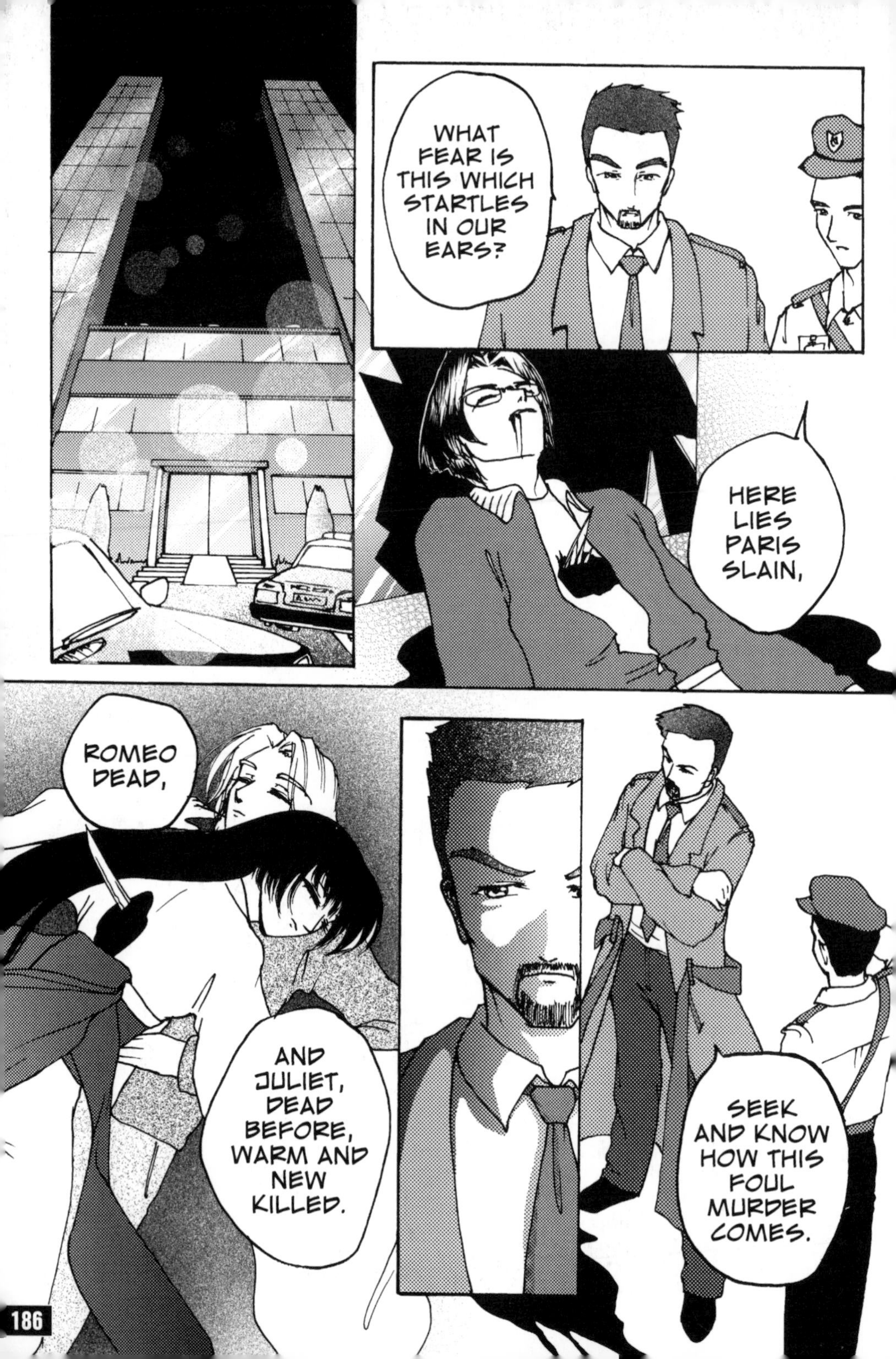
WHAT FEAR IS THIS WHICH STARTLES IN OUR EARS?
HERE LIES PARIS SLAIN,
ROMEO DEAD,
AND JULIET, DEAD BEFORE, WARM AND NEW KILLED.
SEEK AND KNOW HOW THIS FOUL MURDER COMES.

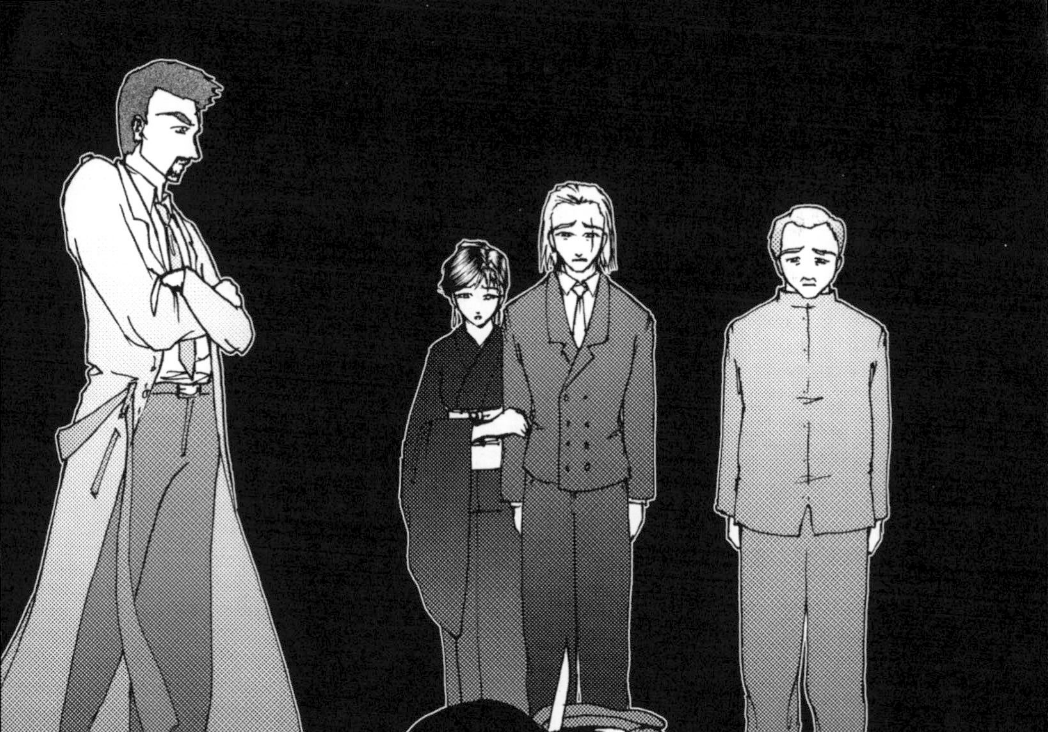

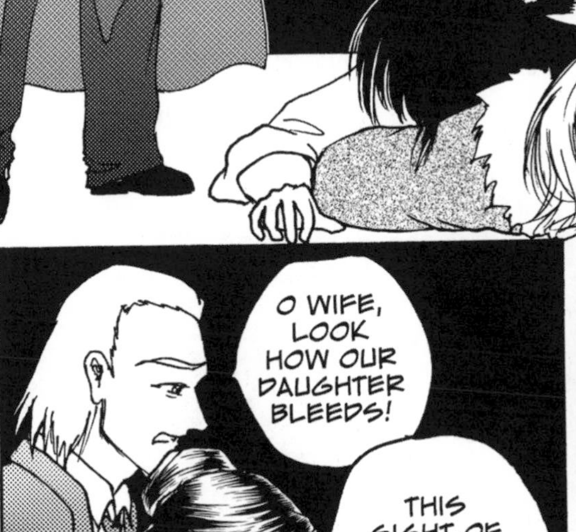
O WIFE, LOOK HOW OUR DAUGHTER BLEEDS!
THIS SIGHT OF DEATH IS AS A BELL THAT WARNS MY OLD AGE TO A SEPULCHRE.

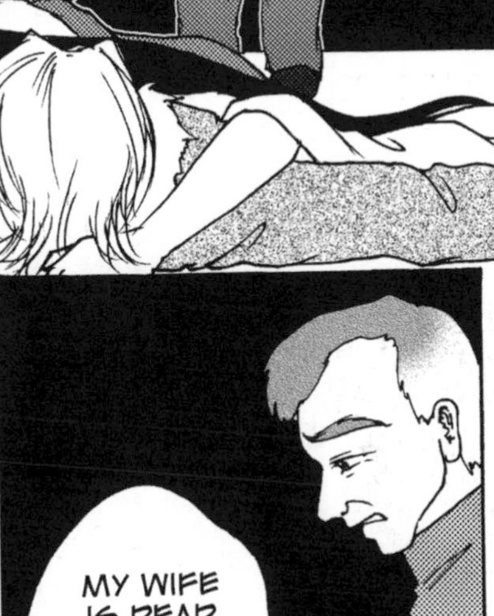
MY WIFE IS DEAD TONIGHT. GRIEF OF MY SON'S EXILE HATH STOPPED HER BREATH.

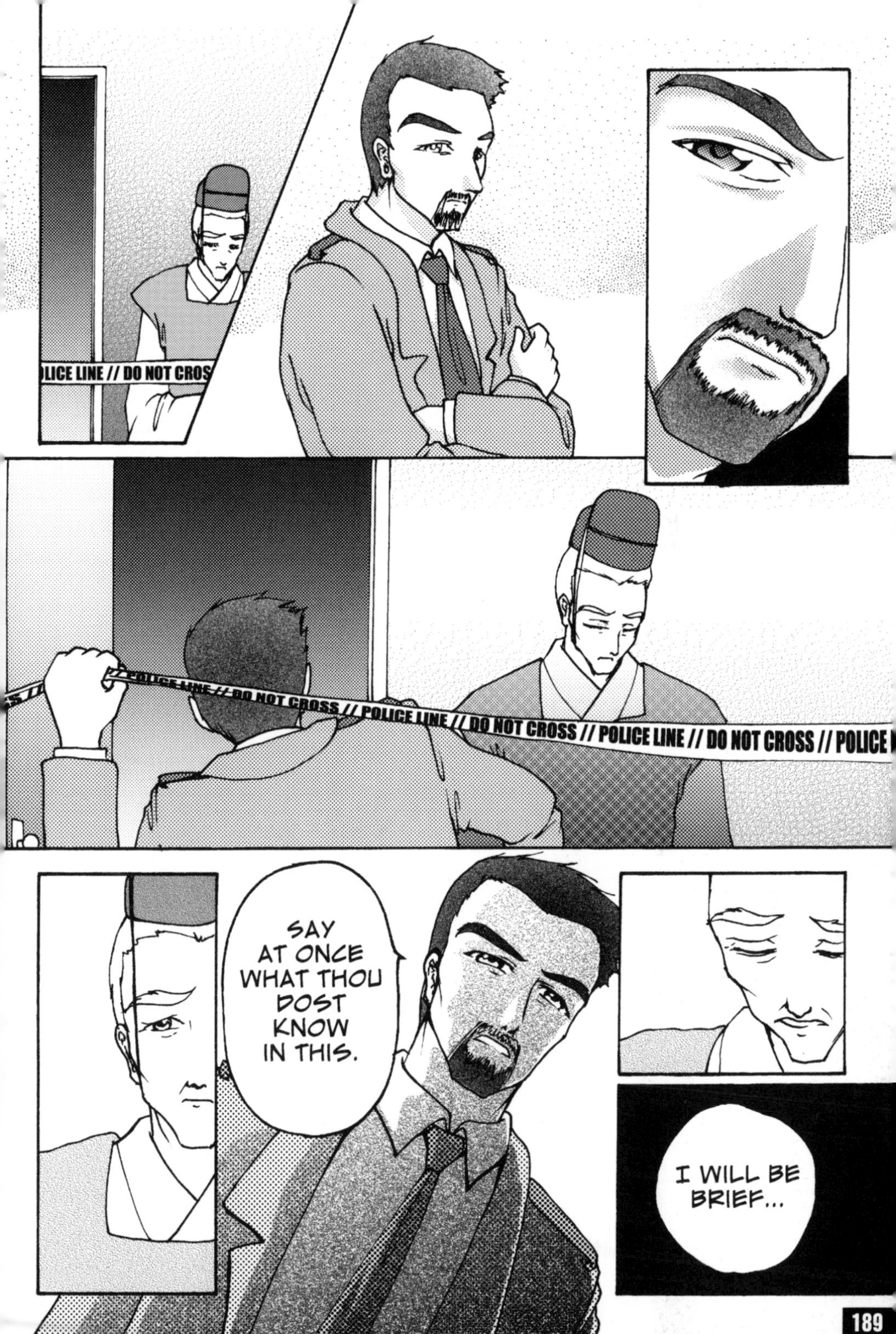
POLICE LINE // DO NOT CROSS
POLICE LINE // DO NOT CROSS // POLICE LINE // DO NOT CROSS // POLICE LINE // DO NOT CROSS // POLICE
SAY AT ONCE WHAT THOU DOST KNOW IN THIS.
I WILL BE BRIEF...

191

PLOT SUMMARY OF ROMEO AND JULIET

The play begins with a street fight between two rival families, the Montagues and the Capulets. Benvolio, Romeo's friend, intervenes but is confronted by the fiery Tybalt who hates all Montagues. The Prince stops the brawl and orders both sides to cease feuding under pain of death. Romeo, brooding on his love for Rosaline, is absent from this fight. Benvolio advises him to end his melancholy by finding another woman.

Lord Capulet encourages the courtship of his daughter Juliet by the nobleman Paris and invites him to a celebration that night. Romeo and Benvolio hear of this party from Capulet's servant and decide to attend.

Lady Capulet tries to persuade Juliet to marry Paris. Juliet's old nurse adds comic commentary. Romeo, his friends Benvolio and the madcap Mercutio, gatecrash the Capulet party — and Romeo falls instantly in love with Juliet. He is recognized by the quarrelsome Tybalt. Later that same night, Romeo climbs into the Capulet garden and overhears Juliet confessing her love for him. They defy their hostile families by vowing to marry secretly the next day.

Romeo obtains Friar Laurence's consent to marry them and Juliet's nurse acts as go-between.

Tybalt encounters Benvolio and Mercutio and provokes a swordfight with Mercutio. Romeo arrives and tries to stop them but Mercutio is killed. Romeo, forced to take revenge, kills Tybalt and has to flee. The Prince imposes a penalty of exile on Romeo.

Juliet's nurse brings news of Tybalt's death and Romeo's banishment. Juliet despairs. Her father meanwhile arranges for her immediate marriage to Paris. Juliet tries to resist her parents' wishes but even her nurse advises her to forget Romeo. Juliet seeks Friar Laurence's help. He gives her a sleeping potion which will make her appear dead. He will summon Romeo from exile to arrive as she awakens in the tomb and they can escape together. But the plan goes badly wrong. Romeo hears of Juliet's death but does not get the Friar's message explaining the trick. He buys poison and plans to join Juliet in death.

Romeo, at Juliet's tomb, is confronted by Paris. They duel and Romeo kills him. Romeo takes the poison and dies as Juliet awakens. She refuses to leave with Friar Laurence but instead stabs herself with a dagger.

The Prince, the Capulets and Montagues are summoned to the scene of the two dead lovers.

A BRIEF LIFE OF WILLIAM SHAKESPEARE

He learned his craft the hard way. He soon won fame as a playwright with often-staged popular hits.

He and his colleagues formed a stage company, the Lord Chamberlain's Men, which built the famous Globe Theatre. It opened in 1599 but was destroyed by fire in 1613 during a performance of *Henry VIII* which used gunpowder special effects. It was rebuilt in brick the following year.

Shakespeare's birthday is traditionally said to be the 23rd of April – St George's Day, patron saint of England. A good start for England's greatest writer. But that date and even his name are uncertain. He signed his own name in different ways. "Shakespeare" is now the accepted one out of dozens of different versions.

He was born at Stratford-upon-Avon in 1564, and baptized on 26th April. His mother, Mary Arden, was the daughter of a prosperous farmer. His father John Shakespeare, a glove-maker, was a respected civic figure – and probably also a Catholic. In 1570, just as Will began school, his father was accused of illegal dealings. The family fell into debt and disrepute.

Will attended a local school for eight years. He did not go to university. The next ten years are a blank filled by suppositions. Was he briefly a Latin teacher, a soldier, a sea-faring explorer? Was he prosecuted and whipped for poaching deer?

We do know that in 1582 he married Anne Hathaway, eight years his senior, and three months pregnant. Two more children – twins – were born three years later but, by around 1590, Will had left Stratford to pursue a theatre career in London. Shakespeare's apprenticeship began as an actor and "pen for hire".

Shakespeare was a financially successful writer who invested his money wisely in property. In 1597, he bought an enormous house in Stratford, and in 1608 became a shareholder in London's Blackfriars Theatre. He also redeemed the family's honour by acquiring a personal coat of arms.

Shakespeare wrote over 40 works, including poems, "lost" plays and collaborations, in a career spanning nearly 25 years. He retired to Stratford in 1613, where he died on 23rd April 1616, aged 52, apparently of a fever after a "merry meeting" of drinks with friends. Shakespeare did in fact die on St George's Day! He was buried "full 17 foot deep" in Holy Trinity Church, Stratford, and left an epitaph cursing anyone who dared disturb his bones.

There have been preposterous theories disputing Shakespeare's authorship. Some claim that Sir Francis Bacon (1561–1626), philosopher and Lord Chancellor, was the real author of Shakespeare's plays. Others propose Edward de Vere, Earl of Oxford (1550–1604), or, even more weirdly, Queen Elizabeth I. The implication is that the "real" Shakespeare had to be a university graduate or an aristocrat. Nothing less would do for the world's greatest writer.

Shakespeare is mysteriously hidden behind his work. His life will not tell us what inspired his genius.